Circumstances of Childhood

John W. Howell

Acknowledgements

Circumstances of Childhood is a piece of fiction written out of the author's imagination. Austin, Texas, Nashville, Indiana, Weston, Boston, the University of Texas, the New England Patriots, the NFL, and the Heisman Trophy are real places and organizations with real people, but the events described, characters developed, and places visited are purely fictional with no intent to depict reality. No personnel from any of the listed cities or organizations were directly or indirectly involved in the development of this story. I want to thank all my beta readers for reading the book in its pre-edited stage and for making very meaningful comments which served to enhance the story. I believe you should be sainted. A special thank you also to editor Harmony Kent, who continues to exercise her craft in such a way as to teach while improving the readability of my story. She is a saint. Finally, as always, a thank you to Molly McCormick for her continued support.

Dedication

Circumstance of Childhood is a book written as a result of reviewing some moments that I have faced throughout my life. Although there have been many acquaintances, there have only been a very few true friendships. This story is dedicated to the two men that I have the privilege of calling friends. The first is my best friend, Bill Given. He has had the patience and endurance in our relationship that can only be described as brotherly. The second is my dear friend, Charles Gruner. Charlie and I had the kind of relationship that continued through years of separation as we each pursued our life goals. Charlie didn't always agree with my choices but never wavered in his support. Thankfully Bill is still available for counsel, support, and at times a new tool. Charlie has gone on to another life and is missed very much.

Chapter One

So, with nothing better to do, I figure I'll stop at Jerry's place and grab a couple a drinks and a burger. Usually, I don't go there on Saturday night since there's a crapload of amateurs taking up what would be considered prime space. I figure since this is a Friday, and close to Saturday, it may be packed but not as crazy as Saturday. It's the kind of place where everyone minds their business. Today's events will, probably, not register with the people in the bar. They're there for a good time and will likely not notice me. Even so, I go through the door, stop, and have a look around, trying not to make eye contact. I hope that the ball cap and large coat will keep me from getting noticed. The bar holds a weekday crowd, all right, hanging on each other like they never had a date before. I tighten my eyelids against the smoke and make out four guys near the pool table and what looks like a couple of girls fetching drinks. I search for a seat beyond the table in the back, but it seems like they're all taken.

A guy bumps into me as I stand here. I say excuse me, and he looks me in the face. "Hey, don't I know you?" he says.

"I don't think so." I make to turn away.

"Yeah, you're the sports hero who lost all his money. I saw you on TV."

"Naw, people always say stuff like that. I'm not him, buddy; trust me."

He gives me a puzzled look but doesn't want to push it in case he has it wrong. I turn away and continue to look for a seat.

Straight ahead lies the bar, and it has a place right in the middle. I move in the direction of the empty place and look over to the other side of the room. The tables look full of happy drunks. Buckets of empties line the bar top, and the barmaid's trying to sell more. She doesn't have much luck since most of these people just spent their last five bucks on this outing. Upon making it to the stool, I hoist myself up and lean on the bar.

"Hey, Greg," Jerry says. "Whadda you have?"

"Evening, Jerry. I'll have a gin on the rocks with a water back."

"Comin' up."

I like Jerry's no-nonsense way of handling things. He doesn't like small talk and gets right to business. My eyes smart from the smoke, and I wonder how Jerry gets away with letting people kill themselves when, clearly, it's not supposed to be allowed in this kind of establishment.

"Here you go. Want me to run a tab?"

"Yeah, I would appreciate that. I intend to have another drink and then a burger."

The guy who thinks he knows me grabs my shoulder from behind. I almost fall off the stool.

"You're Greg Petros, the big fund manager. I knew I saw you on TV. You took a beautiful career in football and ran it into the ground."

Jerry leans over the bar and lays his hand on the guy's shoulder. "Move on, my friend. You made a mistake. This guy is nobody. Go sit down and let me buy you a drink."

"You sure? You called him Greg."

"Yeah, I'm sure. Go get a table, and I'll send someone over."

The guy looks at me one more time but does as Jerry suggests. He believes Jerry's wrong, but the idea of a free drink lets him get away without losing face.

"Thanks. I didn't mean for you to have to jump in."

"No problem. Gimme the high sign when you're ready for another drink."

"Will do. Thanks."

"For you buddy, anything."

I should mention that Jerry and I go back aways. When I fell on hard times, he became the only one that seemed to give a shit. I take a sip of my drink and wait for the burn in my throat, which signals the good stuff. Here it comes. I take a swig of the water and almost believe life is good. The gin needs to get to the brain before making any honest judgment.

While I wait for the warmth to go from my stomach to my head, I check out the folk seated on either side of me. They both have their backs turned to me and sit engrossed in some discussion with their neighbor. I figure it's just as well since I don't want to go through that old "don't I know you?" bullshit again. Also, I don't figure on staying the night, so no use in getting into any long discussions about life.

I look down at my drink and wonder what will happen tomorrow. My daughter Constance wants to come and visit. She lives in New York, and before all hell broke loose, we didn't see each other often. I missed her so much, and it seemed as if I had to beg her even to talk on the phone. Now, it's like she wants to be here every weekend. It's only an hour's flight by the shuttle or three by train, so she can come when she wants. I just can't figure out why she got so clingy. I have my troubles, but it doesn't have anything to do with her. No use in asking her husband either. Though a nice enough guy, I always wonder if he has someplace important to go when I visit. He never sits still and stays busy on the phone or at the computer. He makes a good living, but it seems a person could take an hour to sit and talk. I'd looked forward to some kind of relationship when he and Constance got married. It'll never happen with him.

When I take another pull at my drink, I notice the burn feels less. It happens every time. First sip initiation, I call it. It's like the first puff of a cigarette, hits hard then, after, nothing. I decide to let Constance pretty much have the agenda tomorrow. She and I have not had a chance to talk about anything deep for a while. It could just be that she blames me for her mother running off with that guy with the house on the Hudson. He has a title, and the old gal couldn't resist, but I think the daughter always felt I should have done something. Her mother's sleeping with another guy and what the hell can I do about that?

I'll just go with the flow. If she wants to go out, we will. If she wants to stay in, we can do that too. I better think about getting some food in the house. Of course, we can always order take out. I need to move on to my drink and let this go. Tomorrow will be what it is. I remember the day she was born. I looked down at her in my arms and promised I would do anything for her. I love her more than life itself, and I hope we can somehow get to the root of whatever's wrong. She sounded strange on the phone this morning, and I feel helpless to do anything about it. I hope she opens up when she gets here.

For some reason, I feel tired. Perhaps I'll go ahead and finish my drink. Maybe I'll just go home and forget the burger. First, though, I'll just shut my eyes for a minute. My hands feel good when I put my head down.

"Hey, Greg," Jerry says. I barely hear him. "What's the matter? You taking a nap? Greg?" I can feel him shake me, but I have no interest in waking up. His voice gets further away, and I think he says, "Oh, my God, Sophie, call 911, quick." Now the room goes silent.

Chapter Two

Well, that was something. Looks like old Greg got in a bit of trouble. I'm sure you picked up the fact that something's wrong. Not only is he acting a little weird but that whole thing with his daughter that he mentioned needs to be explained. Oh, I'm sorry; I should introduce myself. The name's Keith. Keith Petros. Yes, that makes me his brother, which is another story altogether. For now, you know all you need to know, so let's move on to the story. I guess you feel confused about what happened back there. His daughter's name, which he mentioned, is Constance. When he gave it to her, I thought it old-fashioned. Her name reminded me of a librarian. I didn't interfere, and Constance it became.

I digress. Where was I? Oh, yes, I should explain my role in this story. Right now, Greg won't be in a position to tell his tale, so it will be up to me to lay it all out. Since I know him about as well as anyone, I shall act as your guide and try to explain how he came to end up in the bar with his head on his hands. I must tell you, the situation of the head on hands makes a tiny part of the whole story, so don't worry about that part too much right now.

Greg had one hell of a life, and I guess we should start at the beginning. I wasn't there at his birth but showed up a little after. The story of his birth got retold a number of times while we were kids, so I almost think I lived it. He was a big baby, according to Mom. She would be the best one to know. Also, he was delayed a little in birth. After almost ten months, he finally made an appearance. We used to joke about his reluctance to leave the warm and wet. Leave he finally did, and his parents were so pleased to have him. His mom and dad wanted the family to be complete with a boy to start off.

His parents named him Gregory, but everyone called him Greg. I won't drag you through all the cute spit up, potty training stories, but suffice it to say, Greg had a normal childhood. I met up with him when we were about four years old. My family moved in next door, and we became fast playmates and friends. I know, I mentioned he was my brother, and we'll get to that in a moment. As I said, the childhood seemed normal up to the point when his dad died. Greg had reached about ten years old, and apparently, his dad had cancer. In the opinion of the family, Greg's dad caught cancer as a result of getting exposed to Agent Orange in Viet Nam. He was an officer and highly decorated.

I remember the day Mom told me about his dad. I don't think the hurt could have felt any more painful had it been my dad instead of Greg's. At his house, he and I found a place under the lilac bush in his backyard and tried to comfort each other. I remember how hard he cried and how hard it proved to get him to stop. His dad was someone any kid would want to know, and to have him as a dad seemed special. I used to get jealous of Greg since his dad was capable of anything. He could make wonderful things out of metal or wood. He had a shop in the garage where we would work on projects under his gentle guidance. He would take us to the places where boys love to play. The forest, creeks, and hills all became fair game. We flew kites, airplanes, and rockets. We ate lunch in the grass and ice-cream in the park. Greg's dad was a god to me.

My dad always seemed too busy to take us where Greg's dad had the time to go. Don't get me wrong, I loved my dad, and he did what he could. His events were mostly movies and ballgames. They were fun but not like living an adventure on each outing.

The news of his dad's passing came like an explosion. One minute, Greg and I were happy kids without a worry in the world, and then reality blew in with some of the miserable facts of life. It was a curtain lifted in a play. Before the news, it all seemed music and excitement, and then the bomb hit. In the fallout, we were left to figure out a mystery of life on our own. How could old man Hampton still be walking down the street with his cane while Greg's dad lay in the casket at the funeral home in his full-dress uniform? We couldn't figure out an answer. Greg's mom couldn't help either. She became someone that he and I didn't want to hang around. Constantly, she dabbed her eyes and talked about how she missed her husband. Other grown-ups told us this behavior was normal, but it kept reminding us of our loss. Also, we imagined she would remain this way forever.

The funeral proved a dismal affair. Quite a lot of soldiers stood around, and everyone kept telling Greg he had now become the man of the house. I told him they lied, and he was still a kid, but I don't think my words stuck as much as the adults'. We all stood out at the grave when the twenty-one-gun salute went off, and taps finished the ceremony. A massive soldier put a folded flag in Greg's mother's arms. She sobbed and handed the flag to Greg. I'll never forget the look of sheer terror on his face. As if someone had tapped him to lead a country. He was only ten, and I could tell even at my young age, his childhood had finished forever. He tried not to cry, but his tears rolled down his cheeks without stopping. Finally, I asked my mom for a tissue and walked over to Greg and held it out to him. He looked at me like I'd gone crazy. He gave a quick shake of his head, which gave a signal for, "get away from me."

I hurt from the loss of his dad, and now began a whole new hurt that I had exposed Greg's crying to the world. It was the last thing I wanted to do. Greg did not suffer fools lightly, and I felt miserable knowing he might never forgive me for my stupid act of kindness. To this day, I think I tried hard to make-up to Greg for that one small indiscretion. It is strange to feel that way, considering I never meant to embarrass him. I only wanted to give him comfort. I still feel that way and would do anything to spare him from pain.

After the service, we all went back to Greg's house. Tons of people attended. I can still recall the dour smells of the food and liquor as well as the closely crowded rooms. Among all those people, I felt a little lost. My folks grew occupied comforting Greg's mother so, more or less, I wandered around on my own. I remember feeling struck by the strangeness of the house without the loud laughter of Greg's dad. I must have stayed overnight hundreds of times and yet I had the feeling I had never gone there before.

I went up to Greg's room and knocked on his door with a gentle caution of not wanting to disturb him. He answered the knock with an invitation to enter that had the sound of reluctance a kid gives to a nosy parent when they want to sit alone. I turned the knob and pushed the door ajar enough to allow my head to go through. "Greg, it's me, Keith."

"Come in. Thanks for coming up."

"You okay?"

"I-I think so. I have a pretty big hurt."

"I loved your dad too, you know."

"I know. I just don't want to keep crying. I'm not a girl but can't help it."

"I'm sorry if I did something wrong before."

"I just didn't want anyone to see me crying. It's okay."

"You still have the flag."

"I want to hold it longer."

He and I talked for a while. We told each other stories about his dad. Greg did stop crying, and we got to telling some of the funny things that we went through. Finally, he decided he needed to take a nap, so I got up off his bed and left him with his dad's flag and little else. I say little else but what I mean is, looking back at him, I got the feeling that when his dad died a little part of him died as well. He looked like a baby curled up with the large triangle of a flag. My eyes got blurry as I made my way back to the adults. I don't think I will ever forget that day and how sorry I felt for him. The thought still makes my head ache and brings tears to my eyes.

For the rest of our lives, I tried my best to keep Greg from getting hurt. I made sure he and I remained inseparable. I did my best to include him in any of our family activities. My parents understood that when we went on vacation, he would come with us. During the summers, Greg and I traded overnight stays at each other's houses. It wasn't a one-night-for-one proposition but more like a stay at Greg's one night and mine for three. His mom never recovered from the loss of her husband. She preoccupied herself with grief, and frankly, it seemed hard staying at his house. His mother started every conversation with some remembrance of Greg's dad. It got to the point that Greg and I gave each other a signal that conveyed a "here we go again" when she began. Those signals helped him understand that he couldn't do much to cheer up his mother. He felt bad about it, and thinking about it now, this lack of control over the situation is probably the core to how Greg turned out as an adult. He always wanted to fix problems even when not at the heart of them. As if he tried to make up for not managing to help his mom. Of course, as kids, we could only react with an eye roll and try to move on.

Greg told me he always felt glad to stay at my house since life ran normally, and it made him more comfortable. My mom and dad never asked how Greg's mom was doing since I think they didn't want to disturb him any more than possible. They knew from neighborhood talk that Greg's mom didn't do well. I remember my mom went over to his house one time and came away in tears. Greg's mom didn't cause the tears. She explained to my dad that she felt so sorry for Greg. I overheard the conversation, and it reinforced my decision to watch over him since it became clear his mom couldn't.

We both joined the Boy Scouts, and my dad became a conscript into a leadership role in the troop. More or less, he got forced to participate by my mom. In the end, I think he enjoyed the experience. My dad's reason for becoming a leader didn't get mentioned again; however, he grew enthusiastic about leading a group of boys. He'd become a scout when he was a boy, and I think the experience all came back to him. Greg and I worked on our merit badges together and achieved various ranks simultaneously. Our work led to a day when it became clear that we had finished all the requirements of an Eagle Scout, the highest honor. We got so excited about the award and especially the ceremony, which would culminate in pinning the Eagle medal on us and we, in turn, would give our mothers an eagle necklace.

The ceremony happened in the school auditorium, and a number of people outside our troop attended. The local newspaper came, along with the mayor and the member of the state house of representatives. The agenda for the evening included a speech by the mayor and House member as well as selections played by the school band. My dad would present the actual medal and then invite us to present our mothers with the necklace.

During the mayor's speech, I could see Greg was in some distress. I asked him what was going on, and he told me his mother hadn't gotten there yet. I hadn't noticed but told him not to worry and lied when I told him she probably got caught in traffic. Since Greg came to the ceremony with us, the lie could have been the truth. About halfway through the House member's talk, his mother made her entrance. I looked at Greg and gave him the "what did I tell you" look. He had a calm demeanor and gave me a nod, which included thanks.

The time came for the presentation of the awards. Our mothers moved up to the stage to join the two of us. We stood at attention as my dad pinned our Eagle medals on our puffed chests. I could see Greg out of the corner of my eye, and he stood smiling from ear to ear. We gave the mayor and my dad a salute, and then gave a smart about-face to present the necklace to our mothers, who stood behind us. My mom looked so pleased to receive the recognition of her hard work, and I took a short step forward and presented her with the box containing the necklace. Immediately, she took it out and put it around her neck. A round of applause followed, and to my total embarrassment, my mother gave me a hug.

Greg stepped closer to his mother and held out the box. It looked obvious that she had been crying sometime earlier, as her eyes appeared quite red. She took the box and gave Greg a weak smile. He moved to help her put it on, and she kind of stepped to the side, and Greg almost fell into her. By now, it became clear something was wrong.

"Excuse me," his mom said. "I've some things to say."

Greg's face flushed, and I knew what was to follow would not go well.

"As you all know, my husband passed away a few years ago. He would have been so proud to be here. Since he's not, I'll have to speak for him." She stopped for a second and seemed to search for the right words. "My shun." She stopped again, and we all saw that Greg's mom was drunk. She looked around, and since no one stopped her, she continued, "My son is one of the best kids a mother could have. He has been by my side since his father left us. He did not deserve to go through the pain of having to live without a dad and to have a mom totally wrapped up in her misery. This night should celebrate the achievement of Gregory and his ability to succeed in spite of the difficulties he has had to face. I'm sorry, my son, but I just can't stand any more of this life without your dad. I don't mean to mess up your ceremony, but there is something I have to do."

You couldn't hear a sound in the auditorium while Greg's mom spoke. Her words bounced around, so it seemed as if the words were made of metal and bounced off the walls. When she became silent, the last trace of the word "do" echoed for a second. Greg went toward his mom to try and prevent whatever she planned to do. She reacted by stepping away from him, and caught her foot on the edge of the stage and tumbled off. A shriek went up from the audience, as it became clear the woman had injured herself severely. Greg leaped over the edge of the stage and knelt next to his mom. She lay there unmoving, and opened her eyes only for a brief moment. Her eyes begged for forgiveness, and then went dim.

The room broke into bedlam. Most of the people left confused and in shock. The few that remained tried to help Greg. He refused to let go of his mom and asked everyone to leave him alone. He shielded his mom's body with his, and I could tell by the heaving of his shoulders he cried hard.

My dad touched Greg on the back of the head, and Greg looked up. "Come on, son," my dad said. "We need to let your mom rest." Finally, Greg eased his mom down to the floor, and my dad picked him up and held him tightly. I could hardly see what went on since the tears pooled so thick in my eyes. My mom came over to me and put her arm around me. I could hear sirens, which sounded far away.

We all just stood there, my dad holding Greg, and my mom holding me. I didn't know what to say or do, so I whispered to my mom and asked if it would be okay for Greg to come to our house. She said it would be okay, and then I wondered if she knew I meant for good, not just tonight. I didn't want to press it, so I thanked her and let the tears fall.

Chapter Three

I didn't need to discuss with my parents whether or not Greg would stay with us permanently. He didn't have any relatives who wanted him. My parents made inquiries, and when they discovered him on his own, they stepped in immediately and welcomed him into our house as if he'd lived there forever.

Greg's mother didn't leave a formal will but did leave a note on her kitchen table, which asked for forgiveness and stated that all her possessions and money should go to Greg. Since my dad practiced as a lawyer, he proved successful in having the document received into the system as her last will. He then oversaw the sale of the house and belongings as well as the transfer of all the assets into a Trust for Greg. A third party would administer the Trust, and Greg would receive funds at eighteen. Until then, he would live with us.

I should explain here that I didn't understand all that went on at the time, but in later years, became aware of what my dad did for Greg.

Our life with Greg in the house took a week or two to develop any sense of normalcy. We had to struggle through the funeral of his mom, and all of us get used to having Greg around full-time. He grieved deeply for about a month. After that time, he came out of his shell and interacted with the rest of us. In some ways, he took to the role of a younger brother, and we both felt glad to have each other.

We started high school, and both went out for the football team. Since we were freshmen, we didn't think we had a chance of making the team. To our surprise, the coach assigned us to the practice squad. To be given any assignment seemed a big deal. It meant we didn't play the games, but we got to scrimmage with the varsity and to sit on the sidelines during the home games. We felt so pleased to have a chance to participate.

Our first practice day arrived at last. Since the opening game happened on Friday of the first week of school, we started practicing a week before school began. Greg earned a halfback position on offense, and I took up a linebacker position on defense. I remember the days as sunny and quite warm. The teams would meet in the morning for a few hours for conditioning, and then in the afternoon for drills and practice games.

Our practice got a lot more unpleasant due to the heat and abuse by the varsity as the day got longer. Although we were the practice team, the varsity players would take the attitude that we were the enemy. A couple of varsity members played on the practice side, but for the most part, we remained unseasoned in the art of pigskin war.

Our coaches would give us plays to run that they figured an opposing team would use in a real game. The idea was to try and fool the varsity. In the beginning, it proved tough to fake them out, but as time went on, we gained experience and skill. I took over the quarterback position, and Greg went to wide receiver. The first time we scored on the varsity came from a simple option play where I could either keep the ball myself or hand it to the running back. In this case, I faked the handoff to the running back and then made it look like I would keep it. Just when I saw the defense committed to a run, I dropped back and launched a long pass to Greg, who stood in the clear. He caught it, and then stepped into the end zone. The varsity defense grew

furious and made Greg and I pay for the touchdown for the rest
of the day with continued hits even when we didn't have the ball.

In the locker room, the varsity guys totally ignored us.
Greg and I smiled to each other since we knew we'd hurt them
bad. The coach came up and asked us to come to his office after
we got dressed. We stopped smiling and wore the concerned
looks of people who knew they'd gotten into trouble. We
showered and dressed without too much more discussion and
went to the coach's office. A light knock on the door produced
the command to enter from inside. Greg turned the knob, and I
swallowed hard as we entered the room.

"Sit down, boys," the coach said. "Any idea why I wanted
to see you?"

"Well, er," I said. "I guess you want to chew us out for
making the defense look bad."

"Is that what you think, Greg?"

"Gee, coach. I don't know why, but that's a pretty good
reason. We didn't mean to make them look bad; it's just. Well,
you see. They are bad."

The coach took a long, stern look at Greg and then
nodded at me. "You think so?"

"I do, sir." I got the feeling that I'd confessed my sins and
sat ready for the punishment phase of the trial.

The coach rocked back in his chair. He had a toothpick in
the side of his mouth, which made him look like a cowboy. Then
he rocked forward and pulled it out. "I agree with you, boys. We
need to make some changes, and you two will help us."

"Help how?" I asked. Greg and I exchanged a worried
look.

"I think you two have the stuff to design plays that will
teach the defense to anticipate anything. I never saw an option
play done quite like that before. What you did was give the
defense the idea you would run the ball, and then when the

defenders committed themselves to rushing in, you passed it instead."

"Yeah, we figured that would work," Greg said.

"So, you did make up that play?"

"Yes, sir, we did."

"Man, this is great. Not only did you give me an opportunity to sharpen the defense, but also, I can use the plays you two design to sharpen the offense as well. That's it. You two are now varsity players. Go to Schmidt and get a new uniform and helmet. We will meet tomorrow before practice to plan out a couple of things. You've done well, boys. I'm proud of you."

"Coach?" After I said it, I wanted to take it back.

"Yes, son?"

I figured I had no choice but to continue, "We are only freshman year. How come you're giving us this responsibility?"

"Great question, Keith. I believe you boys have something we can use. I don't think it's a matter of age but a matter of smarts. You boys are big for your age. Oh, by the way, you both fourteen?"

We answered in unison, "Yes, sir."

"If you can't cut it, no harm, no foul, but I think you can do it."

"Thanks, coach." I felt totally impressed, and I could tell Greg was pumped.

"Pay no nevermind to those jealous ones out there. They will come to respect you, sooner or later."

"Or kill us first," Greg said.

Coach laughed a hearty one and told us to have a nice evening. Greg and I got up and wandered down the hall. We couldn't believe what had just happened. We went from a couple of rummies on the practice squad to varsity players. "Do you believe it?" Greg said.

"What I can't believe is how pissed off the rest of the players will be. They'll have us for dinner."

"Not if we stay smarter."

I shook my head at Greg. "I don't know. I don't think smarts has a lot of room in football."

"Just look what we did already. Those sons of bitches thought they had us, and boom, we laid one on 'em."

"Okay, you're right. We need to plan out a few moves. Maybe they'll come to respect us."

"Well, I wouldn't go that far. In fact, old Moskowitz said he'd kill us next time."

"Let me restate that. Maybe we'll live to see another day like the coach said."

We continued to chat all the way to Schmidt's office. We knocked and heard permission to enter. We went in, and Schmidt sat behind his desk. "Well, well, well, look who's here. The wonder boys."

Greg and I looked at our shoes and mumbled to the effect, "The coach says we should get varsity uniforms and helmets."

"Yeah, I talked to the coach. You guys put it over on the team. Nice job. Follow me." Schmidt rose and let go with a fart, which he ignored. Greg and I followed him, trying to keep from laughing out loud. Still don't know what's so funny about a fart, but under the circumstances, it not only broke wind but the tension as well.

Schmidt piled the new uniforms into our arms and plopped a helmet on top. "Your numbers are offensive numbers. I assume Keith will act as the quarterback and you, Greg, a receiver. You have two sets there. One set for home games and one for away. You'll still wear your practice uniforms for everyday. Try to find someone to clean these after each game. We don't have a washing service here. Tell whoever does the wash to use cold water, so the numbers don't run. Good luck to you."

With that speech, Schmidt sent us to the locker room. "Do we dare leave these uniforms here?" I said.

"You gotta be kidding. Those guys will have a field day messing them up. I'm taking mine home 'til game day."

"Good idea." I opened my locker and pulled out my duffle bag. While I stuffed the new uniforms in the bag, I wondered about the helmet. Greg thought we would wear the helmet in practice, so I put mine in the locker and made sure the lock was closed fully. "I'm done," I said.

"Me too." He looked at the locker as if he didn't want to leave it. I knew how he felt and told him the locker would be there tomorrow. He laughed, slammed the door, and fastened the lock. We went outside and saw our bikes in their proper place. I had thought that maybe those guys would fool with them, but all looked normal.

Always, we both rode our bikes to school and parked them outside the gym, which everyone knew. We always parked there so that the bikes would be close at the end of the day. It made for a bit of a hike to our first class, but certainly seemed worth it when we'd had a tough practice session. It made me happy that no one thought of taking their frustrations out on our rides.

"Let's get home. I'm starving," Greg said. He got on his bike and started off. I told him to wait up while I put my heavy bag on the handlebars. Somehow, I felt different from when I'd come to school that morning. I called out, "You feel any different than this morning?" Obviously, he'd gotten a little too far ahead of me to hear. I decided it unimportant enough to repeat and sure that he would wonder what I was talking about by then. The day just felt special, and for some reason, I felt it was a little bigger than just getting made a member of the varsity team. It seemed more like the beginning of a partnership and producing positive results, which would, potentially, have an impact on our lives. I hoped the feeling would prove not just a wish but more of a reality. I caught up to Greg, and we cruised home without saying much. We did exchange smiles whenever we looked at each other. I think he had the feeling as well.

We got home and rushed the house. We couldn't wait to tell Mom and Dad what had gone on that day. Greg and I both started talking at the same time. Dad held up his hand and bade us each to tell a separate tale. Both parents looked genuinely pleased to hear that we'd become part of the varsity. Dad asked the most questions. He wondered how we'd come up with the plays. Greg told him it came down to a matter of looking at how the defense lined up and to have at least three moves on any ball handle. Dad grew fascinated by the concept. He used his lawyer training to learn all he could from Greg and I that evening and felt satisfied at the end of the briefing that we could duplicate our success, and we wouldn't become just a one-night stand, so to speak. He explained that he didn't want us to end up disappointed when the varsity boys figured out what we were doing and crushed us on every play. He asked more questions than he would have on another subject. "It's not as if I think you guys will fail," he said. "I think you have a solid plan and should go for it."

He made both of us feel good about our plan. We adjourned to the dining room and continued a rather agitated discussion through dinner. My mom even got involved by asking questions on how one reads the defense. Greg explained it was a matter of how they are lined up. If they thought we would run the ball, they lined up a certain way. An anticipated pass would have another configuration. Mom seemed interested in the strategic part of the plan. She also felt satisfied that we would, in all probability, prove successful.

By the time dessert got served, the meal had taken on all the appearance of a victory celebration. We beamed and took the honors with a sense of grace that only comes from knowing you will do well. That evening felt magical, and it made the beginning of a long line of successful collaborations between Greg and me.

The next morning saw us out of bed early and hunched over the dining-room table. "Here's one that will get 'em," Greg said. He looked almost electric with enthusiasm. Consumed with drawing a few plays on our tablet, he didn't stop to get a breath.

"What about doing a run?" I said.

"Yeah, that will work." He made notes on the page. "I see we can do any number of things from this position."

"You've got the quarterback way back where the fullback should be. Don't you think they can blitz and get me?"

"The beauty of this formation is if they come rushing in, you just step forward, and they will all go by you. You can then toss long or short. It's beautiful."

"I have to admit, you called it right; it is beautiful."

My mom came into the room just then and reminded us we needed to get going, so we wouldn't arrive late. Greg gathered up the playbook, and we both grabbed our books, said goodbye, and went out the door.

We got to school and parked our bikes near the gym. While we walked to class, a couple of the varsity players came toward us on the sidewalk. They wouldn't move, so Greg and I had to get onto the grass. They laughed and made a point of the fact we were not men enough to push them off the sidewalk. We simply smiled at them. "They'll be kissing our shoes before it's over," Greg said. We both laughed and went to class. The day dragged on forever. Finally, the three o'clock bell rang. Greg and I almost killed each other getting out of that classroom. We pushed our way down the hall to the exit. We cut across campus and got to the gym before any of the other players. We dressed quickly and got out on the practice field first. The coach stood waiting. "Afternoon, boys," he said. We returned the greeting. He then asked us to give him an idea of a couple of the plays that we had developed. Greg showed him six plays that when used as options, were, in reality, eighteen plays.

"So, you're telling me that our team can use the six plays and have eighteen separate moves with the ball?"

We nodded vigorously, and he seemed impressed. "We'll have to try these. I assume the blocking assignments will need to change depending on the option?"

"No, sir," I said. "The blocking assignments all remain the same. It will be up to the quarterback to read the effectiveness of the offense and the skill of the defense before deciding what to do with the ball."

"What quarterback can do that?"

"I can."

The coach looked at me, and then broke into a wide grin. "I'll be damned. You planned to play all along, didn't you?"

"Well, Greg and I are a good team, and we thought we could convince you to use us for a little more than practice."

"Okay, here's what we shall do. I will take these plays and keep the defensive coach completely in the dark. The offense coach will work with the line on these six plays. We will be ready to run some sessions tomorrow. If you guys continue to outfox the defense, you'll play Friday night. If they catch on, you'll ride the bench. Deal?"

"Yes, sir, a deal. As long as no one rats us out to the defense, we'll be good."

"That will be my job to make sure it doesn't happen. Good luck, boys. Here comes the team. You better get into the callisthenic program."

Chapter Four

The practice went okay for the day. Greg and I felt excited to see tomorrow come. It did, eventually, and the day crept by until it came time to suit up for practice. Greg and I were the first on the field again. After a round of exercise, the time arrived to run some practice plays.

I convinced the coach that, because of the simplicity of the plays, it was not necessary to huddle. Each of the plays had pretty much the same assignments. Instead of a huddle, I would simply tell each a number out loud during the count between one and six for the play. The coach also agreed on the word that would signal the center to hike the ball, preassigned by quarter. The first quarter had animal words. So, the center knew to hike the ball on an animal name. The team also knew that the animal word would be the next word after the number of the play. Let's say that the play was number one; the signal to hike would be an animal word after the number one. I could then have a series like "Stroke stroke even seventeen one tiger crash crash." All the stuff before and after one and tiger had no meaning, but the defense would not pick it up until too late. The important part would be that our team knew what was going on and worked in unison when the time came to begin the play.

The first play of the quarter was a number six. I counted off, and one of the defensive players jumped the gun. He got thrown off by the double-word opening. We started again after the five-yard penalty got walked off. I started the count and saw that the defense looked very weary of going offside again, so I pulled a quick six and alligator. The ball came back to me, and I looked for Greg out of the corner of my eye. He had made good progress down the field, so I kept the ball instead of handing it to the fullback. It became clear that the players up front thought the fullback had it since they crushed him as he went through the line. My second option was to throw a short pass to the receiver crossing in front of me. I saw him covered, so I faked a throw, which caused the downfield defender to pause for a step. I then threw the ball toward Greg. It was a long pass, and I timed it to land a little ahead of Greg. He sprinted, and I placed it so that he could run into it. He made a perfect catch and kept going into the end zone.

The defensive players pounded the ground in anger. I think the thing that got them the most was the fact that we didn't huddle, and the cadence dragged them across the line early. The coach whistled and told us to run another play. I chose number three, a classic run. The ball would go to the fullback, but the difference lay in that I would accompany him into the line so that the linemen wouldn't feel sure who had the ball. I began to call the signals, and then stopped. I pointed to several players and said something like, "Kill them." I wanted the defense to think it would be a pass play and that I would need plenty of protection. My guess was that they would hold back a little in order to knock down the ball. I made my count again. Purposely, I dragged out the count until the snap. The right side of the line came rushing in like a freight train. The fullback came alongside me, and he and I went toward the line. Right then, I could see Greg totally in the clear, about twenty yards out. I kept the ball and flipped a pass to him. He ran like hell and got caught about five yards from the goal.

We did not huddle, and I called a four, which meant a dive over the line. Another long count kept the defense on edge, and then I had the ball. I gave it to the running back, and he vaulted over the pile of linemen for a touchdown. The coach blew the whistle. "Okay, team. That's enough for today. Keith and Greg, stay with me."

The rest of the team did the usual jog around the track outside the field to warm down. Greg and I stayed beside the coach as ordered. "You two have revolutionized the game. We need to teach the defense what they need to know to defend against your plays. I can see us going to state this year. I'm so proud of you two."

Greg and I looked at each other, and then broke into wide grins. "Thanks, coach," Greg said. "We think we have a good shot too."

We walked back to the gym slowly. The coach grew all excited about drafting the defensive plays. We told him we would be more than happy to do it tonight. He looked at us with some degree of surprise on his face. "You can do that?" he said.

We told him we thought we could at least rough out a few plays and show him tomorrow. "If it looks good, we can run them with the defensive players," I said. The coach agreed. We left him a happy man and went into the showers.

***

Greg and I worked on the plays, and sure enough, the next day, we showed them to the coach. He liked them immediately, and so we went out on the field. Greg and I walked the defense through some simple setups. We ran a couple of plays, and the defense stopped us cold. The coach was all smiles. He gathered the team together after the practice and gave us a pep talk on the importance of doing our best and the value of teamwork. He let us know he felt we were ready for the opening game on Friday and that we should feel proud of where we were. The team gave a cheer and jogged off the field.

Nothing much changed in the veteran player's attitudes regarding Greg and I. They did have more respect but seemed to keep us at a distance. Greg summed it up with a guess that they felt jealous, which I supposed covered the situation perfectly. At least they didn't shove us against the lockers anymore.

Friday night came all too quickly for my comfort. I had a big mass of butterflies in my stomach. The coach talked to the team in the locker room. He reminded us that the game of football was just a game. Though serious, at the same time he had a tone of confidence in his voice that seemed to calm me. I kept thinking of the fact that Greg and I were only freshmen and not the biggest guys on the field. Finally, I went to the bathroom and got rid of my lunch. When I got back to the locker room, I felt better. After about a half hour of dimmed light and soft music, we got ready to take the field.

The experience of running out of the gym to the roar of the local fans was something I had not anticipated. I'd expected some people in the stands but not half the city. Greg came up to me and whispered that he felt scared shitless. I could not help but laugh out loud. Greg joined me, and the laughter took us to a point where we got over much of our fear. After some warming up, it came time to play. The visitor team won the toss of the coin and elected to kick. We would have the first possession. I told Greg that at least we wouldn't have to stand around and become scared again.

"We're in deep yogurt," he said. We laughed some more. The coach came over and asked if we were okay. We both told him that we felt more than ready. He told us that he had the utmost confidence and walked away.

The kickoff proved predictable. Their kicker jammed it into the end zone, so we took the ball on the twenty. Greg and the team took the field. The visiting fans screamed for defense, and I thought that there was nothing their team would manage to do to stop us. We lined up in a shotgun formation, and I pulled a long count, which I could see had the other team confused. They set to thinking about not having a huddle, and I'm sure felt totally distracted. The ball shot to me, and I rushed forward like I planned to keep it, which drew all the defensive players more toward me. I flipped a short pass to the fullback, and he fired a long pass to Greg, who stepped into the end zone. The crowd erupted into a mass cheer. My allowing the fullback to make the pass proved a good political move. He got so excited with the touchdown, and the rest of the players patted him and Greg. The play was an eighty-yard, ten-second play. Never before in our high school history had it been done on purpose. Oh yes, plenty of flukes had happened where someone would intercept a pass or something, but this sucker got done on purpose and was repeatable. We kicked the extra point, and the kickoff team held the other team to the ten-yard line. The defense did not allow any headway, and their punter, who had a magic leg, kicked a sixty-yard punt.

We took over on our thirty-five-yard line. Three plays later, we scored again. So, this is how the game went all night. We scored on each possession and ran the score up to sixty-five zip until the coach decided to give some others a chance. Although the defense pretty much held the other guys to about fifty yards, they managed to score late in the fourth quarter. It went as the papers said the next day: *A ROUT.*

I don't want to bore you too much, so let me say the season went the same way, and we took the state title. Greg and I got awarded a Varsity letter at the banquet, and the rest of our teammates gave up their attitude at last, and we all became close. Greg and I went to all the big parties and became welcome teammates.

I have to say here that it all felt too easy. Before we reconstructed the team playbook, we were nothings. After, we became big men on campus and enjoyed every minute. The balance of our high school career mostly went the same way. We took the team to a state championship for the next four years running. During our junior year, after the season had finished, various universities contacted us, who wanted us to come visit during the next summer. Our coach stood in the center of the hubbub, and he grew a little overwhelmed by the attention. A couple of schools asked him to consider bringing Greg and I with him as he took over a new coaching position on their team. Greg and I had made the decision that we wanted to go to the same university. We also agreed that we needed to do what we wanted academically and that football would remain secondary to our life goals. Greg wanted to become a successful business person. He always had his nose in Fortune and Forbes magazines. He lamented that some of the big business deals were being made without him. I, on the other hand, wanted to become a lawyer.

We both accepted offers to join the football team at the University of Texas at Austin. We figured Texas was about as far away from our hometown of Nashville Indiana as we could get. Besides, the UT football program could lead to a pro draft opportunity. Greg and I used to sit up and talk about getting into the pros. We both agreed it would be a good thing for the money but, ultimately, not something that would make for the end result on our goal path. It might seem fun for a while and could set us up for the future. I put our decision to go to UT down as what seemed the right thing for the present.

***

We arrived on campus and immediately got swept up into the grind of practice and exercise. We stayed there a full four weeks before classes started. It proved a different kind of practice. The team members' names got into the news. They were the guys the announcers named for their good plays. Greg and I had caught a few games on the network during the last season, and we more or less stood around with our mouths open as the team ran drills.

"Hey, Keith," the offensive coach said. "You know the playbook?"

"Yes, sir," I said. "I have all the plays in my head."

32

"Yeah, we'll see, won't we? You and Greg go ahead and join the practice team and run a few."

We jogged over to a bunch of guys standing on the practice field. "Coach says to run some plays." I put on my helmet and stood in front of some big guys, who hadn't moved. "You got a problem with that?"

I guess no one had a problem since we huddled up. I called an option play, and we broke the huddle. The center hiked the ball, and immediately, I saw stars. The whole line simply let the defensive players rush in unopposed, and at least four huge guys sacked me. I lay in a heap on the ground for a minute, trying to get my breath. I felt sure I had no broken bones, but catching my breath seemed harder than you would believe. Greg came over to see if I felt okay.

"What the fuck happened?" made for my first words when I had enough air to speak.

"I think these boys did have a problem with you running a few plays." Greg extended his hand to me and, when I took it, yanked me onto my feet. I looked over to the team, who stood smiling broadly. "Sons of bitches did that on purpose." I turned to Greg and gave him the look. He knew the look from high school. The "teach someone a lesson" look.

We returned to the team, and I yelled, "Huddle up." They all ambled over as if getting paid for slowness. I called another option, and we broke the huddle. I lined up in the shotgun position so that, at least, I would have a little room when the defensive players got allowed through to cream me. The center hiked the ball. I took a couple of steps back. The linemen rushed in without getting touched by the offensive line. Immediately, I charged forward and passed the ball to Greg. The linemen seemed confused with my aggressive move toward them. Finally, they figured it out and buried me. As I got up, I could tell Greg had made it to the end zone. My breath stayed with me, and I could see a different expression on the faces of the linemen.

Their countenances had more respect in them. One guy walked over and told me his name was Jim and that things would go differently from there on in. I called for another huddle, and this time, the team jumped into action. We ran another play, and the players all did their jobs. Greg and I had survived the first test. I felt unsure whether all freshmen went through the same rigor, but for then, we had become part of the team.

The first year, Greg and I worked with the practice team. We would play the varsity and attend the games. We didn't see much time on the field. I got in for one play when the regular quarterback lost his shoe, but that lasted for about ten seconds' of play time. Greg and I found out that we were getting kept in reserve. Officially, we didn't make part of the team the first year. The arrangement would allow the team to play us for four years if they wanted, with the last being after we graduated. All in all, the coaches and team members made us feel as if we had a job to do and that we did it well.

The next year proved totally different. The varsity quarterback had graduated and was no longer eligible, as he'd played his four years. I became the starting quarterback and played every game. Greg played in rotation with another receiver. I always did better when Greg was on the receiving end of a pass. He and I had a connection. The team did okay but didn't make any playoffs. When the season ended, we'd grown plenty tired of football.

Greg and I lived off-campus in an apartment. We both decided not to join a fraternity. We didn't feel we could afford the time. The funny thing was, we always made the invite list for the major fraternity functions. As football players, we were well known on campus and good to have to stand around when it came time to impress potential members and peers. Greg and I liked to attend the functions. We stayed careful not to get toasted, as our scholarships stipulated good behavior. We also had too much pride to allow alcohol or other substances to put others in control of our well-being. Besides, we enjoyed the functions and the co-eds without having to suffer the next day.

Speaking of co-eds, Greg and I had the greatest dating life possible. We would walk across campus, and virtually every female would say hello. We always said hello back and, sometimes, a conversation would spring up from the greeting and another person would get added to our circle. Greg and I agreed we wouldn't get serious with anyone until after graduation. We didn't think we could support a relationship, study, and play ball all at once. Our pact worked pretty well. Greg fell in love maybe twenty times, and me probably as many. We had a regular discussion when it was clear one of us was getting serious about someone. The session usually ended promising to be honest with the person and trying to break it off without hurt feelings. A few times it was easier said than done.

I remember one time Greg and I were held captive in our apartment by a young woman who camped outside our door. She said she had a knife, and we did not open the door to find out if she was telling the truth. "Thought you said you would handle it without hurting feelings." I was talking to Greg while listening to the poor soul pounding on the door demanding Greg come out and fight like a man.

Greg told me he thought he had handled it. "I never even had sex with her," he said. It was obvious that she did not feel it handled and stayed in front of our door for two days. When we were finally free, we went outside and hoped we wouldn't run into her again. Knowing the odds of doing so kept us on cat feet for several days. Only later did we find out the woman had left school and returned east. Although we felt relieved, we also felt a degree of remorse in not being able to successfully not cause someone any pain. We decided that we should probably set up some new rules of engagement. Certainly, at the top of the list was having a way to spot someone who might be a little unbalanced. Greg had the tendency to align himself with women who hinted at the need for a little support. They weren't full-fledged dependency cases but just a little needy. We decided he should go after only those people who exhibited a real positive self-image. He agreed not to date anyone who would not be capable of kicking him in the nuts on the first date. We both hoped this would be enough to keep us free of trouble relationship wise.

Chapter Five

Our new-found criteria for selecting dates worked quite well for the rest of our Sophomore and junior year. We managed to make it through the last summer without any incidents either. We came close a couple of times but managed to keep out of any serious trouble.

It was time to return to school for our senior year, and Greg and I grew pumped to get back to school. It felt hard to explain but, when in college, being away not studying and playing football felt as if time got marked with insignificant activities until the real purpose of life came around again. So it was with Greg and me during the summer. Sure, we worked at summer jobs, but it didn't feel the same. Greg had a job in the best men's store in town. He made an excellent salesperson, and the owner appreciated having him for the summer. Greg figured it would look good on his resume having not just a summer job but one where he learned the ins and outs of selling. I worked with my dad in his law firm. Most of the work was clerical, but he did allow me to sit in on some trial strategic planning sessions. My dad also required me to attend the trials as a spectator. The experience would come in handy someday when I became a lawyer myself.

Greg and I saved some money and bought a car. Though not a babe magnet, the four-door 87 Toyota Celica was serviceable. We liked it not for the color, green, or type of car, but because it was the year we'd graduated from high school. We packed it up and headed to Austin, Texas. A routine drive, although when we reached Austin, we'd grown sick of the car and every song on every radio station along the way.

We moved into our apartment and began the routine of getting settled. Greg sat reading the local paper that we'd picked up at the supermarket on the way into town. We needed a few things to survive the evening and next morning—nothing special, just chips, salsa, beer, and some Captain Crunch cereal. "What you looking at?" I felt a little perturbed because I stood unpacking a bunch of boxes while Greg had stretched out on the couch reading the damn paper.

"There will be a big welcome back party downtown tonight." He looked up from the paper with a picture of joy on his face that you only see on a kid looking into a candy store.

"Yeah, so what?" I still couldn't get over my peevishness.

"We need to relax after that long trip, and a good ole mob party is just what we need." He now had the look of a teenager presenting a case of staying overnight to a doubtful parent. "Besides, practice doesn't start for two days, and we don't have any responsibilities until then."

The last point made some sense. I settled on a deal with Greg. If he helped me unpack and we got it done, we'd go. He jumped off the couch and grabbed a box. It amazed me at how quickly the work got done. After a couple of hours, we had finished. At the time, I felt grateful for the party since it got Greg off his butt and the work done. Greg was one of those beautiful people who had a laid-back attitude about when or why things needed to get done. He would have been happy to continue to pull stuff out of boxes as he needed it. I always admired his point of view, as I couldn't rest until everything was in its place.

He and I could not have been more opposite in priority setting. He, more or less, took care of important things like food and sleep. The unimportant stuff like studying, class attendance, and paying the electric bill always fell subject to the availability of Greg's mindset. When the lights went off, or an exam would happen the next morning, Greg would jump into action. He would set whatever he was doing aside and handle the crisis. I wanted to avert crisis and tried to plan ahead most of the time. I used to yell at Greg whenever his lack of attention caused me stress and threatened to take the task away from him. Greg always grew contrite, but to his credit, he kept the task and usually did not repeat the error. He got most upset when he realized his lack of attention came to haunt me.

We decided to get dressed up in our finest Texas gear. To look at us, you would swear we came from Lubbock, Texas, instead of Brown Country, Indiana. We took the Toyota even though we figured it would prove a bear to find a parking place. Finally, we found an all-night garage structure and paid five bucks for parking. The walk only covered a couple of blocks, and when we arrived at the big party, I had to admit it seemed massive. A couple of bars had permission from the city to block off one of the streets. It was wall-to-wall students in various stages of feeling happy.

I noticed the relative preponderance of men and thought that maybe this might have been a waste of time. Greg seemed unconcerned. He told me that all it took was one, which also formed part of his general philosophy. He never got discouraged when the odds looked not to be in his favor. A couple of bands did their best to sound like Willie Nelson or Garth Brooks. The night turned out warm, as it usually did in Austin, and with the music, people, and beer, it felt magical. Greg and I caught up with a couple of the team's members and shared some laughs about summer exploits. A couple of sorority girls joined the group, and before long, we all got to line dancing. It didn't take long for more to join us, and we dominated the party space. Of course, someone came around with a bottle of tequila and shot glasses. The shots started immediately. Greg and I always avoided this headache maker. We behaved no differently this time. It always amused me the way people would purposely plan to trash themselves with stuff guaranteed to cause pain, not to mention throwing up. The way no one seemed to notice the fact that Greg and I were not partaking also seemed humorous. If they did, they never mentioned it. I guess they had a certain amount of respect connected to our decision not to overdo it.

The party progressed to the point where those of us left standing needed to get something to eat. We adjourned to the all-night slider joint. After a few burgers and a couple of pounds of fries, we called it. We said good night, and all promised to get together again real soon. Greg and I walked to the car.

"You okay to drive?" I knew Greg was okay but wanted to see if he preferred for me to drive.

We got into the car. "Yeah, I'm fine. What a party, huh? I think this was the best night in a long time." Greg started the car and pulled out of the garage. We merged onto the freeway, which took us back to the apartment.

Since it had grown dark, and I didn't want to distract Greg, I waited until he got on the road before I engaged in conversation. "I agree. It was the best. How about those two guys, doing shots and handstands?"

"I know, right? Could you see you and me trying that and swallowing the shot glass?"

"That would be my luck. I agree this was the best night. Uh, Greg, do you see that car in our lane?"

"Holy shit. I see it. Where the hell can I go? Help me, Keith. Look around. Find me a fucking way out."

The car drove in our lane and came at us full speed. Greg tried to avoid it but came up against a wall on the freeway and couldn't pull off the road. He yelled at the top of his lungs, "Oh, my God, that guy is going to hit us. Hang on, for Christ's sake."

The car hit us full force; I hit the dash, and everything went black. I could hear Greg yelling at me to wake up. He sounded frantic. I could feel his fear, and it made me shiver. Although I tried, I couldn't answer him. My teeth chattered, and I opened my mouth to speak, but nothing came out. The bile in my throat burned, and I wanted to heave. Then, wishing to end the feeling, I forced my head to the side, but couldn't get sick. I wished I could make Greg feel better and wanted to tell him everything would be fine, but I couldn't find the words. Greg continued to call my name, and his voice got further and further away until I couldn't hear him anymore. I felt so glad that he'd survived the crash, although I didn't know how. I hated to leave him, but at the time, I couldn't fight anymore and had to give in.

Oh, I guess I should explain, and I know it was a little dishonest of me not to tell you earlier, but I didn't survive. I know, I know, the dirty trick is not admitting this before. I wanted to say I was a spirit upfront but thought better of it since I felt you should get to know a little about Greg, and a story coming from a dead guy might not work right. So, now you know, Greg and I played football and grew up together. The rest of the story that leads to Greg in that bar is one that needs telling by someone who can describe all the circumstances from an objective point of view. The nice part of being dead is that the power of objectivity is a given right when crossing to the other side. I think if you stick with me, you'll see that I did it for the best.

So, let's get back to Greg. He bled from a broken nose but hadn't gotten badly hurt and, finally, got us both out of the car. He laid me on the side of the road, crying so hard that the tears diluted the blood running from his nose. The other driver slumped dead behind the wheel. The investigation would later find him dead drunk. Greg took a field sobriety test and passed. The EMTs arrived and told Greg there was nothing they could do to save me. He wouldn't believe them and refused to let go of my body. He went with me to the hospital and only gave up when a doctor told him I needed to rest now. Greg felt like he had on the day his mother walked off the edge of the stage. My dad told him it was time to let his mother rest, and those same words made Greg understand. The doctor escorted Greg to the waiting room and held him as he gave up and accepted the fact that his brother and best friend was no longer with him.

Greg felt totally alone. He called my parents and broke the news to them. Then he told them to stay in Indiana and that he would bring me home. My father broke down completely, and it is the kind of thing no child should witness. Parents are not supposed to bury their young. It's supposed to work the other way around. Greg couldn't say anything to make my dad feel better, and my mother took the phone. She cried softly but told Greg that she loved him and to be careful coming home. He told my mom he was sorry, and she tried to comfort him instead of him comforting her. The attempt to comfort the children is what parents do even if feeling a deep hurt themselves.

When Greg hung up, he stood in total shock. I think the full impact of what had happened hit him then. The full impact of how much I loved him hit me. I would have liked to give him a hug or something, but of course, in the spirit state, I found it impossible. All I could do was stand by and give him mental support. I hoped that maybe a chant or song would get through and give him a reason not to feel so alone. The feeling proved painful to me, as I'm sure it did to him. I had made him a promise when his dad died that I would do everything possible to see that he didn't get hurt. Right then, I stood helpless to keep that promise. The cruelty of the situation hit me below the belt. I wanted to be sick all over again but had no way to do it. I had become a spirit and confined to the agony of being a spectator. I couldn't even cry and felt that God had finally figured out a way to punish me for whatever sins I was guilty of committing.

Greg stayed at the hospital until they released my body. My parents arranged for a car from the local funeral home to come and pick up the remains. I say remains because I didn't think the word body was any longer part of me. It felt like looking down at a wax figure. It didn't seem real, and since I've never seen myself from all the angles that I became able to observe the body, I didn't think it looked like me. The fairly large wound on the face didn't help, but it still looked like someone else. They allowed Greg to come in and visit before they closed up the transportation package. In silence, he stood looking. He cried without making a sound. The tears rolled down his cheeks like they did when his father died. I can tell you that the ache and sadness of seeing someone you love in pain do not go away simply because you're not a part of the living world. I had a lump in my throat not curable with tears. It seems there is no crying in the afterlife, which is not a blessing. I could feel my throat getting tighter without relief and wished I could bawl my eyes out.

I reached for Greg and, as you would expect, my arms passed through him. Funny thing, though; he seemed to react to my touch. It came as a shiver, and I'm sure he could tell when I touched him. He didn't know it was me, and maybe he thought it just a chill or cool breeze. But I did it a couple of times, and each time, he had a reaction. I hoped I would be able to refine this to do some good, or at least manage to communicate with Greg when he had some stressful moments, as he was having then.

The funeral home people came in, and Greg laid his hand softly on the remains. He bowed his head, and for the first time, I felt him pray. He asked God for forgiveness and made a promise that he would make it up to my family. It was then that I knew he felt totally responsible for the accident. It wasn't his fault, but he took all the blame. I saw him going down the same path as when his mother died. He blamed himself for not being a good enough son to somehow make his mother happy. That spiral was what I'd promised him I would try and protect him from feeling. This time, I tried shouting at him that it wasn't his fault. The police even told him that he could have done nothing, as the other guy was drunk and had probably passed out behind the wheel.

John W. Howell

Finally, Greg said an amen to his prayer. The two workers closed up the container and rolled it out to a hearse. Greg got into the other funeral car, which waited in front of the hearse. He left the door open, and so I moved in beside him. I guess you might say I passed through him. Yes, he did shiver, so I made up my mind not to do that too many times. One of the men closed Greg's door, and we set off to the airport.

I hadn't thought about how I would get around in my current state. In fact, I felt so concerned about Greg that I didn't give much thought to my state at all. I grabbed this ride, but since it looked like I'd entered the afterlife, it would be logical if I could simply transport myself to wherever I wanted to go. I felt unsure how that would work, so I decided to hang with Greg and take the same transportation he took. Hopefully, a guide or something would appear that could give me a little help on what I should do. Being dead is one thing, but being all alone and not having a clue as to what happens next is quite another. I had to push down a rising panic that the afterlife was simply being without any means of controlling what happens to those you love and yourself. I flashed on the idea that maybe I'd fallen into hell after all. I had to swallow hard and try to remain calm.

We arrived at the airport, and the hearse went to the cargo area. Greg and I went into the passenger terminal. My parents had made a reservation, which Greg picked up at the counter. He had no bags except the cargo in the hold of the airplane. The people at the counter were sympathetic and wished him a safe journey. Greg went totally inside himself. He answered questions and thanked the counter personnel, but I could tell he'd gone on auto-pilot. He shuffled through security and fell into a seat at the gate. He didn't look around, deep in his thoughts. When the boarding announcement came, I felt sure Greg would continue to sit there. He surprised me by getting up and joining the line to board.

On board, all the seats around Greg were taken. I had to stand until it became clear that a seat two rows behind him remained open. He had taken off his jacket and settled in. I hoped he would get some rest. We had been up all night, and this was the first time he'd sat down. The flight would take about two hours, so maybe he might get some shuteye. I closed my eyes to see if sleeping was allowed over here. Predictably, I found no such thing. In fact, the longer I stayed up, the fresher I felt. There must not be a thing called tired on the other side. The experimentation around sleeping caused me to wonder again if I would meet up with any others on this side. I also got into a reverie about coming to the pearly gates and thought that maybe a golden road would lead to magnificent structures manned by a guy with a long white beard and wings. He would open a book and check me off as I went in. The reality I found myself in made me more depressed.

Obviously, the thinking of foolish thoughts was not outlawed, and I had to snap out of it. I had landed in some afterlife situation, and no storybook perception covered the situation. There came no flash of light or my life passing before me. Only a blackness followed by becoming aware that I no longer occupied Earth. Speaking of the planet Earth, I needed to find out what held me to the surface. Was it gravity or some other force that allowed me to sit in this seat on an airplane without drifting around the cabin? I decided to try an experiment in levitation. To that end, I closed my eyes and thought hard about rising off the seat. Although I couldn't feel anything, I had a sense of floating. When I opened my eyes, I saw I hadn't moved. I remained in the seat. So much for the idea of being capable of flight or transportation on my own. I had hoped that some of the myths of being dead would prove true. I could imagine floating above the populations and taking some hyper-speed trip to all parts of the world. Unless some of these powers came later, I seemed no better off than the living population. The only advantage I could see was that I'd become invisible, and I guessed I could pass through things. I figured I should try it out, so I got up and walked down the aisle into first class. A real test would be to walk into the cockpit of the airplane. The door stood closed and locked, and this would offer the perfect test. I held my breath and went forward. Sure enough, I went right through the door and had to stop myself from going through the windshield. Once stopped, I looked down at my feet for the first time and could see they were different in relation to the floor. They had gone almost into the floor. In fact, I more or less floated, not above but in the floor. I took a breath and clenched my arms to my body, let the breath out, and then sank through the floor. I got almost halfway to the cargo hold before I stopped the descent by inhaling again. Clearly, I could control my ascent and descent by holding my breath. It seemed like being under water. The longer I held my breath, the higher I rose. The longer I let out my breath, the lower I went. When I breathed normally, I stayed at equilibrium.

For the rest of the flight, I practiced and became quite good at moving around. When in a seat, I could float up by inhaling deeply. And letting out the air caused me to lower once again. No doors could stop me. I didn't go into the restrooms since I had no desire to come face-to-face with some hapless person on the pot. I did go through the bulkheads in front and rear. Also, I went into the hold and found I could pass easily through all the cargo as well. To see what would happen, I stuck my head through the fuselage. It felt quite interesting to see the Earth from that height. I didn't feel the air rushing by, which I did expect. I suppose I passed through it, and so met no resistance. I got a little queasy at the thought of falling completely out of the airplane and had no idea if I would be able to keep up and come back in again, as traveling at five hundred miles an hour is not something I'm sure I could do.

I decided to halt further experiments and take no more chances. When I rose back to the main cabin, I checked on Greg. He sat staring out of the window, and I imagined he thought through the situation. I wondered if he made plans on what to do about school and the team now that I was no longer there with him. Hopefully, he would just go on with his life and continue to play and maybe get picked by the pros.

Immediately, I had a flash of an idea. If I put my head inside of Greg's, could it be possible to read his thoughts? Greg would feel it, but I just had to find out. So, I stuck my head inside of Greg's and, straight away, regretted doing it. Greg jerked as if on the receiving end of a cattle prod. I, on the other hand, could see his insides, and it gave a sight I never want to repeat. The answer to the mystery brought a definite no. I felt more than thankful that it hadn't worked, as I didn't think I could repeat that move. Greg sat wide-eyed, and I hoped he just figured he'd dozed and had some dream. The guy next to him asked if he felt okay. Greg told him that he'd just had a bad dream. The guy said, "The way you twitched, it must have been a beaut." Greg shook his head and went back to looking through the window.

I couldn't help but feel he knew it was me. When I went in there, I could tell it was Greg. It wasn't the sights, exactly, but more a feeling of being in Greg's head. It seemed almost like Greg's head bade me a welcome. I shivered at the thought and went back to my seat. Another feeling I got was one of despair and contemplation. Not a positive thought or feeling. Greg was giving up. Now I needed to figure out a way to reverse that kind of thinking.

While pondering Greg's issue, the plane started its initial approach to the Indianapolis Airport. Before long, we rolled along the ground. When we got off the plane, a guy from the Brown County Funeral Home stood waiting. He had Greg's name on a poster card. When Greg reached him, he expressed his sympathies and directed Greg to follow him. We all walked to baggage claim and, since Greg had no bag, straight out into a parking area. A large silver hearse waited in the lot. The man directed Greg to get in the passenger side. I looked and saw no other car. It appeared that this hearse was it. I moved through the side and into the back.

The hearse moved to a restricted area, and the driver showed some identification and then got directed to a cargo area. A casket sat on some pallets. The funeral guy knew what to do. He pulled a carriage-like thing out of the back of the hearse and lifted the casket one end at a time and put the carriage underneath. Greg asked if he could help, but the guy told him not to worry and that he had it. When he pulled a lever, the carriage popped to waist high. He then rolled it to the back of the hearse and eased it in. As he did so, the carriage collapsed under the casket. The whole thing took two minutes.

Greg and the guy got back into the hearse. I had no choice but to get in the back. Despite not having much room, I managed to lie down and take some space below the remains in the casket. The trip would take about an hour, so I knew I could do it. I made sure to breathe evenly so as not to pass through the remains accidentally. Although the body was me, I had no desire to see any of my old insides.

The ride took over an hour due to heavy traffic on the south side of town. The driver tried to make small talk with Greg and got mixed results. Greg answered questions with single word responses but didn't add anything extra. The driver gave up after a while, and we finished the trip in forced silence. Upon pulling into the funeral home, I could see my parents in the parking lot. They must have just arrived themselves because they were getting out of their car. My dad came over to the hearse, and the driver rolled down the window.

"Is that my son?" Dad said.

The driver nodded, and then Greg opened his door and got out. My mom wrapped her arms around him, and they both had a good cry. My dad came to them and put his arms around both. I would never have imagined how hard it would be to see your parents suffering as much as they did. As I mentioned, there is no crying in the afterlife, which makes it hard. I passed through the hearse and went up to the three of them, wanting to join and feel the comfort. However, I thought I'd better not since I might cause the same reaction like the one in Greg. Instead, I stood close without touching, and finally, they broke apart and went into the home.

The hearse pulled around to the back, and I assumed the body would get unloaded and processed in the rear. It struck me how I used a term you would associate with an animal carcass. I felt a little guilty, as it seemed obvious I had no feelings for my old corporeal self. Was this a normal reaction once a body and spirit separated from each other? A little twinge of regret came at knowing I could not go to the internet to Google this kind of thing and obtain the answer. I would have to be satisfied with finding out the answer on my own.

Deep in thought about my personal problems, I realized that just because I had died, the process of self-centeredness hadn't gone away. I also realized that I had a lot to learn about being a spirit if that's what I'd become. It grew clear that I would have to pick carefully through a trial-and-error method of problem-solving, as I didn't think there would be a class on spiritualism.

Then, shaking off the thoughts, I went inside the funeral home. I found my parents and Greg talking to the director and arrived to hear some of the arrangements. Greg wanted to deliver the eulogy, and my parents told him he didn't have to if he didn't feel up to it. He assured them he did. I, for one, believed him since he had a certain air of resolution about him. He may have come to peace with what had happened. I hoped this would prove true, as seeing him suffer felt too much to bear.

The conversation finished, and the director told my parents that they could begin the viewing tomorrow morning at ten o'clock. My parents thanked him, and with my dad's arm on Greg's shoulder, they rose and left the home. I passed through the wall and beat them to the car. My dad got in the front, and my mom insisted that Greg should ride in front with him. My mom got in the back, and I did too. I looked at my mom, and her eyes brimmed with tears. She used her lace-bordered handkerchief to catch them before they could roll down her cheeks. How I wished I could have helped her get over her pain, but I knew I could do nothing. "It will be okay, Mom," I said. "I'm not hurting, nor do I believe I'm in hell, so I think, all in all, it could be worse."

I stopped talking when she looked me straight in the eye, and I swear she could see me. "Oh, Keith," she said. Her voice came out soft and filled with sorrow. "I so wanted you to be healthy and happy, and now you're gone."

"I know, Mom, but it's just one of those things that none of us could have predicted."

My mom paused and continued to look at me. She didn't look out through the window but straight into my eyes. I felt so sure she could see me that I reached up to touch her face. So much, I wanted to caress her and tell her I loved her. My hand passed through her skin, and I pulled it back. She didn't jump like Greg, but she did reach up and place her hand where I'd touched her. Her eyes overflowed, and this time, she didn't try to stop them. After whispering, "My son," her mouth turned up at the edges, and a peaceful look came over her. She leaned back in the seat and continued to look over to where I sat. I still believe that we'd made a connection and that I'd provided some comfort. I would hope that, someday, I will have the chance to find out for sure. In any case, I felt so good about following Greg to my home and getting involved in this last farewell. I had a thought after thinking of the word farewell. Would I get released to go where spirits go after the ceremony was over? I had heard some people talk about spirits hanging around until they felt sure their loved ones were okay before going off to the permanent, eternal place. I supposed that this would be another mystery which would become solvable over time. Of course, at that time, I had no idea that I would be present when Greg put his head on his hands in the bar, making the supposition of release doubtful.

Chapter Six

The next morning saw us all in the car heading for the funeral home. I had checked in on Greg, and he had a good night's sleep, which pleased me. My mom and dad proved less fortunate. They were up and down most of the night. They talked a little but mostly lay in the bed looking separately at the ceiling or the wall. I wished they had more comfort for each other but, apparently, this kind of grief is a solitary thing.

The night provides a long period of inactivity for a spirit. Since they have no need to sleep, they have little to do when others are so engaged. New to the whole concept, I didn't have much experience in how to fill the time. I learned that a state exists that, with practice, a spirit can enter. I called it a suspension. It's where the mind can clear and time becomes an unconscious thing. I can compare it to the nap state a dog goes into when its owners leave it for any length of time. When the owners return, it is almost as if they never left, as the dog had no idea of the relevance of time. The owners were there at one time, gone, and then came back. In between remained a blank. It took me a while to master the technique. The first night in my parent's home lasted forever. I felt so glad to see the sunrise since I knew there would be movement, at least.

The funeral home proved empty except for the director. He showed Greg and my parents to the parlor where the remains stood on display. The room looked quite large and seemed way too big for three people. I didn't think anyone else would show up. The three walked to the casket, holding hands. I went around to the other side, and it amazed me at how peaceful the expression appeared on the face. Truly, I looked like I was sleeping. The technicians had done a marvelous job on the facial wound. Almost no way remained to tell there ever was one.

Greg and my parents grew tearful and appeared frozen while they gazed down. Greg reached out and adjusted the tie slightly. He explained to my mother that I always liked the knot with a little dimple and wouldn't want anyone to see it the way it was. Greg started crying again, and both parents joined him. I couldn't stay any longer and went out to the lobby. The home had three other showings. I went from parlor to parlor to see if anyone like me hung around. Nope—just little ole me. A few of the other deceased's relatives had arrived, and most looked in a similar condition as my parents.

This death thing is hard for the ones left behind. Was I getting punished for some reason by being forced to watch Greg and my parents suffer so? I could do nothing to help them, and as a result, I suffered right along with them. Since there were no other spirits around, it must be that I had gotten singled out for this torture. Upon returning to the room with my remains, I arrived just as a few people filed into the room. My parents and Greg formed a little line to welcome them. A book lay open near the door, and people could sign and leave messages. How many families go back and read all these expressions of sympathy? For the first time, I became aware of the flower smell and looked into the room to see a number of flower sprays. Then, walking further into the room, I took a closer look. The scent smelled wonderful, and the roses especially beautiful. A large spray sat at the head of the casket with the card turned outward, so I could read it. It came from the University, expressing sorrow for my parents' loss. A few of the others also had visible cards. I felt shocked at how many came from various organizations at UT. The team bouquet seemed especially touching, and I believed I'd died way too early. Yesterday, I was pretty much okay with the way things were, but today had a feeling of loss. The outpouring of sympathy, from those who I would never have expected to notice my passing, awoke this feeling.

More and more people filed into the parlor. I saw my high-school football coach and his family. The coach hugged Greg, and the two of them had a good cry. I had to believe they felt the same sense of loss that I now did. A lot of the people, I didn't know and assumed them my parents' friends. Several old teachers made an appearance. They told teacher stories to my parents, which seemed to cheer them all up. I had to laugh when the auto mechanic teacher related how he suggested I find a different class. He knew I wasn't adept mechanically and had been kind enough to point it out. He pulled out a big red handkerchief and wiped his eyes after the story. I always thought his heart was large, and now I could see it as so.

The day passed with more of the same. It pleased me to see a few of the old high-school gang show up. Since college hadn't started yet, I guessed the timing of my passing had proven perfect in terms of those who'd arrived in town. Greg and my parents finally called it at around nine o'clock, and we all left. The ride home passed in total silence. The three seemed exhausted. They'd only had brief breaks to grab something to eat and never left the home all together. They hadn't wanted anyone to arrive and not manage to find at least two of them. Tomorrow, the showing would happen in the morning, and then the burial in the afternoon. At least after, they would get some rest. The only good part of this ritual was that it kept their minds off the obvious grief each had inside. Besides that, I couldn't see how this burial process was useful or necessary.

When Greg and I sat down one time and talked about our funerals, we'd both decided we would just like a quick ceremony and do the take-and-bake option. Cremation sounded like the perfect way to handle the whole mess. An urn and some ashes spread around, and it's over. I wanted mine spread wherever I'd felt happiest. I believed it would be near or on the ocean, but I left the exact location up in the air. Greg wanted his to get released from the top of the World Trade Center so that he could haunt Wall Street forever. I guess he figured he would be a big man on the street and would have a symbolic presence. He did detail his made-up news story in the Wall Street Journal regarding the halting of trading for a minute in his honor while the ashes drifted down from above. We both laughed mightily at the vision of New Yorkers looking up only to get a load of ash in their eyes.

When we had these fantasies, we always thought we would be a couple of old codgers and never contemplated not making it past twenty. Clearly, they didn't plan a cremation, and my parents would go through the traditional ceremony because they didn't know any different. I also believed that the thought of not being able to go to a place where the body rests gave a degree of separation neither could handle.

The night got taken up with my parents answering the phone and door. People kept calling and dropping off food. Our refrigerator soon filled, and my mom stressed over the quantity of food that could go to waste. My dad assured her that even if the food went to waste, it was what people felt they could do to help, and we should be grateful.

By the time the lights went out, it had gone past midnight. I couldn't detect if Greg or my parents still cried. I reckon, exhausted, they had no more tears to shed. How I wished I could have told them to drink plenty of water to rehydrate. Of course, rehydration would probably lead to more tears, so maybe it remained best I couldn't communicate with them.

The dawn broke at long last, and I could hear my parents moving around in their room. I passed into Greg's room, and he still lay in bed. I sat in the chair across from his bed. While watching him sleep, I thought of what would happen after the burial. Would this make for the event to cause me to go off wherever I was supposed to go? I wished I had an answer. While I sat thinking, Greg's eyes popped open. "Keith?" he said. I jumped off the chair and asked him if he could see me. He gave no indication that he heard the question. He laid there, staring at the chair, and finally rose on one elbow. I could have sworn he heard or felt something. It could have been that he was having a dream, but why say my name just as I sat thinking of where I would go? I couldn't believe it a coincidence and still thought there must exist some way to bridge the gap between our worlds. Greg jumped out of bed and went about getting ready for my body's last day above ground, and I had no time to continue with any experiments.

The visitation at the funeral home went well. It gladdened me to see a number of classmates from UT make it. Probably, they used the funeral as a good excuse for a monumental road trip. I sure hope they had a little fun mixed in the serious business of mourning. My coaches also turned out. The head coach, offensive, and defensive coach all came to my parents and Greg to express their sympathies. A few team members all came in at once. They wore their game jerseys. The sight of them caused my dad to fall apart completely. The realization that I used to lead this team must have hit him along with the reality that I wouldn't do it anymore and taken him like a wave. Honestly, I thought he would pass out. Greg came over and helped him to a chair. The team gathered around him, and each placed their hand on him as if about to heal his deep wounds just by touching. In unison, they recited the Lord's Prayer, and my father gathered strength and looked from one to the other with gratitude in his eyes. The rest of the people in the room seemed struck dumb by the show of solidarity and love from these young men. As they say, there wasn't a dry eye in the house except for mine.

The graveside ceremony proved moving. Greg said some beautiful things about our love for each other. He also drew an analogy to running a relay race. He told everyone that he would now need to run the race alone and would feel challenged to continue, lacking the support we gave each other. For the first time, I saw in Greg's eyes a fear of the unknown. He'd always been the most confident between the two of us. He always took the "what is the worst that could happen" road. I now saw that he felt unsure of himself and would require more time to pull himself together. I said a little prayer that whatever powers that be would allow me to stay with Greg until he felt like his old self. Although hard to explain, I had a funny feeling that my prayer would resonate. I didn't pay attention to what others said about me. Finally, it came time to leave, and we all went back to my parents' house. A few of the neighbors had set up a spread of food and drink. I thought it a fitting end to the day and hoped everyone would get drunk and move on. Specifically, I wished peace for my parents and Greg.

The next morning, Greg told my parents he wanted to head back to school. My dad took him to the airport, and he and I caught a flight back to Austin. Greg kept to himself on the flight, and when we arrived, he got a cab to our apartment. I knew coming back to the apartment would prove traumatic, but Greg took it all in with a degree of calm that I hadn't expected. He closed the door to my room, and then sat down and wrote a note to my parents, asking what he should do with my stuff. I could almost guess they would tell him to pack it up and send it. I think that writing the letter gave Greg a way to put off packing for as long as possible.

Before long, word got out that Greg had returned to school. A constant flow of our friends visited. Classmates and team members. Greg looked like he appreciated all the company. Most of the time, they told stories about me, and this cheered Greg immensely. When all of them left at the end of the day, Greg ended up alone again; not a good time for him. He had serious guilt that he needed to offload. I hoped time would take care of it.

One morning, about two days after Greg got back, the coach paid a visit. Greg grew surprised to see him at the door when he answered the knock.

"Greg, may I come in?" the coach said.

Greg apologized for standing in the doorway and, with a wave, invited the coach to enter. "It was such a surprise seeing you at the door. I didn't mean to keep you standing in the hall."

"No problem, Greg." The coach came in and took one of the easy chairs.

"Would you like something? Coffee? Water?" Obviously, Greg felt flustered in the presence of the coach.

"I'm good. I came by to see how you're doing and to find out when you think you can make practice?"

This caught Greg off-guard, and he didn't say anything for a moment. He took way too much time to answer, and the coach got a little unsettled waiting for a response. Finally, Greg said, "I'm not sure I'll stay on the team, coach."

The coach and I both sat upright. "What do you mean, you're not sure?"

"I have all these feelings inside, and I'm not sure I can go out there with Keith gone."

"Do you think Keith would want you to quit?" I had to hand it to the coach. He hit the nail right on the head, and Greg reacted like the coach had slapped him across the face.

"I-I haven't thought about what Keith would like. He's not here anymore."

"I understand, Greg, but you and he were so close, and I think maybe it's time that you do consider what Keith might want you to do."

"Coach, it's my fault Keith died. How can I live with that?"

"A dumbshit, drunk out of his gourd, killed Keith. How can this be your fault?"

"You can say that, but you weren't in the car. You don't have your best friend's last breath on your conscience."

"You're right. I cannot hope to understand your feelings. I just know logic tells me you should go out on the field and work this shit through. What could it hurt?" The coach made some serious strides. I don't believe that Greg had a comeback for logic. He'd gotten so wrapped up in the emotion and all geared for self-punishment.

"I guess it can't hurt, coach. I know playing without Keith will be a big adjustment, though."

"Yes, it will be a big adjustment for all of us. We don't have a quarterback. I'm afraid I put all my eggs into the Keith basket."

Right then, I thought hard about having Greg take over as quarterback. He knew the plays better than anyone. Hell, he was the brains behind many of them. I said out loud, "Why doesn't Greg do the quarterbacking?"

The coach looked over to where I stood as if he heard me, although impossible. "Greg, would you consider taking over as quarterback?"

"M-Me? I never thought of myself as a quarterback. I'm not sure I could handle it."

"Of course, you can. You know every play and each person's responsibility in those plays. This kind of knowledge is what it takes to make a good quarterback. You might need some passing instruction, but you're a natural leader, and I'll bet you'll be great." The coach might just have begun to convince Greg.

Greg looked down, and I found it hard to tell what he sat thinking. In the past, he would look down, and then, usually, he'd look up and say something like, "Let's do it."

After about a minute, Greg looked up and said, "You make a good salesman, coach. Let's do it." Then he broke into a wide grin, which matched the one on the coach's face. They both got up and shook hands, and then the coach pulled Greg into a hug.

"We have a practice this afternoon at two o'clock. I'll meet you on the field."

Greg nodded, and I could see he felt a little choked up. He cleared his throat. "I'll be there."

The coach gave him a couple of pats on the back and set off toward the door. "I think you're doing the right thing, Greg. I know you'll do great."

"Thanks, coach." Greg walked the coach into the hallway, and after he'd gone, he leaned against the closed door and wiped a trickle of tears from his face. "I hope you're right, coach," he said. Greg never talked to himself much, but I could understand it under the circumstances.

Greg then got himself ready to go to the practice field. He gathered up his bag and checked to see if he had everything there. He noticed he had no deodorant and went into the bathroom. A container of mine sat on the counter. "Keith. May I borrow this?"

"Of course, you can," I said.

"Thanks."

The interchange spooked me utterly. Though not real, it seemed so natural. Ready to go, Greg stopped by the open door to have a look around. "Wish me luck, Keith." He closed the door, and the idea that Greg had adopted a coping mechanism struck me. He talked to a spirit. I grew convinced he wasn't of the belief that I was there, but counted on the spirit for support.

I had to hurry to catch up. Upon passing through the door, I saw that a pretty co-ed had stopped Greg. Because I came up when they'd almost done talking, I could only catch a little of the conversation. The co-ed told Greg to take care of himself, and Greg assured her he would. "Give me a call later," she said as they separated.

If I were still on the Earth, I would badger Greg with a bunch of questions about who that girl was and what did she mean to him. Since I'd landed in this never-never land, such an interrogation remained out of the question. I had to content myself with hanging out until Greg gave her a call later. It frustrated me to be out of control. So far, I hadn't seen much advantage in being a spirit floating around and watching everyone else live their lives without any interaction. Maybe this was what hell was supposed to be. I couldn't imagine having done anything to warrant going to hell. I'd never so much as harmed anyone. Certainly, I hadn't stolen anything nor coveted anyone's wife. Well, I had better slow up a minute. There was that time when I mowed Franklin's lawn, and the wife came out into the backyard in that bikini. Oh, come on. That can't give enough to warrant sending a soul into eternal damnation. I only thought about what she would look like without the suit. I never did or saw anything.

We got to the field house, and Greg went in to change into his practice uniform. I took the opportunity to wander around and listen in on some of the other players' conversations. The majority opinion held that Greg would make a good quarterback. This support seemed a good thing, as Greg would need the team on his side if he were to be successful.

He jogged out to where the coach stood. The coach gave Greg a pat on the back, and they laid the plan for practice. The coach wanted Greg to warm up his arm and assigned one of the backs to run some patterns. The drill was for Greg to take the ball from the center and pretend he was getting rushed, and then toss the ball to the receiver, who would run a pattern down the field. The first three or so passes didn't make it far enough for the receiver to get his hands on the ball. A look of concern settled on Greg's face. I had seen it a hundred times. If he didn't get his worry under control, then things would get worse.

The center snapped the ball, and Greg faded back. I screamed for him to take a step forward and let the ball go. To my amazement, he did just as I'd yelled. The ball hung in the air forever and arced beautifully into the receiver's hands. The toss must have been a fifty yarder. The coach couldn't contain his joy. He jumped straight up into the air and threw his hands up with the classic touchdown sign.

The rest of the practice went well. Greg got into a groove and threw about twenty down and long passes. He seemed an even better passer than me, ever. His distance amazed me, and he would just need some practice in the fundamentals like throwing out front or behind the receiver, depending on the defense. All the skill of the position would come when he got more experience. For now, the fact that he had distance remained the most important thing.

The coach called it a day, obviously pleased. He and Greg discussed the finer points, and the coach told Greg he looked forward to the first game. Greg looked a little nervous at the mention of a game. "Relax," the coach said. "The game is over two weeks away. You'll be ready for the pros by then."

Greg laughed and thanked the coach for his help. The coach told him it was his pleasure, and Greg turned to jog into the locker room. "Greg," the coach said. Greg looked back at him. "It will turn out okay. Trust me."

"I trust you, coach. I just miss Keith."

"We all do, but we gotta go on."

Greg nodded and continued to the locker room. I hung back to hear what the coach thought. His assistant coaches gathered around, and he told them that Greg had the makings of a first-rate quarterback. "We'll need to help him get over Keith because, right now, he's fighting guilt, and his biggest problem will be feeling bad about playing better than Keith, which I see as a real possibility." The assistant coaches all pledged to help any way they could. Satisfied, the coach signaled the assistants to follow him into the field house.

Greg took a few more minutes but finally came outside. We walked back to the apartment. Would Greg go to the dining hall for dinner? Right then, it looked like he didn't plan to go there straight away. We entered the apartment, and Greg flopped on the couch and pulled out his cell. "Hi, Terry, this is Greg."

I now understood the reason for coming straight home. Greg wanted to call that girl who had the name of Terry. I didn't know he felt interested in a girl. He'd never mentioned her, and I don't think he ever went out with her, but here he sat, talking like they were old friends. I should amend that—they talked like they were dating. Of course, Greg looked happy while they chatted. I guess he'd gotten serious and never let me know. I'll bet he missed her during the funeral. He talked to her as if they had been apart for months instead of a few days. In the end, they agreed to meet for dinner and hung up. Greg went and changed his shirt. Him missing her gave a real tangible sign of a serious thing between them. Greg hardly ever gave his appearance a thought, and to get him to change would be like you asking him to remove a foot.

At dinner, Greg seemed as relaxed as he used to before all this unpleasantness. He and the girl laughed and enjoyed each other's company. The conversation remained all about what was going on at school. My name didn't come up in the first half hour, and it would have been great had that continued for the rest of the evening. Of course, Greg had to throw a small clinker in the conversation. "You know, I miss him," he said.

I wished that Terry had asked who Greg was talking about but realized she had way too many manners for that kind of statement. Instead, she said, "I know it must be awful to live where Keith lived since there are reminders everywhere."

"That's just part of it. I'm taking his place on the team, and I wish I felt good about that."

"Maybe you should find someone to talk to about this."

"What do you mean, someone to talk to?"

"I mean a professional who can get to the bottom of what bothers you and give you some advice on how to overcome it."

"I suppose you're right. It might be a good idea."

"The University has councilors on staff."

"I reckon I need a full-fledged shrink. Those psych majors and Ph.D. candidates are half nuts themselves."

Terry threw back her head and laughed loudly, exposing her long white neck. Greg joined in the laughter, pleased with her response. The subject of Keith never came up for the rest of the evening. The two finished dinner and walked back to Terry's dorm. Stood by the front door, Greg grew a little hesitant about what he should do next. "Can we go out again?" he said. I must say that struck me as the dumbest thing he could have said, and Terry's response proved so predictable.

"If you ask me out, I would say we could."

Greg's face turned red. "Would you like to have dinner with me tomorrow?"

"I would be delighted."

Greg felt so pleased that he grabbed Terry in what could only resemble a bear hug. "Easy, cowboy. I'm a girl, you know."

Greg let her go and apologized.

Terry put her fingers on his mouth to stop the words. "No need. I love your enthusiasm." She kissed him on the cheek and turned to go inside.

"I'll call after practice is over."

"I'll be waiting." She then disappeared through the big oak door.

Greg had a big smile on his face and walked home with a spring in his step. He whistled while he walked. For the first time, I heard some funny messages. Words spoken as if over a poor long-distance connection.

I could make out certain words but had trouble with the context, as there were no sentences. I moved closer to Greg and, suddenly, realized the words came from him. When I looked closely, I couldn't see his lips move. There could only be one answer; I could read Greg's mind.

Chapter Seven

Greg got up early and ready for his day. I kept close and listened for more words. He didn't disappoint me when he got to thinking about practice. He went over the plays in his head. Although he used no sentences, I could make out the total context. Greg thought about Terry a couple of times and wondered what she was doing right then. He had fallen for her. When he looked at the clock, I could have sworn he said, "Whoops, quarter to ten. Gotta go." He never moved his lips, and this made for the first time I could make out a complete sentence. I hoped this meant the mind reading skill would get better over time.

We walked to practice, and while on the way, I picked up a bunch of different thoughts from Greg. He appreciated the beautiful morning, which seemed good to me. He had a nasty thought about a car that ran through the crosswalk. He also had an appreciative feeling about a group of students, chatting excitedly about one of their classes. I never realized how many thoughts went through the mind at any one time. There must be a hundred a minute. Even something as obscure as a loose dog produces a thought on what to do or not do about it. The mind seems like a computer processor, spewing out lines of code by the second. My big fear was that I wouldn't manage to get the important messages out of the clutter. I would have to practice selective mind reading.

So far, the powers that I had accumulated in my current state had produced more problems than solutions. I hoped time would be the secret sauce used to sort out some of my lack of capability. No manual came with this condition, and I felt sure I wasn't meant to come out of the box with all the answers.

We got to practice, and Greg spent the rest of the morning running drills and working with the offensive team. So far, everything looked on target. The coach let Greg know that the afternoon would be a practice game with the defense. The game would be the test of whether Greg could run the plays under pressure. Everyone hoped so because the backup quarterback was a first-year freshman and no one believed him ready to run the team.

The afternoon came around quickly, and Greg kept wiping his hands on a towel. The wiping of hands gave a sign of his nervousness. He used to do it as a receiver. In fact, some teams believed that every time Greg wiped his hands, he would be the one to get the ball. After a while, Greg used the towel on each play to throw them off track. I listened to Greg, and he had a number of self-doubts running through his head. He beat them down, but for how long, I couldn't be sure.

The first two plays against the defense went well. Both times, the defense put on a tremendous blitz, and Greg ran back a couple of yards. He managed to avoid a tackle, and then stepped forward into the pocket and got off two nice passes. Unfortunately, the next couple of plays didn't go all that well. The first saw Greg bobble the ball, and luckily, he fell on it. The next was an option play, and Greg handed the ball to the back, and that player got tackled immediately. The coach halted play and asked Greg if he felt okay. Greg assured him that the last two items were a fluke. The coach walked back off the field and blew his whistle for play to resume.

Greg huddled up with the team and told them to forget the playbook. He designed a play that he called a triple option.

They broke, and the ball snapped on the count. Greg dropped back as if to pass. The defense all rushed forward to sack him. He then flipped the ball behind him to the halfback, who ran toward the sideline. The halfback stopped, which drew the pass defenders off their coverage. Then he fired a pass to a lone receiver standing in the end zone. It gave a touchdown for the offensive team. The coach blew the whistle and came running back to the field. "What the hell was that?" he yelled.

"I call it a triple option." Greg stayed cool.

"I've never seen anything like it. Brilliant." The coach smiled broadly. "How many more tricks like that do you have?"

"I guess I can make up some more. Making up plays is what I do."

"I heard about that but didn't know there were any more plays to get invented."

"It depends on how the defense lines up. That triple came out of the fact that I noticed the pass defenders got lazy. If they thought the play was a run, they let the guy they were covering go. I faked a pass to get the line to commit to a pass rush, which took them out of the field of play. I then gave the halfback the ball, so the pass defenders would assume it was a run and stop defending the pass receivers. As you can see, it worked. In a game, I could call this play if I saw the defenders behaving the same way."

"Okay, we need to get some of these down, so the team will know what is going on."

"Right, but they also work if the rest of the team does what they normally do. The line needs to block, and the receivers need to go down the field. So, that leaves just three of us who need to know what's going on with the running back, the center, and me."

The coach called practice for the day, and he and Greg went into the team conference to diagram some plays. They worked for about two hours or so, and when finished, the coach seemed pleased. The coach told Greg he could hardly wait to try the plays. Greg felt pleased as well. He felt he had made a real contribution, and that made him feel good. He and the coach called it an evening, and Greg called Terry. We all met for dinner, and Greg dominated the conversation for an hour or so. Terry never took her eyes off him, and I could tell she had an interest in what he said. She asked about the prospect this year, and he expressed a thought that the team would take the Big Twelve championship and go on to the national championship as well. Terry couldn't help but join in with Greg's enthusiasm. They chatted and laughed until the dining room personnel asked them to leave so that they could finish cleaning. Greg looked at his watch, and I think he knew he'd better get back to the apartment since he needed to get a good night's sleep before tomorrow's practice.

He shuffled his feet and hemmed and hawed about saying goodnight.

"Is something wrong?"

"No, erm, I just. Well, I pretty much dominated the conversation tonight. I didn't even ask how your day went."

"Please, I had a lovely time and got so interested in your discussion that I didn't give it a thought. It's okay. Believe me."

Greg searched her eyes for an indication of hurt feelings. He gave no evidence that he thought she was anything but truthful. Greg gave her a hug and walked her back to her dorm. They said good night with a quick kiss and went their separate ways. I figured I would stay with Terry a minute to see if, in fact, she had any hurt feelings.

She went into her room and called a friend. I got from one side of the conversation that Terry felt okay about the evening and a little confused as to why Greg believed he had somehow behaved selfishly about the conversation. She loved hearing all about his exploits. This friend seemed impressed that Terry had begun seeing the quarterback.

"What do you mean catch of the year?" Terry said.

She listened and then had to admit that her friend had it right. She repeated the fact that if the team did make the national championships, Greg would become a hero. Then she gave the opinion that he would also get a professional contract. Terry wondered aloud to her friend what it would be like to be married to a football player. Her friend asked a question, and in response, Terry said that Greg wanted to go to business school for his MBA and thought maybe he could probably do that in the offseason. In the discussion, no question arose that she wanted to be part of Greg's life and she seemed fairly sure he reciprocated. The phone call ended, and it became obvious that Terry felt happy but tired. I slipped away before she got ready for bed. I felt unsure how the powers would take a spirit becoming a voyeur and wasn't about to find out.

When I got to Greg's place, it became obvious that he'd gone home and immediately to bed. He lay sound asleep, and I wondered at the time if he'd given any more thought to his discussion with Terry.

Greg did, indeed, lead the team to a Big Twelve championship. They won eleven games and faced Alabama, ranked number one, with UT as number two for what would turn out to be the national championship for the winner. Greg also got entered into the running for the Heisman Trophy.

The day before the game, my parents came to Austin and got a hotel room. He wasn't sure they would make it and so grew surprised when they called and told him they had arrived. He apologized for not being able to meet them for dinner and explained that the team had gotten locked down until the game. The parents felt disappointed, but Dad said, "Don't worry, son. We can meet up after the game. Your mother and I don't leave until Monday, so we can have dinner Sunday night."

"That sounds great, Dad. I'm sorry."

"No problem. You take care, son, and good luck tomorrow."

"Thanks, Dad." Greg hung up and set to thinking that maybe his dad felt more disappointed than he'd let on. He hoped not. An idea came to him that if he couldn't have dinner with them, maybe Terry could. He dialed Terry's number.

"Hello?" Terry sounded as if she was in a good mood. It pleased Greg that she didn't feel bummed out by not seeing him tonight.

"Hi, Terry. Greg."

"Gee, I recognize your voice." Greg could hear the good humor in her words. "What's going on?"

"I just got a call from my parents."

"Oh, Greg, what's wrong?"

Greg paused for a moment thinking back on referring to Keith's parents as his parents. Somehow the transition had happened where he thought of Keith's parents as his. In fact, he hadn't mentioned the circumstances of his background to Terry. Not that he intended to hide something; the opportunity never came up, and now it didn't matter. Time made his silence awkward, so he needed to answer her question. "Nothing. Everything's fine. It's just they've arrived in town, and I can't have dinner with them and wondered if you could stand to do the honors for me."

"You mean they're here in Austin?"

"Yes. At the Best Western Motel."

"Well, this will cost you." Greg heard the slightest beginning of a laugh.

"Anything. I will owe you big time."

"I was just having some fun at your expense. I would be glad to have dinner with them. It won't be too awkward for them, will it?"

"Awkward? How?"

71

"You and I are good friends, and I would hope by having dinner, they won't read any more into it."

"Is there any more to read?"

"Other than I would like to stay with you forever, I don't think so."

"Ah, I just wanted to make sure. No, it won't be awkward for them. How about you?"

"Me? I'm like a Rhino when it comes to thick skin. I shall charm them and answer any questions they have with nothing but straight lies."

Greg and Terry shared a laugh. He asked her to remain by the phone while he called his parent to make sure they felt okay with the plan.

"Hi, Dad, it's Greg."

"I do recognize your voice. I'm glad the medication is finally working for me."

Greg laughed at the joke. "Although I can't meet you for dinner, I have a nice substitution. I told you about Terry, and we're seeing each other."

"Yes, you did. How is she doing?"

"Just fine, thanks. How would you feel about having dinner with her tonight?"

"I think the honor would be ours. How'll she feel being in the company of a couple of old folks?"

"I think she will love it. How about if I have her meet you at the motel. She can then take you two to a nice place."

"Okay, she chooses the place, and I got the bill."

"Okay, Dad. She'll come get you at seven-thirty."

"Can we make it seven? Your mom and I haven't had anything since breakfast this morning."

"Okay, but promise you'll have a little snack. That's almost three hours from now."

"Okay, son. Take care. We'll look forward to it."

Greg hung up and called Terry. He let her know the arrangements and said to get a cab. "I know you don't have a car, and I didn't want my parents out late trying to drive around. I forgot to ask them if they had a rental car, but I guess it doesn't make any difference."

"Everything will be fine. Yes, I'll get a cab and then take them to a good place. I'm thinking of Antoine's. What do you think?"

"Great. They'll love it. Thanks, Terry."

They said their goodbyes. Greg didn't mention anything about the butterflies in his stomach. The full impact of tomorrow's game had come down on his head a couple of hours earlier. He sat watching a news broadcast, and before he knew it, his picture came on the screen. The commentator listed some of the good and bad points of his seasonal performance that the Heisman voters would take into account. He sat mesmerized by what the guy had to say. The announcer pointed out Greg's penchant to hold the ball too long. Holding the ball led to a number of sacks, which his competition didn't have. Greg always tried to convince himself he didn't think the Heisman would get given to him. And seeing some of his weaknesses broadcast to the world gave him a sinking feeling that his belief might just come true. Greg hit the remote and took solace in the dark screen.

Since watching the show, he'd started acting funny. I'd seen this situation a hundred times growing up. He must think that he didn't belong there, leading his team to a championship. I imagined his inner voice did its best to sneak up and kill him. I saw by his expression and furrowed brow that he rolled over how he should have saved his mother, and then he set to worrying about killing me. Finally, he got up and stood in front of the mirror in the bathroom and repeated over and over, "I am the champion. I am the champion and deserve the Heisman trophy."

This little pep talk helped. He felt a little better. His face took on the countenance of a winner. To get placed in this position wasn't something Greg had planned. I know from being a witness that he went to each game as if going to play his best. If the situation came around that they lost then, as he told his teammates, he wanted to make sure it came down to a matter of the other team playing better and not that he or the rest of the team didn't do their best. This year, losing became a moot point, so he dismissed his feelings for the time being. Tomorrow could be another win or the first loss this year. Either way, he would play his best.

Greg decided to join the team for dinner. He felt good that Terry would take care of his parents. The team meals always proved fun. The guys would have a bunch of good jokes, and the coach would join in. Various members took the opportunity to poke fun at each other. They roasted everyone who had made significant contributions the week before. Greg remembered when he got the ball and kept it for a run that should have only lasted five yards or so. He'd picked up a couple of blocks and avoided a few tacklers and, eventually, made a touchdown after a thirty-five-yard run. At the team dinner the next week, he had picked up the nickname of Crazy Legs Petros. The kicker in one game made a fifty-one-yard field goal and got labeled Golden Toe. All in good fun. The only downside came from the hurt feelings of those who didn't receive a razzing. I left the boys and went see how Terry and the parents were doing.

Chapter Eight

I arrived in time to see that Terry got out of the cab and asked the driver to wait. She walked into the motel. An elderly couple waited across the lobby. She went directly to them. "Hello, Mr. and Mrs. Petros. I'm Terry." Both had kind smiles, and Ned rose, extending his hand.

"Please, call me Ned," he said. Terry took his hand and felt amazed at its softness. She had expected a little more roughness given that Ned stood at six foot three. "This is my wife, Marie."

"Pleased to meet both of you. I hope you're ready for a good dinner."

"We are indeed, dear," Marie said. "We come from Indiana, and sometimes we appreciate having new things to experience."

"I will act as your guide, then. Are you ready?"

Both nodded, and Marie rose, so Terry led them to the door and pointed to the cab. "Our chauffeur awaits." The parents seemed a little surprised with the cab. "This is the easiest way since neither Greg nor I have a car."

The parents got into the back seat, and Terry pulled up one of the jump seats and joined them. She gave directions to the cab driver, and they pulled away.

"Tell us about yourself," Marie said to Terry.

"Now, Marie," Ned said. "We don't want to put Terry on the spot the whole night, do we?"

Terry waved off his concern and said, "Don't worry about me. I'm more than happy to tell you anything you want to know. After all, I *am* dating your son."

"You and Greg are a couple, then?" Marie took the initiative while Ned gave her a stern look, which she failed to acknowledge.

"Well, couple is a hard term. We prefer to say friends, as we haven't made any plans. I feel so excited to be with you tonight. I do have some questions about Greg's childhood."

Marie and Ned looked at each other, and Terry saw that something wasn't getting said.

"Did I say something wrong?"

Ned spoke up, "No, you haven't said anything wrong, it's just that I wonder if Greg told you about us?"

"He thinks you're terrific parents but hasn't mentioned much else."

Marie took the opportunity for a follow-up question, "Has Greg told you anything about his background?"

"Background? I'm not sure."

Ned held up his hand to signal Marie that the subject should be dropped. "This cab driver certainly seems to know his way around."

Terry and I picked up that Ned wanted to divert the conversation. I dreaded the next question, which I felt sure Terry would ask.

"What about his background?"

Ned dropped his chin and gave Marie a stern look. He sighed loudly, and then began, "We are not his birth parents. He lost his when in grade school and has lived with us ever since. He even changed his last name to ours."

"N-no, he didn't mention that."

Ned leaned forward and took Terry's hand. "It doesn't matter. We think of him as our son."

Marie felt Terry was a little upset at the lack of information from Greg. "You see, dear, Keith Petros was our son, and he got into a car accident and died. Greg was driving." Then she added quickly, "It wasn't his fault. A drunk driver hit them. We more or less adopted Greg. I'm sure he meant no harm in not telling you. I just wish men were better at expressing their feelings."

"That may be true, but it does seem a little weird hearing this from a third party. I wonder why he chose not to tell me."

Marie smiled, "Greg feels responsible for Keith's death, and I think any subject reminding him of that fact is hard for him."

Terry nodded, "I can see that. It's just if you trust someone, you feel okay about telling personal and painful things."

Ned let go of Terry's hand and sat back. "I knew it was meddling to tell you about things Greg didn't mention. We didn't know Greg hadn't said anything, and maybe Marie should have paused when she asked the question about background. By then it was too late. We probably should have asked Greg first before talking to you. The cat's out of the bag now, and I hope the damage isn't irreparable."

The cab pulled up in front of the restaurant. Ned paid the driver, and we all went inside. The dinner passed in a pleasant manner, but Terry had lost her enthusiasm for conversation. Once or twice, she seemed to come back into the conversation only to fade back into silence. Though she didn't try to broadcast her unsettled nature, it proved hard to miss. Each course brought out superfluous talk about how good things looked, but nothing of substance got discussed.

When the coffee arrived, Marie said, "You all right, dear?"

"Yes, fine. Just a few stray thoughts that I'm trying to shake off."

"Marie and I feel horrible about talking about Greg's background in that he didn't talk to you first."

"He must have a good reason, but for the life of me, I can't think of what. I have a feeling that Greg isn't quite ready for a deep relationship. Well, no matter, I'll talk it over with him and see where we come out."

"I hope Marie and I aren't the cause of any trouble," Ned said. He knew full well that trouble would come, given the distance and preoccupation with thought Terry had demonstrated since she found out. Though he could do nothing to help the situation.

"Please, don't worry," Terry said. "Y'all ready to go? If so, I need to have the restaurant call a cab."

"Yes, I think we're ready," Ned said. He looked over at Marie, and she nodded once, confirming that the time to go had come.

Terry left the table to order the cab. "Well, Marie, you and I messed up this one."

"Oh, Ned, if their relationship is as shallow as it sounds, I don't think Greg was having any long-term thoughts about her."

"I have to agree, but I still don't like to be the catalyst for a breakup."

"I would get it out of your mind. You need to quit worrying about it. You're starting to obsess. They will be fine together or apart."

"Okay. You know best." Ned signaled the waiter that they were ready for the check. Terry came back and let them know the cab would take about ten minutes. Ned poured himself another cup of coffee from the carafe. "I called for the check."

Terry nodded but didn't say anything. Caught in her thoughts, she couldn't help but stare off into the distance. The waiter arrived. Ned didn't look at the check; he just handed the waiter his credit card. I could tell he wanted to ensure that there would be no more of a delay since Terry's preoccupation with her thoughts had become uncomfortable. He must have thought he would try some other discussion, as he cleared his throat in preparation for saying something. Marie made her eyes grow larger with the obvious message of "shut up." Ned caught himself and looked down into his coffee.

The waiter returned, and Ned signed the statement. They rose and moved to the foyer. A bright yellow cab waited outside the double doors. Ned guided Marie and Terry out to the cab.

The Petroses dropped Terry off at her dorm. It seemed logical that they would get home last since they would pay for the cab.

Terry said goodbye and thanked Ned and Marie for dinner. Quickly, she went inside the dorm and to her room, with me close behind. She'd barely gotten through the door when her phone rang. She answered.

"Hello, Greg." Terry didn't know how to approach this call, so she said coolly, "I recognize your number. What do you want?"

"Gee, Terry, is something wrong?"

"Wrong? How come you didn't tell me the Petroses were not your parents?"

"I guess I didn't think it important to us."

"Not important? Do you know what it feels like to find out something about the person you're dating from someone else?"

"I don't understand why you are upset. It never occurred to me to get into who my parents were."

"It shows a lack of trust and of wanting to share information with the one you lo—. Oh, I see, now. You're not in this relationship for the long haul. I almost said the L word, and I have to be honest when I say you have never indicated we had any more between us than friendship."

"I didn't think about it is all. I think it is that simple."

"Oh, you do? Well, then, simplify it for this incredibly complex person."

"Seriously had I even had a hint that it would cause you concern, I would have mentioned it."

"I guess I don't have an answer for that. Oh, wait. Yeah, you did it to show me how little I mean to you."

"I think you are now showing signs of having some self-esteem issues."

"What would you expect, getting treated like I'm nobody special?"

"You are very special to me."

"You have a funny way to show it."

"Okay then. How about we get married?"

"What? What the hell is wrong with you? Marriage is totally off the question here."

"You think I don't care about you? Well, would someone who wants to spend the rest of his life with you not care?"

Terry put the phone on speaker as she pulled down her hair. "I suppose it would show you care. No, I don't want to get married. I want to have a normal relationship filled with trust where we each tell everything to the other and no secrets. Is that so hard?"

"Do you have me on speakerphone?"

"Yes, I need to get ready for bed and, after all, you called me."

"Fine. I do hate the speaker, though."

"I would try hard to get over it."

"You're right. I don't feel in any position to make demands."

"I think you are finally getting it."

"I want to tell you everything and not hold back."

After a pause, she said, "Then, do you think you could be a little more forthcoming with some of your thoughts and events in your life?"

"Can we drink beer while we are talking?"

"You're impossible. No, I don't want to have a beer while we chat. You need to get your rest. I'll see you after the game tomorrow."

"That does sound more encouraging than how this call started."

"Don't push it, buster. You're still in the dog house."

"Think we can get a dog?"

"Good night, Greg."

"Goodnight, Terry. Oh, and one more thing. I hope yours is the last face I see on this Earth when it is time to leave."

"Okay, Greg. That was a good one. Sleep and play well."

"Goodnight, Terry."

Terry hung up. I think she felt much better as a result of talking. My opinion was that it could be that Greg just didn't think his family life all that unusual. Once all this football stuff was over, I felt sure that real progress could be made on their relationship. Until then, though, I hoped she understood that she needed to stay supportive and not raise issues where there could be a misinterpretation of intent by either of them.

My work done here, I would try to get back to Greg before he went to sleep. I tried a new technique of transportation—to wish myself to a spot, and I wished I had done this earlier. I visualized Greg's bed, and that's where I ended up.

Greg still sat staring at the phone, so I knew the whole trip had taken only seconds. Sat hunched over, he contemplated calling her back and felt bad that she'd taken the information about his family so hard. Knowing Greg the way I did, had he thought this would be the case, he would have told her before now. Although I felt sure it had no importance to him, he must by then have realized he'd created a huge trust issue by allowing this information to come from someone other than himself. Greg wouldn't want an issue like this to get between him and Terry. Without a lot of analysis, it looked like he'd come to a realization a few months ago that Terry was the perfect person for him. I don't think he was kidding when he asked about marriage. In Greg's mind, if getting married would push away all the problems of trust, then he would do it. However, getting married before graduation might not be the best thing, but like other couples, they could make it work. I think he had made up his mind to remain with Terry, and now he had to concentrate on making sure he acted like the kind of person in which she could place her trust.

Greg lay on the bed, and it looked like he rolled a few thoughts around on how he could become more engaged in predicting the things on which Terry would want some active discussion. At length, he closed his eyes, and sleep halted any more consideration of the problem.

Chapter Nine

The game went pretty much as expected. Greg proved spectacular and led the team to a two-touchdown victory over Alabama. The victory celebration and the press conference took the time to well past ten o'clock at night. Greg met up with Terry and his parents at the motel. They took a quiet booth in the restaurant. Not the best place, but at least relatively private. A few fans passed through and spotted Greg and asked for autographs. He graciously signed what the folks gave him, and they chatted a little and moved on.

Ned spoke up when they sat alone, "So, what did it feel like to win?"

"I'll tell you, Dad, it was an interesting experience. From the first minute on the field, I knew we would win. It felt like a vision but so real."

"You played an exceptionally controlled game. The announcers said you stayed so calm and collected."

"Yes." Marie nodded. "They even said you looked like a pro quarterback."

"You guys are making me blush, but you can keep it up."

They all laughed. Ned then asked if Greg planned to enter the NFL draft. Greg surprised them all by letting them know he hadn't made up his mind. He turned and looked at Terry and said, "I have a few considerations, and I think that Terry and I need to talk out some things beforehand."

Terry smiled and reached for Greg's hand. She gave it a squeeze, and he knew he had now gotten on the right track and felt good about including Terry in the decision. Ned continued to talk up the prospects of being a pro football player. He mentioned a couple of things like fame and fortune but then paused.

"You know, son, you have one more year of eligibility at Texas."

"Yes, I know. That's another consideration. Should I pass on the draft and play that last year after I graduate, or enter the draft now?"

"Well, if you pass, you won't be certain you'll get ranked as high, and there's always the prospect of injury."

"I know." Greg laughed at the idea that his dad thought these things hadn't occurred to him. "These are the things Terry and I have to weigh before I make up my mind, or rather, before *we* make up our mind."

Ned seemed to take comfort in the fact that Greg had given the situation the proper weight. He fell silent.

The discussion on Greg's future gave way to wondering what looked good on the menu. The rest of the time, the group engaged in a normal family discussion. Greg commented that Terry and his parents interacted well and seemed to genuinely like each other. No one raised an objection, and all agreed vocally. After dinner, Greg's parents begged off Greg's suggestion to go for a walk since they had an early flight tomorrow. Greg gave them a big hug. They hugged Terry as well and said their goodnights. Terry and Greg walked them to the elevator and waited until the door closed.

"So, you think we need to discuss your future, do you?" Terry said.

"Yeah, I think so."

"What part do you want to discuss? I thought you had it all decided."

Greg led Terry over to the lobby bar and took a seat. She sat beside him and turned so that she could look into his eyes. "Well, what part?" she said.

"Since that unfortunate situation with me not telling you about my parents, I've given some thought to you needing to be part of the decisions."

"This bothered you?"

"Of course, it bothered me. I understood why you got upset and don't want that kind of thing to happen again."

"I appreciate that, but you have to understand I have no reason to warrant you feeling the need to include me in decisions about your life."

"All right, then." Greg took a deep breath. The next few words had deep importance to both of them, "As I said the night before the game, I want to spend my life with you, and you should help with the decisions that will affect us both."

Terry looked into Greg's eyes for a hint of fabrication. Upon seeing none, she said, "I want to spend my life with you, too."

Greg let out the breath he'd held and took Terry's hand. "This is a major decision on your part, and I want to make sure you feel good with it."

"So far, I'm good with it. Of course, you could talk me out of it."

Greg laughed and leaned back. His look confirmed that he felt Terry to be priceless. "No, I won't try to talk you out of anything. Once I have you, I plan on keeping you."

Terry leaned over and gave Greg a kiss on the cheek. "Good. Now, let's leave all the discussions for tomorrow. Buy me a drink and tell me how much fun you had in the game today."

Greg gave Terry a hug, returned the kiss, and signaled the waiter. They ordered an Irish coffee, and Greg spent the next half hour talking about the game. Terry could see the excitement in his eyes when describing the various plays. Her look made him pause.

"What is it?" he said.

"I've made up my mind."

"Made up your mind? About what?"

"No matter what, I can't deny you your destiny. I believe football is key to your overall happiness."

"No, I think you are key to my happiness."

"Be that as it may. Oh, and don't get me wrong, I happen to agree, but still and all, I approve of the idea that you pursue an NFL opportunity."

"I thought we needed to discuss each aspect."

"We do, but I want you to know I want what will make you happiest."

"You are the best, you know that?"

"I know, darling. Now, I feel so tired I could fall off this stool. Let's call it a night."

"Okay. I'm with you. Also, I'm feeling a couple of those hits today."

Greg helped Terry down and called for the bill. He paid quickly, and they left to return to Terry's dorm. Greg gave Terry a sweet goodnight kiss, and then headed back to his place. He explained to Terry that he planned to get up early and see his parents off at the airport and figured he should get to bed.

The next morning, Greg rushed to the motel and arrived just as his parents stood checking out. "Hey, son," Ned said. "We didn't expect you to go with us. You need your rest."

"Don't worry. You guys came all this way, and I didn't spend much time, so I figured the trip to the airport would give us time we could spend together."

"Great idea," Marie said. "I, for one, have questions about Terry."

"I'll just bet you do." Greg laughed as he grabbed the bags and took them out to the cab.

Once in the cab, Marie looked at Greg, and he could tell she had a few questions. She started with, "So, how long have you known her?"

"We met last semester in a class. We only started dating this semester."

"How serious is it?"

"I'd like us to get married once I know what I'm doing after graduation."

"How does she feel about it?"

"The same. I haven't asked her to marry me, exactly, but I think if I did, she would say yes."

"When will you have the wedding?"

"Mom, we haven't even gotten engaged yet. I don't know."

"She certainly seems a lovely person. I think you'll be happy."

"Thank you. That means a lot to me."

Ned had little to say but did add that he thought Terry would make a fine addition to the family.

The airport came up quickly. They gathered at the passenger drop off and said their goodbyes.

"I'm glad you could make it, and I hope you didn't get too put off with my unavailability."

"Oh, son," Ned said. "We understand how busy you are. It felt a joy just bearing witness to your moment."

"Aw, Dad, I wish you could stay longer."

"Your dad has a bunch of court dates."

"I understand. Can't stop me from wishing, though."

"Maybe when your dad retires, we can come and stay until you get tired of us."

"That would be swell, Mom."

Ned and Marie gave him a big hug, and then went into the terminal. Greg watched them until they disappeared into the crowds heading for check-in.

Greg got into the cab cue for the trip back. A couple of fans congratulated him and asked for an autograph. Greg liked that others wanted his autograph. He always took care to remain most gracious to those who asked. He asked questions about where they came from and what brought them to the game. He had signed autographs for about three years, so he felt quite used to getting interrupted to respond to the request. He signed their programs and, finally, reached number one in the line for a cab.

Greg went back to his apartment and gave Terry a call. They decided to meet for lunch tomorrow and finish the discussion about their choices for the future.

***

I have to break in here for a minute. The remainder of the story needs to move along, but I have a few facts that you need to know. Unfortunately, you and I don't have enough time to live through the next twenty years of Greg and Terry's life. I shall give you an abbreviated version but will ask your indulgence. This will not read like an action sequence but is what the literary folks call more tell than show. I think it is important, so let's begin.

***

Terry and Greg had their discussion. Terry wanted to go on to grad school and specialize in early childhood development. She had a plan to get a Ph.D., which would take another three or so years from graduation. Since she and Greg would graduate this year, she figured her work and his would finish at about the same time if he went right into grad school. The timing of both getting finished with their education made for one of the reasons she had originally favored Greg going to grad school even though she knew he wanted to play football. Deep down, she felt uncomfortable getting married until after all their schooling had finished.

Greg suggested that he could do grad school in the offseason and still accept the NFL draft. Terry told him she had thought of the same tactic. He also mentioned that he could stand to get a contract worth more than five million dollars. Terry took a final turn of opinion in favor of the NFL solution, knowing that Greg wanted to do that and the money was so good. She also changed her mind about marriage. She thought the money would remain too tight to allow them both to stay in school. Greg laughed out loud when he heard about the money concern. He made the point even if they had a financial concern, why would not being married solve it? Terry had no answer, and so they wrapped up the discussion, and both felt pleased with the result.

They decided that Greg would enter the draft and that, depending which team he chose, they would enroll in a grad school close to the team city. Once in school, and Greg a member of a team, they would get married. Since her parents lived on the East coast, they could have the wedding there, as Greg's parents could travel easily. They both agreed they would foot the wedding bill so that they wouldn't have the usual overdone, stressful occasion most of their friends went through when the parents paid for the ceremony.

Yes, Greg won the Heisman, so his NFL contract went into the twenty million category. He also found an agent, and for the first year, he had about sixty million in endorsement contracts. He and Terry felt more than dumbfounded at the turn of events. In the first round of the NFL draft, the New England Patriots grabbed him. During the first season, he didn't get much time playing until the first string quarterback got injured. Greg finished the season by playing the last three games. He won all three, but since the team had lost six in the season, they had no playoff opportunity. Terry had enrolled at Yale in the Ph.D. program for early child development. Greg enrolled in a special program at Harvard, a five-year MBA and Law degree combination. The class met through the fall and winter, and he had a requirement to attend classes in the spring and summer. It all worked, and he graduated with an MBA and Law degree. Terry had also graduated and worked as a developmental psychologist.

They still hadn't married. They had no real reason other than that they had become busy and felt happy. The subject came up a few times, but neither wanted to tackle the arrangements. They did buy a nice house in Weston, a suburb of Boston. They paid over four-million dollars but got the house and grounds that both wished to have.

Greg led the Patriots to the Super Bowl after three seasons. They played the Seattle Seahawks and won the game as a result of a late fourth-quarter pass from Greg to the wide receiver. The announcers went insane in their praise of Greg, as it looked like there would be a sack, and Greg moved out of it and threw a pass on the run.

Terry and Greg, finally, got married. They had a huge wedding at their home. It was all you could imagine. Tons of photographers stood outside the grounds, and off-duty police kept order. Many stars of the NFL and Hollywood attended. The papers said the price of the wedding cost over a million, but I can tell you since I was there, it came closer to two. The happy couple paid for all the travel of their family, and since the house had eight bedrooms, they had no problem with housing everyone. All the bridal party and groomsmen also received transportation and got put up at a local hotel. The reception got held on the five-acre grounds and, by all accounts, was the best. A huge tent provided the venue for the wedding dinner and dance. The food and drinks proved superb and never ending. After cutting the cake, the band kept the guests dancing until well past midnight. The couple left for their honeymoon by helicopter. The shots of Terry throwing the bouquet from the door of the chopper looked classic. The wind from the whirling blades blew the bouquet into a hundred pieces. At least more than one hopeful managed to catch a piece.

The honeymoon in Barbados went well, and the couple returned in time for Greg to report to practice camp. The nice thing about a honeymoon was that it offered the perfect atmosphere to concentrate on activities that became the first child. A girl was born about nine months later, and they named her Constance. In a couple of short years, another child was born, and this time, a boy. They named him Jackson Keith Petros. I have to say; I felt quite pleased with the prospect of having a namesake in the living world.

The next years passed as one would expect for those who have obvious privilege. Greg continued to quarterback the Patriots for another ten years. The team visited the Super Bowl one more time but lost. Greg decided to retire. Certainly, he had enough money. Most of his endorsements stayed with him the whole time, so he had banked in the neighborhood of a hundred million. For the next ten years, he commentated for Fox Sports. He formed part of a team that handled the Monday Night Football duties. His name and face became a household staple.

In the meantime, his daughter and son grew up and embarked on their college careers. Neither ended up particularly good at sports, but both proved extremely intelligent and got courted by every top-level college. Constance chose Harvard as her school. Two years later, Jackson Keith chose Yale. Greg gave each school a bunch of money for an active endowment. Harvard established a chair in the business school in Greg's name. Yale established a Chair in the Psychology department in Terry's name. In addition, Greg gave gifts to Indiana University Law School in honor of Ned, who'd passed away. Marie followed Ned in less than a year. Terry's parents needed close support for about ten years before they each passed as well.

It became a tough couple of years for Greg and Terry, but in the end, peace finally came to the household. Greg decided he'd had enough of football and resigned his position with the network. He wanted to get a business career started at long last.

At nearly forty-two, he figured he'd better get on with it if he were to have any possibility of success. Terry felt a little apprehensive, as she had become fond of her life as celebrity spouse and comfortable.

Greg set up an equity fund, and with his worldwide contacts, it didn't take long to collect a portfolio of clients. His fund grew quickly to over a billion dollars under management. He remained conservative on the investments side, so the fund carried a portfolio of blue chips, highly rated bonds, and carefully selected real estate EFTs. His instructions to his employees were to manage the fund with the idea that everyone could get a good night's sleep; client and employees alike. The fund delivered a consistent year-over-year return of about eight percent, enough to keep everyone happy. He invested over a hundred million of his money at the start, so he also had a vested interest in seeing the fund do well.

Although Terry felt apprehensive in the beginning, she soon became comfortable since it didn't appear anything had changed. Greg remained the media darling of football and now of business. His fund received the highest ratings on Wall Street, and he became a frequent visitor on several of the Wall Street talk shows. His "goodnight sleep" philosophy struck a chord with the media, and his firm continually received sound bites from the commentators. Greg had the logo of the company redesigned with a depiction of what looked like someone sound asleep. More and more clients got attracted to the fund, so Greg became even more respected and, of course, made more money.

His two kids graduated from college and started their careers. Jackson became a worker in a Psychological treatment center while he went to grad school. Constance joined a start-up as an intern while still in college. She worked at a debit card company that barely made it. The company had dependence on venture capital funding, and so it had no frills. She stayed with the firm after graduation and received a promotion to the position of Risk Analyst. The funding remained a feast and famine situation, so her paychecks came sparsely at first. Finally, the concern became a viable entity, and the paychecks, as well as stock options, became a regular feature to those who'd suffered in the beginning.

Greg asked each if they would have any interest in joining his company. Both felt appreciative of the offer but wanted to make their way on their own. In discussions with Terry, Greg admitted he felt incredibly proud of how the kids had turned out and especially their independent spirits.

Greg and Terry did a lot of entertaining at their home in Weston. The original home covered eight thousand square feet, but Greg expanded it to sixteen. He felt the extra space made it possible for their guests to stay overnight without feeling like they were putting Greg and Terry out. Greg also had a corporate jet, which he would use for business as well as to ferry some of their friends around. Greg and Terry had homes in Telluride, Colorado, and West Palm Beach, Florida. The jet made it easy to go to each at almost a moment's notice and to take their friends with them.

This lifestyle was one which became familiar to Terry and Greg. It became one of life's pleasures for them to decide to go skiing on Friday and be on the slope Saturday morning. If the weather in Boston became too terrible, a quick call to the hangar and a few hours were all that separated them from the warmth of Florida. Usually, they had a couple of friends who could drop everything and join them as well. In fact, life with Terry became so nice that Greg took less of an active role managing the fund. He would get reports daily but, for the most part, spent his time on the boat in Florida or on the slopes of Colorado and, sometimes, both in the same week.

So, this is the life of Greg, Terry, Jackson, and Constance. They all had supreme confidence that life as they knew it would continue forever. They had no foreshadowing of what was in store for the next phase. You can trust me, though, as I'll tell you all about it.

I also had a number of things happen to me while this life of Greg's progressed. Finally, I got to meet with the spirits in charge of guiding the conduct of folks like myself. It proved an emotional session, which left me a little weak in the knees. They asked what I wanted to do about Greg. When I didn't understand the question, they explained that I could move on and leave Greg to his own devices. They told me that to do so, though, would in all probability jeopardize my eternal good standing with The Leader. It appears that when one has love for an Earthly being, some kind of vested responsibility goes along with the feelings. I would never have abandoned Greg but, as they explained, it remained in my best interest to keep a watch on him and make sure all went well. So, it seemed that I'd have a reward for staying behind with Greg. I asked how long the commitment would last for, and the only answer I got was, "Until Greg comes over."

I felt quite happy to oblige. Also, they told me that, under no circumstances, should I interfere in Greg's life. I was not to use any information not known to him to assist him in any way. They explained the importance of spirits not altering any aspects of history or potential history. To do so could disrupt the balance of what were to be logical and natural outcomes.

Several powers got explained. I had a hint at it, but they showed me how to travel from place to place in an instant. The trainer gave me several exercises in thought monitoring that allowed me to sense what people thought. Not exactly reading minds but close. This skill took an immense amount of practice, and not until later did I become good at it.

So, it appeared that I would not only be able to help my friend but earn my way to an audience with The Leader.

Chapter Ten

Greg sat at his desk, looking out of the window. He explained to his assistant Ms. McCormick when he came in that, for some reason, today didn't seem like the kind of day where he would get anything done.

"Mine and Terry's twenty-fourth wedding anniversary is coming up, and I've not yet decided on a present for her. My mind got too focused on what would make a great present. I want to knock her socks off and only have less than a month to figure it out."

"How about a trip?" Ms. McCormick said.

"I thought of that, but no, we travel all the time. No, it has to be something beautiful and from the heart like a ring or necklace. Something she can look at and always remember that I gave it to her for our twentieth. It needs to have engraving as well. Terry always gripes about the fact I never engrave the gifts of jewelry I give her."

"Wouldn't we all like something like that?"

"I've got it. I could buy a real nice watch and have the back engraved. A great watch may provide the solution."

"Yeah, that would work. Excuse me; do you want me to get that?"

The ringing phone got his attention, finally. He picked it up and said, "Yes."

His chief financial officer sounded a little out of breath. Ms. McCormick left, and Greg put the caller on speaker phone, then took off his jacket.

"Slow down, Ralph. What's the problem?"

Ralph explained that irregularities had gotten uncovered in the latest audit by the Securities and Exchange Commission.

"There are always irregularities. What's so important about these?"

"Greg, I need to come see you. These do not look good, and I'm afraid the SEC will want further explanation."

"Okay. Come on up." Greg hung up and buzzed his assistant.

She opened the door and said, "Yes, sir?"

"Mr. Torrence is heading up here. Show him in when he arrives."

"Yes, sir. Would you like coffee?"

"That would be nice, thank you."

"I'll bring it in after he gets here. You might need a break after all."

"Good thinking. Thanks."

The assistant closed the door, and Greg had forgotten about the anniversary. He remembered the last time the SEC got their panties in a knot. It happened over disclosure irregularities. Some of the brokers didn't get the standard disclosures signed in a timely manner. The firm dodged a bullet in terms of fines by putting in place an electronic terms and conditions sheet that needed the signature of the client and the broker before any sales or purchases could get made. The real problem, in that case, came down to a few of the brokers having the power of attorney on some of the clients' accounts. The power of attorney meant they could buy or sell without the client's permission. The brokers assumed the standard disclosures as not mandatory. The power of attorney status became the lawyers' argument, but the SEC still insisted on individual disclosures on individual transactions. Although this meant extra paperwork, it did protect the client from any untoward activity by an unscrupulous broker. All in all, the settlement seemed satisfactory to both sides.

A light knock on the door interrupted Greg's thoughts. "Come in."

The assistant swung the door open and said, "Mr. Torrence to see you, Mr. Petros."

"Thank you. Hi, Ralph. Have a seat. You can close the door, Ms. McCormick."

Ralph looked around, not knowing where he should sit. Greg rose and walked over to the conference table and pointed to a chair. Greg took the one opposite Ralph and sat heavily. "Now, what is this about?"

"Well, sir. I got a call from the lead auditor as a courtesy alerting me to the effect that there have been some substantive findings on this audit."

"What kind of findings?"

"He wouldn't tell me. He just wanted me to know that some of the findings are quite serious."

"When will we find out?"

"Not sure. It's not commonplace that the SEC spells out their findings. They usually send a subpoena and request an appearance to answer the allegations."

"We had better get Mathews up here as well. This sounds like a legal issue."

"I agree. I just wish I had more information."

"Maybe Mathews can give some of his friends a call and find out what's going on." Greg rose and returned to his desk. He dialed a number without sitting.

"Hello, Jack. I need to see you right away. It looks like some trouble with the SEC."

Greg returned the receiver to the cradle without any further discussion with the lead attorney. He moved back to the table. I could tell that the whole thing bothered Greg a lot. This news had a sinister tone to it. Maybe that came down to the way Ralph presented it. Not knowing the problem made it appear much worse than it might be. Greg concealed any escalating concern beyond his frown but failed to quiet the rumble in his stomach.

A light knock at the door drew his attention. "Please, come in, Jack."

To his surprise, not Jack but Ms. McCormick stood there with coffee. "I thought you would like this."

"Thank you. We would. Also, Jack Mathews will be joining us."

The assistant set the coffee on the table, nodded, and turned to go. Even though Greg had told her of his arrival, she looked slightly startled by the appearance of Jack Mathews, who came into the room without making a sound. "Mr. Mathews," she said.

"Ms. McCormick," he answered.

"Jack, come in and have a seat. There's coffee here if you want some."

"Thanks, boss. I could use a cup. What's this all about?"

"Ralph, here, got a call from the lead auditor of the SEC saying they found irregularities on the last audit."

"What kind of irregularities?" Jack grabbed a cup and poured steaming coffee.

Ralph said, "They won't say. They just gave me a courtesy heads up."

"Is that usual?" Jack took a sip of coffee.

"Not really. I think they wanted me to know there was something serious, but that's all they could say. My team and I worked with them for over six months."

"Did I know about this audit?" Jack took a seat at the table.

"I assume you did. I sent an interdepartmental memo when it started."

"No, I mean, did anyone come and talk to me about this audit?"

Greg spoke up, "I don't think so. I know I didn't."

"Damn, Greg. I have asked someone to keep me in the loop on all of these audits."

"Easy," Greg said. "Ralph gave a briefing at least once a month on the progress at our leadership meetings."

"I don't mean briefings for public consumption. I'm talking about the discussion of the risks and what we do with them."

"Ralph, were there any risks known prior to today?"

"No, sir. All looked normal, and I didn't hear a peep about irregularities. None of my team reported any suspicions either."

Jack sat back and said, "Okay, I may have gotten a little ahead of myself. I had assumed that you guys picked up some skinny prior to this. My apologies."

Greg looked at Jack, and then turned to Ralph, "Okay, now that we're all squared away on who knew what and when, what's the next step?"

Ralph and Jack looked at each other, and then Jack spoke, "We need to find out exactly what's going on over at the SEC. They might have found something and have decided to take it to the justice department."

"What does that mean?" Greg sat forward in his chair.

"I'm making a guess, but normally, when they find anything, we all sit down and figure out how to correct the issues. Like when they found our brokers weren't getting the proper sign-offs. Right, Ralph?"

"Yeah, exactly right."

"So, what's different with this?" Greg's brow developed a deeper furrow.

Jack sat back in his chair and looked like he selected his words carefully. "It sounds fishy that they would give Ralph a heads up. Sounds like they can't say anything due to an investigation, and they gave Ralph some info to reserve him as a friendly witness."

Ralph sat upright. "Witness? Witness to what?"

"Not *what*, Ralph, but who."

Greg put his cup in the saucer with a rattle. "What do you mean, who?"

"Hypothetically speaking, it's always good to have the CFO as a witness for the prosecution."

"Okay," Greg said. "Let's get out of the hypothetical and move to the practical. What are you saying?"

"I'm saying, I think these guys have some evidence of securities laws broken and they will want to come after you and will want Ralph to testify for them."

"Well, that's great. Why me?" Greg slumped in his chair.

"Well, if you think for a moment. Who's the head of this company, and who has more money than God?"

"Those the only reasons?"

"If laws get broken, who would you want to bring down? Which would you choose, the dumbshit clerk or broker who broke the law or, perhaps, the head man himself? Which choice would say more to the public about how they protect the citizens?"

Greg smiled. "Sounds like politics to me, and all political problems can get worked out."

"Unfortunately, since the Madoff thing, there hasn't been much tolerance for mistakes."

Greg frowned. "Yes, but I haven't knowingly done anything wrong."

"Sorry to disagree, boss, but you have committed the biggest offense of all. You are rich and famous and, in Washington, that equates to being evil incarnate."

Greg's frown got even deeper. "Come on, Jack. There has to be some justice thrown in here somewhere."

"Justice in the Justice Department? Excuse me, but my job is to take the worst point of view and try to protect you. I smell a witch hunt, and Ralph doesn't know it, but he will be the one to light the pyre."

Ralph stiffened, and his face flushed. "Why the hell do you say stuff like that? I have no intention of being disloyal."

"Oh, I know your intentions, Ralph. Just wait 'til the prosecuting attorney waves an immunity document under your nose. It will be your choice. Ten years in a federal prison or some co-operation. I bet on the co-operation. Greg, I would lock down all information and not have any discussions with any of your leadership team without me being present. I can assure you that these people will turn on you as if a pack of wolves. By the way, Ralph, this whole conversation is under attorney and client privilege, so no one outside this room needs to hear any of this. Understood?"

Ralph looked calmer but had an edge in his voice, "Yeah, I understand. I must say that you paint a pretty poor picture of loyalty. What's to stop you from turning sides?"

"Ethics. I'm Greg's attorney, and my job is to protect him from threats inside and outside the corporation. If I don't do my job, I could lose my license. What would you lose by co-operating?"

Greg sat low in his chair, his face darkening. "I think we've had enough infighting. I respect what you say, Jack, and rely that you will help clear this matter up. Ralph, I don't think for one moment you will be disloyal. Since you have already said that you don't know what this is about, I'll ask you to leave Jack and me now. We need to talk strategy, and you don't need to be part of that, as you're innocent of any wrongdoing."

Ralph rose. "Thanks, boss. I hope it all is nothing."

"Yeah, Ralph, I do too. Thanks."

Ralph turned and left the room, closing the door behind him. Greg looked at Jack for a moment. "Okay, Jack, what do we do?"

"You did a good thing to get Ralph out of the conversation. I meant it when I said to eliminate talking about any of this without me present. You will need a corroboration witness to any conversations around this so-called irregularity. I don't mean to alarm you, but the idea of not presenting an audit result means something bigger is afoot. I have worked in the prosecutor's office and can tell you this kind of thing is what makes prosecutors drool. To bring down one of the big names on the Street is something these guys dream about all the time. It could provide their stepping stone to Congress or a judgeship. If this is anything at all, these guys will build it up until it looks like a major case of fraud. I have some friends and will try to find out more. If nothing turns up, it means they have probably gone to a Grand Jury already. If so, the only thing we will be able to do is answer the charges and hope for the best."

Greg wiped his forehead with the back of his hand. "What can I do in the meantime?"

"I would go about your life as normal. There is no percentage in worrying. They could go to a Grand Jury and come out with nothing. So, don't spend too much time on this. Watch who you talk to about this as well. If Ralph or anyone wants to know if anything has changed, ask them to call me. That is the easiest thing to do."

"Thanks, Jack. Did you mean what you said to Ralph about being my lawyer?"

"Sure did. I just hope your money doesn't run out. I hate pro bono work."

Greg couldn't help but laugh out loud at Jack's macabre joke. They got up, and Jack took Greg's hand with a firm grip. "Hang in there. We'll figure it out."

Greg showed Jack to the door. "I hope you're right," Greg mumbled his response, as Jack took his leave toward the elevator. He asked Ms. McCormick to come into the office. She smiled and moved around her desk.

"Please, close the door and have a seat."

Ms. McCormick's smile dissolved. It must have been the worried look on Greg's face, but now she produced a frown of her own. "Anything wrong?" she said.

"No, nothing. At least, not from your perspective. It's just some difficult business decisions have to be made. I always hate to ask you to do anything that might appear to be a personal favor for me."

"Please. I never mind doing anything that would take some worry off your shoulders. What do you need me to do?"

Greg thought for a minute. "I wondered if I should ask for help on my anniversary gift. The last thing in the world I want to do is forget or become too busy to get a nice present for Terry. I'm going to become busy and may need some help in getting the gift together."

"I would be glad to help. Do you know what to get?"

"Yes, I have made up my mind. The idea came to me this morning, and since my meeting with Jack, I'm convinced this gift will be perfect. I even have a picture of it. It's here in this magazine. Hold on a minute, and I'll find it. Here it is."

"Oh, my, that will be a nice gift. A Patek Phillippe watch."

"Yes, and I will need it engraved on the back."

"Do you know what you want to say?"

"Yes. You ready?"

"Yes, sir."

"To Terry AMLFEAE, and the date, 4-18-2017."

"That's it?"

"That's it. Thanks for not asking what AMLFEAE means."

"I don't think it any of my business."

"What the heck. It means All My Love For Ever And Ever."

"How sweet."

"Order it and have it gift wrapped. You can use my credit card."

"Yes, sir. Is that all?"

"Thank you, Bella."

She got up and looked relieved there wasn't anything serious about this meeting, which caused me to tune into her thoughts. Bella always liked to spend big money, and this watch would run around thirty thousand. She saw herself going into a fine jewelry store and playing the part of a big spender. The completion of the purchase could take a half-day away from the office. "Oh, Mr. Petros, I forgot to ask. I might have to take office time to get this done."

"Don't worry. Take all the time you need."

With a smile, Bella went through the office door and sat in her chair, taking my attention with her. She planned her attack. Lunch first, then a shopping trip. She figured to stop by a couple of stores before going to the best Jeweler in town. It would be fun to turn up her nose at some expensive but inferior items. She could almost see the clerks' faces when she asked if they had anything of a little better quality when they had produced the best they had. Few stores carried watches in this category, but still, it would give her some fun acting like a rich bitch. I left her and returned my attention to Greg.

Greg sat at his desk and couldn't seem to think of anything but the conversation of the morning. Glad now to have the gift taken care of, he worried about what the feds had in store. His phone rang, and Greg grabbed it before the second ring. It was Jack, and obviously, he wanted to come to Greg's office. "Come on up. I'll order us some lunch." Greg knew from experience that Jack never wanted to talk on the phone. He had the belief all his calls were getting recorded. Given the amount of federal work he did, Greg wouldn't be surprised if they were.

Jack arrived just as Greg finished the lunch order. "I got us a grilled tuna salad. Hope it's okay."

"Yeah, that's perfect. I love rare tuna."

"So, what's up?" Greg tried to sound casual, but Jack had on his game face. This couldn't be good.

"Let me be direct, Greg. It looks like the justice department is seeking an indictment."

"Indictment? On what?"

"They think there was illegal movement of money."

"Illegal movement of money? What the hell is that all about?"

"It looks like some money got taken from the company and moved offshore."

"Okay, so let's find out who did it and turn them over."

"It's not that easy. It looks like whoever they were, they used your house account to cover their tracks."

"What? How the hell could that happen?"

"I still don't know, exactly, but I suspect one of these wunderkinds got your passcode somehow. The important point is that the feds believe you took out about twenty million in company money."

"Holy shit. Word of this could ruin me."

"I would be more concerned about the fifty years in the penitentiary."

"Talk about looking at the dark side."

"I'm extremely concerned. In fact, we need to take defensive action. The first thing you need is outside counsel. I think we ought to hire Bronson and Bronson as your defender. These guys have a lot of experience with white-collar crime and have ex-prosecutors on staff."

"Yeah, I think they're good. I read a lot about some of their cases."

"Also, I think you ought to give them a healthy retainer. You need to protect some of your money for use in your defense. I would do it as soon as possible, so there is no accusation of trying to hide assets."

"Can we go see them today?"

"That would be wise. I won't be able to be present but will set up the meeting and go over with you."

"Jack?"

"What?"

"You jumping ship?"

"Hell, no, but you need to have a confidential relationship with your defense lawyer. I'm a company employee, and eventually, there could be a conflict of interest."

"I'm feeling pretty much alone."

"You are not alone. After your discussion with the lawyers, you'll feel better. My concerns here are all to save you from having to explain any unusual actions since you found out about the audit. Another thing I hate is the way the so-called heads-up got given. It just means that, from this morning on, everything you do will come under scrutiny. Okay?"

"Yeah. I appreciate what you're doing."

A knock on the door announced the arrival of lunch. Jack and Greg said nothing while the waiter set the food on the conference table. Once he'd left, they moved over and sat.

"Jack, do you pray before meals?"

"No, I don't."

"Okay, then I will say one to myself."

Chapter Eleven

The next day, Jack took the lead, and Greg followed him into the conference room of Bronson and Bronson. The firm obviously did quite well. The furniture and appointments all seemed the luxury types and done by professionals.

"Would you like coffee?" Jack pointed over to a sidebar, heavy with fruit, cookies, sodas, and a nice-looking coffee urn. Greg shook his head, and then sat heavily in one of the leather chairs. Jack went over to the bar and poured a cup for himself. "You sure?"

"Yeah, I'm sure. My stomach doesn't feel the best right now. I'll take a rain check."

Jack returned to the conference table just as a thirty-something guy walked through the double doors. "Mr. Petros?" he said. Still walking, he put out his hand. "I'm Peter, Mr. Bronson's legal assistant. I will be helping Mr. Bronson support your case."

The two shook hands. "Nice meeting you, Peter. This is Jack Mathews, our corporate counsel."

"Very nice meeting you both. Mr. Bronson will be in shortly. He's on the phone with the District Attorney. I'm a big fan of yours, Mr. Petros. I've followed your career since I was in grade school. I feel quite pleased to have the honor to serve on your case."

"You should call me Greg, then. I'm sorry we couldn't have met under different circumstances."

"Yes, I agree. We will do everything we can to get this matter cleared up. Ah, here comes Mr. Bronson."

"Jack Mathews," Bronson said. He grabbed Jack's hand and gave him a slap on the back. "Jack and I used to work together. My name is Franklin Bronson."

"Greg Petros, and I'm glad to meet you."

"Would you like coffee or something else before we get started?"

"No, I'm fine, thank you."

"Okay. Let's get into it then, shall we?" Bronson sat opposite Greg. He asked Peter for a file, and he opened it but only gave it a brief look. He also asked Jack to step outside for a few minutes. Jack took his coffee and left.

Once the doors had closed behind Jack, Bronson started talking, "My understanding is that the District Attorney thinks he has a strong case of securities fraud against you personally and your company. I don't have all the details, but he seems pretty sure he will get an indictment. I talked to him today, and he is glad you have retained counsel. He believes it will make it easier down the road. This kind of case usually comes down to how much evidence they can collect and, if not enough, maybe getting a plea deal."

"Plea deal? I'm innocent."

"I believe you, but in certain cases, it is better to say you've done one little thing wrong than to try and fight the big things and lose. My job will be to give you the best defense possible and try and keep you out of jail. After the indictment, I will be able to look at the evidence against you and better provide you with a solid path forward. You understand?"

"Yes, of course, I understand. I don't like it, but I do understand."

"I know this isn't the best of circumstances, and I believe you are innocent, but we need to keep an open mind. I have a question about your net worth."

"Yeah?"

"How much cash do you have?"

"How much do I have, or how much can I raise?"

"I mean, how much can you put your hands on today?"

Greg took out his iPhone and pulled up his accounts. "I have about five million, give or take."

"Okay. How much of your net worth does this represent?"

Greg looked at his phone again and made a rough calculation. "I'd say about one percent."

"That's good. I need to have you deposit all but your necessary living expenses with my firm. We offer a retainer account that earns interest. A deposit like this will protect your legal funds from seizure. The fact that the cash is a small part of your net worth means it won't appear that you're trying to hide funds from the feds if they come looking. Another thing, if there is an indictment, there will be legal proceedings that will include a full audit of your assets. You should not do any unusual selling of assets or any sheltering activities. As of today, you must assume you are being watched."

"Did the District Attorney say anything else? Like how long the indictment will take?"

"No, he said he felt confident that the Grand Jury would return an indictment, and that was about all. We are just going to get forced to wait."

"What about the people who set me up? Is anyone going after them?"

"I understand there are some questionable transactions done under your name. Jack tells me there are some forensic computer people working on identifying them, but so far, no leads. If we do get a lead, then we can present the information to the District Attorney for follow up. I have requested the DA's office keep this out of the public eye as long as possible. Once an indictment comes down, that will prove pretty hard."

"So, the forensic team should hurry."

"Yes, that sums it up beautifully. Now, unless you have more questions, you don't need to spend any more money with us today. Peter will give you the instructions on wiring the cash. Good day to you, Greg, and try not to worry. You are in good hands, and I have told Peter to send Jack back in."

Greg and Franklin rose and shook hands. Franklin turned and went through the doors. Peter handed Greg a form. "This has the wiring instructions. Once received, we will set up an account, and you'll get a statement each month." Greg nodded his understanding and tucked the paper into his portfolio. Peter rose and said goodbye as Jack came back.

Jack said, "So, what did you think?"

"Think? It sounds like I'm going to be the poster boy for all the ills of Wall Street."

"It may appear that way, but trust me; these guys are the best, and if anyone can get the government to take it easy, it's them."

"Doesn't it count that I'm innocent?"

"I guess it does in the long run. In the short run, it doesn't mean a shitten thing."

"I don't know what prevention measures we should have put in place."

"I would say you should have had a forensic internet person on staff full time. He could have detected a system hack and maybe stopped it before any damage."

"This is great hindsight. Let's go back to the office."

Greg headed for the door, and Jack followed. Jack could see that Greg was in no mood to talk any more right then. He thought he wouldn't want to be in Greg's shoes. Someone decided to go after Greg, and not only did they get away with real money, but they'd also they left Greg holding the bag. A real tough position to be in, for sure.

Greg and Jack made it back to the office. Jack suggested that they bring in the forensic guy to see if he'd made any progress. Greg brightened at the suggestion and made the call. "You want lunch?" Greg said. He still had the phone in his hand. Jack nodded and asked for a sandwich and soda. "What kind of sandwich and soda?"

"How about ham and cheese on rye and a Coke."

Greg rolled his eyes as he placed the order. Jack asked him if he planned to have anything. Greg declined and got a glass of milk. "Stomach still feels a little queasy."

"Have you told Terry what's going on?"

"No. I don't want to bother her until I know more about the whole thing."

"I suppose that makes sense. I wouldn't wait until it hits the news, though."

"Yeah, it would not be good to have Terry read about it in a news story."

"For sure. You'll have to tell her yourself."

"I tried last night, but I just couldn't bring myself to ruin her good mood. She sounded so happy talking about a girl's trip to Telluride. It hit me while she sat there bubbling over with excitement that the government could seize our place, and I guess, most everything else."

A knock at the door stopped the discussion. Ms. McCormick sent in the forensic computer technician. "Have a seat." Greg waved toward the conference table. "Have you had lunch?"

"Yes, sir, I have. My name is Robert, and I work for an outside firm."

"Yes, Robert. My name is Greg, and I work here."

"I know who you are, sir. It's a pleasure to try and help out."

"You know the problem?" Greg's surprised look showed his concern, as he'd thought the thing had remained hush-hush.

Jack jumped in and explained that Robert had signed up under a non-disclosure agreement and was trustworthy.

"So, to answer your question. Yes, I'm aware that someone hacked into your system and posted some trades on your account."

"Do you have any idea who?"

"Not yet. The hack looks like a professional job. They used no less than three surrogate servers to mask the Mac ID. It will take a while to trace all the permutations."

"Do you think you'll have any success?"

"Well, sir, it's like playing blackjack. You can have a great system and all the skill in the world, but if you pull bad cards, you still lose. The key will be staying with it until the traces all come to dead ends or a successful score."

"Let me ask, can you definitely prove there has been a hack?"

"Oh, that's a no-brainer. A number of markers show system breaches."

Jack asked, "Would this evidence be well understood by an expert that the government could hire?"

"This evidence is almost universal in its indication of a hack. So, from that perspective, I would say anyone who knows anything about computers would have to agree the system did get hacked."

"Wow, that's terrific." Greg brightened. "At least we'll be able to argue the point of unauthorized access."

"I must say that this makes me feel a little better as well," Jack said. "So, what more do you have to do, Robert?"

"I just need to keep following all the strings until I rule out those that are not leads."

Jack rose. "Okay, then I think you should get back to work."

Robert got up and smiled at Jack and Greg.

"Good work, Robert," Greg said.

"Thank you, sir. I try my best." Robert crossed to the door and turned around. "You want to hear when I find the source?"

Greg and Jack both told Robert to call them the minute he found the source. He nodded, and then disappeared.

"That sounds like reasonably good news," Greg said. He stood rubbing his hands together and smiled broadly. "Don't you?"

"Good news. I couldn't be more pleased. We shall need to get the information over to the DA as soon as we find out the source."

"Even if Robert can't find the source, don't you think this is a good thing?"

"Of course, but having the source would give the DA another duck to hunt, so to speak. They don't like it when their quarry gets away. I could fully imagine the DA still trying to find some infraction as a result of the hack. You know, some law of hacking prevention that you guys failed to follow."

"Is there such a thing?"

"No, but these guys are like bloodhounds. It's difficult to get them off the scent once they pick it up."

"I can understand that, I guess. Okay, let Robert do some more work. I would like to head this off before anything hits the newspapers, though."

"I'll try to get wind of anything before it gets made public. I asked the DA to give me a courtesy call once they know what's going on."

"Good."

Ms. McCormick opened the door after a soft knock and let in the server. He placed the lunch on the conference table and left with haste. Ms. McCormick pulled the door closed.

Greg said, "We might as well try to go on a business-as-usual profile until we know more. You okay with that?"

"Yeah, of course. I think it might offer the best way to get our minds off this thing. You going to tell Terry?"

"I'll let her know we have some problems but won't go into detail."

"Sounds like the best way. Unfortunately, our loved ones get scared easily."

"She's having the time of her life. She sits on the boards of several non-profits and has her days filled with meetings and speeches. With the kids out on their own, she also has the freedom to visit them and give help where needed."

"I would say she has the perfect life, and I don't blame you for not wanting to disrupt it."

Greg finished his glass of milk and went back to his desk. Jack wolfed down the rest of his sandwich and took his Coke with him as he got up.

"Call me if you hear anything," Greg said.

Jack gave him an okay sign and went through the door. Greg picked up the phone and called Terry's cell. His call went to voicemail, and he hung up. He didn't feel in the mood to deliver some kind of warning message on her voicemail. It would have to wait until he got home. He tried to remember if they had planned to have dinner at home tonight or some dinner out. He called Ms. McCormick and asked if he had anything on the agenda for tonight. She checked and told him she saw nothing listed. She also told him that the operations group waited to come in and present a new client application. He sighed and thought that this made for the last thing he wanted to do this afternoon. The operations guys always took up a bunch of time to explain stuff that he never understood. "Take them to the boardroom. We'll have more room in there. I'll join them in a minute." Greg disconnected and tried Terry one more time. The phone went to voicemail again. This time, he left a message to the effect that he understood they would be having dinner at home and, if this had changed, to let him know.

Greg put the receiver on the cradle and, reluctantly, pulled himself away from his chair. Though not sure, it felt like he might be coming down with something. His whole body ached as if he ran a fever. He stopped in the private bathroom to check the mirror. Other than the deep frown, he looked normal. His cheeks showed no flush in the slightest. It must be the stress, he decided, and went to the boardroom.

After almost five hours of technical discussion, the meeting broke up. Greg told the team that they'd done a great job and looked forward to seeing the app in service. For his life, he would not be able to tell anyone what the app did for the client. His mind didn't stay on the subject long enough to absorb the details. He had to excuse himself a couple of times when he became so distracted that it became obvious that he hadn't followed the conversation. Several times, he ended up in the embarrassing position of asking that a question get repeated. On each occasion, the team leader smirked and made the query again as if talking to a five-year-old. Greg caught several eye rolls and smirks that passed between young people who had full awareness that the information went right over his head.

Finally, he told the group that he understood how brilliant they were and that it wasn't necessary for him to understand all the details to approve their efforts. The effect of putting them all down as smartasses worked. They all grew respectful and dumbed down the discussion so that he could keep up with the information. In the end, he believed the team felt appreciative of his comments and that they'd had a good meeting.

As the rest left, he asked the team leader to remain behind. The leader looked like he regretted his disrespect, as clearly, Greg didn't feel happy. "Sit down," Greg said. "I want to make sure that this kind of meeting doesn't repeat itself in the future."

"Yes, sir, but—"

"Please, let me finish. You and your team should engage in the product enhancements of a company I founded, and do so at my pleasure. Do you understand this fact?"

"Yes, sir, I do." His eyes looked at the floor to avoid Greg's.

"This idea of mocking the head of the company simply because you're younger and brighter is something you have to try and correct."

"I don't think we were mocking."

"Well, I don't know what else to call it. It seemed clear that I had a poor grasp of the technological discussion. I am a CEO, for Christ's sake, not a techie working in a cubicle. There is no way I can keep up with your team."

"We didn't mean any disrespect."

"I believe you, but actions speak louder than words."

"Should I resign?"

"Hell, no. Just knock off the arrogance with upper management. Do you think you can do that?"

"Yes, sir. I will also speak to my team."

"Great. That's all I ask. You do good work, and I would hate to see you get sideways with some of the other officers. I can assure you; if any of them had been in this meeting, you would experience vaporization. That would have been a loss for the company."

"Thank you, sir. I totally apologize."

"Thank you, son. Now, let's get back to work, shall we?"

"Yes, sir."

Greg reached for the young man's hand and gave it a shake. The guy smiled, and Greg could tell that he felt bad about leading what had become an insubordinate attitude. Greg showed him to the door, and then walked back to his office. He said goodnight to Ms. McCormick and gathered his things. Tonight, would not prove easy.

Chapter Twelve

Greg pulled up to the garage and, absentmindedly, watched the door as it rose and disappeared overhead. The noise of the garage door opening would have alerted Terry that he'd arrived home. With no going back, he must proceed with what he needed to do tonight. All the way home, he'd rehearsed what he would say. It more or less came down to saying upfront that they had nothing to worry about, but some trouble had arisen with the firm. He figured he would keep it generic to a business problem rather than drift into the dangerous territory of personal. Later, he could always declare more trouble than he'd originally thought.

He turned the off the engine and sat for a second before opening the car door. Greg let out a deep sigh and pulled himself out of the car. "Here goes nothing." It shocked Greg that he'd spoken out loud. He'd better be a little more careful. With a sigh, he entered the door into the mud room. "Terry," he called out at volume, but received no response.

He moved into the kitchen and put his briefcase on the counter. It looked like no one was home, and Greg couldn't recall whether or not he'd seen her car in the garage. He'd gotten so preoccupied with what he would say that he hadn't noticed his surroundings. Perturbed and annoyed at himself, he retraced his steps and looked in the garage. Her car sat in its place, raising a slight alarm inside him.

Maybe she was in the bedroom or the shower. Given the size of the house, it seemed feasible that she might not have heard his greeting. He went through the living room to the rear wing and their bedroom. He called her name again. Still no answer, and now his nervous feeling turned to resentment, as it became apparent that Terry had something to do and hadn't let him know what was going on.

He returned to the kitchen and pulled a beer out of the refrigerator. After pouring the brew, he gave Terry a call for the third time that day.

"Hello, sweetheart," Terry answered on the first ring. "What's up?"

"Hi, honey. Just trying to figure out if we planned to have dinner home tonight."

"Why, yes, we did. I have a beautiful dinner arranged. In fact, I'm picking it up right now."

"Your car is here. Who are you with?"

"Our library board meeting ran late, and Joseph volunteered to give me a lift since Cynthia had to leave early."

"Joseph?"

"Yes. On that other thing, I can't talk now, darling. I will give you the details when I get home."

"Uh, okay. What other thing?"

"Oh, you silly. You're embarrassing me. I have to go. Goodbye, dear. I'll get there in a half hour. Be a sweetheart and make me a drink, will you?"

Greg, finally, got that she spoke in code, as Joseph whoever sat in the car with her. "Okay, love. See you in a half hour. Martini okay?"

"Marvelous, my sweet. Bye."

She switched off the phone, and he now felt better. Of course, Cynthia had to leave early. She had a couple of kids, and they needed to have their mom home after school. The idea of mixing a pitcher of martinis came as a good thing. A little bit of gin would help the story go down easier. For the first time today, Greg felt his stomach relax a bit. It could be the beer that he now saw he'd finished. He reached for another and reminded himself of the old poem governing mixing drinks. "Whiskey on beer never fear. Beer on whiskey very risky." Another beer wouldn't hurt, and then he would semi-numb-out on the gin.

His thoughts turned to the character named Joseph. He couldn't recall ever hearing that name before. In fact, he didn't recall hearing of a man on the library board. He thought back to the board Christmas party and still couldn't recall a male member. The whole board was made up of women, who had a common interest in the health of the place. Nope, he felt sure no man had an involvement except as a spouse of those in control. When Terry got home, she would give him the whole story.

Greg found the gin and vermouth along with his special pitcher. He must wait until the right moment to mix the martinis, but he wanted to get ready. When Terry walked in the door would make the perfect time to put the soothing syrup together. He took the last drink of his beer and walked the bottle and glass to the sink. He rinsed out the glass, put it in the dishwasher, and threw the bottle into the recycle bin. Headlights swung into the driveway and pulled up to the service door. Greg went across the kitchen and reached for the knob.

As the door opened, he caught sight of Terry laughing and saying goodbye to the driver, who must be Joseph. She came into the light, and Greg saw she carried two bags from the deli. "Let me help you. Does Joseph want to come in for a drink?"

"Oh, thank you." Terry handed Greg the bags. "No, he said he had to rush off. Some kind of dinner engagement."

From the configuration of the taillights and distinctive sound as he pulled away, Greg saw that Joseph drove a Porsche. Greg took the bags into the house and put them on the counter. The martinis needed mixing, and he'd better get to it.

"So, where did Joseph come from?" Greg made small talk while he poured the gin into the pitcher. "Too bad I couldn't meet him."

"Oh, Greg. You are a poor dear. Don't you know you scare the crap out of most people, and their natural tendency is to run away."

"Me? Scare people?"

"Yeah, you. Major football and TV announcer star as well as a big-time fund manager. My drink ready?"

Greg poured the clear liquid into two martini stemware glasses that immediately showed signs of the chill as the cold gin hit the glass. He dropped two olives on a pick into each. "Here you are."

Terry came over and took her drink. She sipped and complimented Greg. He smiled at her and wondered what she had in the bags.

"I asked for the finest standing rib they had. We'll have twice-baked potato, the rib, and some nice, fresh green beans. It's all ready to go, and the man said it would stay perfect for at least an hour. Let's go and sit down for a minute, and you can tell me about your day."

Greg swallowed hard at the thought of his day. He took a deep drink of the martini and grabbed the pitcher. They went into the living room and sat in one of the conversation areas. Greg put the pitcher on a coaster on the side table. "Today was a real challenge." He stopped and took another sip of his drink. Terry looked no more concerned than normal, so he decided to get to the point. "I have been informed there are some irregularities at the firm."

Terry sipped from her glass. "What irregularities?"

"The SEC did an audit, and apparently someone did some fraudulent trades."

"Do they know who?"

Greg realized he had waded halfway into the swamp. Either he must pull back or go forward. Another gulp drained his glass, and he poured another. Terry noticed that he acted abnormally. A slight blink of her right eye usually marked the beginning of a nervous reaction to a situation. "They don't know who. It's a little more complex, as the person used my trading account."

"They what?" Terry almost spilled her drink and caught the gin on her lip with her finger. "They think you did it?"

"Well. Not much else they can think."

"Greg. Tell me you didn't do anything illegal."

"Terry, I swear, I didn't do anything, period. Someone hacked into my account and did the trades. We have a forensic technician looking into it, and he says he can prove that a hacker has compromised the account."

"Oh, my God. What a relief. I've always worried about the trading rules and how easy it would be to break a law without even trying."

"All true, darling, but it looks like I'm the victim here."

"I'll be right back. I need a cracker or something. For some reason, this martini is hitting me like a ton of bricks." Terry got up and went back to the kitchen.

Greg sat back. He'd gotten it all out, and it looked like Terry would be okay. Of course, she would need time to process what he'd told her. He'd best mention that he'd hired the best lawyers and that they believed this would go away without too much more inconvenience.

Terry returned with a small plate of crackers and some cheese that she set on the table between them. "I checked the dinner, and it all looks good." She reached for a cracker and took a small bite. "May I have another drink? Mine's getting warm."

Greg leaned forward and poured fresh gin into her glass. "I want you to know I've hired the best lawyers."

"Oh, Greg. You already said you were innocent, and the person looking at the situation said someone hacked into your accounts. I have the belief that this will go away. I don't think you should worry anymore."

"I don't want you to worry, is all."

"I shall put my faith in the fact that you're a good man and you'll get to the bottom of this."

"I appreciate your faith, but a lot could happen."

"Like what?"

"Oh, I don't know." Greg sighed. "Maybe someone has it in for me and have set me up for a fall."

"That sounds a little paranoid. Who would do such a thing?"

"Yeah, you're right. I guess I feel a little spooked, is all."

"Have some more of your drink and let's talk about something else."

"Okay." Greg took a sip. "Who's this Joseph who brought you home?"

Terry laughed. "Hmmm, jealous are we?"

"No. I just wondered how a man got roped into the library board. I thought it was a women-only club."

"He's the Baron de La Rossis, and he donated a bunch of money to the library foundation. We invited him to become part of the board so that he would have a little say so in how we spend his money."

"Baron?" Greg wrinkled his nose. "Who gets a title of Baron?"

"His family is from Italy, and the title goes back generations. They came to the US in the nineteen hundreds. They still have a winery back in Italy."

"How does the Baron make a living?"

"He and his brother are importers. That's about all I know."

"Seems you know a lot."

"Well, we do have a bio on him, and I read it, is all. Are you getting hungry?"

Greg looked at Terry for a second. He tried to see any hint of untruth on her face. It sure seemed odd that she would pay attention to anyone let alone this mysterious Baron. Maybe that made for the reason she showed interest—him being a mystery man. "Yes, I think I could eat some of that delicious dinner you prepared."

Terry gave him a large smile. "With my two little hands. Want to eat in the dining room?"

"Sure, why not. I'll go get us a nice bottle of wine."

"That sounds great."

Greg's mood had improved. He thought maybe it came down to the gin, but in retrospect, it was the fact that his bad news hadn't seemed so bad to Terry. The last thing he wanted to do was give her cause for concern, and it looked like she felt fine. He picked up the martini pitcher and his glass. Terry took hers with her to the kitchen, and he followed. She looked in good spirits, and that made him rise to the occasion.

The wine cellar stood off the kitchen, through the butler's pantry. Though not a cellar, the room had wall to ceiling coolers. It also held a little table and two café chairs, and at times, he and Terry would share a bottle in here. The atmosphere felt conducive to conversation and enjoyment of the wine. The glass-fronted coolers allowed the bottles to provide the décor, and the wine itself the subject matter for discussion. Greg opened one of the red-wine coolers and selected a bottle that he knew Terry liked.

Upon entering the kitchen, he found Terry on her cell phone. When she saw him, she told whoever it was that she had to go. Greg never asked who was on the phone and figured that if it were someone he knew, she would tell him. She turned back to the meal preparation without saying anything. Normally, he wouldn't give it a second thought, but given the strangeness of the Baron thing, it bothered him not knowing who she'd spoken to. "Who was that?"

Terry turned and gave him a look that broadcast the fact that his weird behavior had continued. "Just Sally checking to see if we're still on for tomorrow. Greg, you need to relax."

He now felt like an idiot and smiled weakly. Greg opened the wine without any more comment and took it to the dining room, where he poured them each a glass and sat in his normal chair. Terry came through the swinging door with two plates. She placed them on the table, and then went to the light switch and dimmed the overhead chandler. Then his wife lit the tapers closest to them and took her seat. "Isn't this much nicer?" she said.

Greg had to agree, and in the candlelight, Terry's face took on a glow that he always found enchanting. He loved his wife deeply, and moments like these felt precious to him. He lifted his wine glass. "Here's to us." Touching her glass with his, he gave her a smile that she returned warmly. They each sipped their wine to seal the toast and then turned their attention to the prime rib dinner.

After the meal, they relaxed in the living room and, before long, it became clear that both needed to get some sleep. Greg had a tough time keeping his eyes open, and Terry kept suggesting he go to bed. He didn't want to go without her, and finally, she decided she could sleep as well.

Greg got ready for bed, slid under the covers, and took his book off the nightstand. He lay reading but had to give up since he couldn't keep his eyes open. Vaguely, he recalled Terry sliding into the opposite side of the king bed, but fell sound asleep before they had any further conversation.

Terry read her book for another half hour before sighing and turning off the light. She still lay awake, thinking of what Greg had told her earlier. Visions of the press finding a good story in a local football hero tumbling off the pedestal plagued her. Did any way exist that they might manage to protect their family from the scandal? Terry decided that she needed to take one step at a time and allow Greg to resolve this thing without further worry on her part. After a while, she fell asleep but woke sporadically during the night with more thoughts of dire consequences.

The alarm shattered the peace that seemed only seconds old. Terry and Greg couldn't believe that the night had been so short, as both could have slept more. Here, morning had come, and not too welcomed by either of them. Terry could feel the puffiness under her eyes from the sketchy on-and-off-again sleep pattern of the night. She hoped a shower and splash of cold water on her face would get rid of eye luggage.

Greg groaned and pulled himself out of bed and felt as if he had played a full sixty minutes of football. He ached from head to foot and felt sure he had contracted a flu bug. Once in the shower, he realized it as nothing but tension. Today would be another day of hell, and he could feel it in his bones. The news about the hacking evidence, which yesterday had felt good, had now given way to the dread of the unknown. He would have to face another day no matter what lay in store. The reality of the situation seemed more noticeable in the daylight than being warm and comfortable with a good dinner, nice wine, and Terry.

He finished dressing and told Terry goodbye. Greg didn't feel like breakfast and planned to grab coffee at the office. He wished he could stay home, but unlike most everyone else, there are no sick days for a CEO.

Chapter Thirteen

The elevator took forever, and Greg regretted not having a cup of coffee before heading to the office. He couldn't tell if he had a caffeine headache or felt the results of the martinis and half bottle of wine. In any case, the coffee called his name. Finally, he reached his floor and stepped into the plush entryway that let anyone know they had entered a suite of offices of important people.

Greg stepped through the doorway and looked at Ms. McCormick, who detected, immediately, the low-warning sign on his coffee reservoir face. She hurried to the carafe, filled a big cup, and carried it into his office.

"Thank you. I need this." He looked at Ms. McCormick as he lifted the rich coffee to his lips. He wished it didn't brew so hot that he couldn't drink it down quickly for more immediate relief.

"Your agenda looks light today."

"That's good. Not feeling tip-top just now."

Ms. McCormick took an unconscious step back from his desk. "You sick?"

"No, I just missed the coffee this morning and had a little too much wine last night."

"Well, that's my special Columbian blend. Guaranteed to fix anything wrong."

"Hope so." Greg took another large sip and breathed in the aroma of the rich brew. He'd read somewhere that the aroma of coffee had curative benefits. After another sip, he felt the caffeine reach his brain. His headache faded fast. "Who do I see today?"

Ms. McCormick took a seat and opened her portfolio. She passed today's schedule over to Greg. "The first one up is Robert, the computer guy, along with Mr. Mathews. I don't have Robert's last name."

"It doesn't matter, but his name is Given. Did Jack give you a subject?"

"No, Mr. Mathews just said they needed to see you for an update."

"Okay." Greg leaned back and took a bigger drink of his coffee. He supposed that Robert had some news on the hacking.

"Next is your favorite, Mr. Torrence."

"Am I that obvious about my feelings for Ralph?"

"Well, I know you, and I don't think Mr. Torrence has a clue."

"I suppose he didn't say what he wanted?"

"No, he said it was urgent, but I explained that Mr. Mathews and R-um, Mr. Given were ahead of him. He didn't seem pleased."

"I'm sure. I see I have a lunch with some analysts."

"Yes, that's been scheduled for a while. You, Mr. Torrence, and Mr. Mathews will meet with them in the boardroom. I've arranged to have lunch brought in. I hope a salad with grilled tuna will be okay."

"Fine. That's Jack's favorite. The tuna is always good. I'm sure they'll enjoy it. I know he will."

Ms. McCormick smiled at Greg's sarcasm. She had grown used to his dry sense of humor. It took some time, but she now enjoyed it when he made a joke or two, as it usually signaled that he felt good. Today, his humor gave a definite sign that he felt on the mend. "After lunch, your schedule stays fairly full 'til five.

You have a capital meeting that starts at two. It may take three or so hours."

Greg groaned loudly, and Ms. McCormick smiled and paused. Then she continued, "Tonight, you have a dinner at the opera house. The patron recognition dinner. Mrs. Petros will meet you there because she has a meeting just beforehand. Cocktails run from six to seven, and the dinner at seven. It should prove a nice evening. A string quartet will play throughout. I understand the dinner will get served on the stage, which should be interesting."

"Yes, that does sound interesting. I wonder if Mrs. Petros plans to drive. If so, I won't need to drive over and can take a cab."

"I'll give her assistant a call to find out. I would suggest you use a driver anyway. The night could run late, and the last thing you need to do is worry about driving home. In fact, let me set up the transportation with Mrs. Petros' assistant."

"That would be great, Bella. I appreciate it."

"No problem. If you have nothing else, I'll get you another cup and show Mr. Given and Mathews in."

"Yes, thank you." Greg handed over the cup and looked out through the window. He still didn't feel a hundred percent and didn't look forward to a whole day and then a night filled with people and things he had no interest in meeting or discussing. He realized that the strain of the last day had had an effect on his outlook. Normally, he attacked each day as if it were his last. The last twenty-four hours had him dragging around as if underwater. Greg loved going to the opera patron dinner since so many talented and interesting people always attended. He remained of the belief that anyone who was anyone in Boston would go there. Tonight just felt like it would be a chore rather than a treat. Greg didn't notice Ms. McCormick when she placed his cup on his desk. She cleared her throat, and he looked at her as if he didn't know who she was.

"Mr. Mathews and Given are here."

"Thanks, Bella. Show them in. Sorry, I got lost in thought."

"It's fine, sir. You have a lot going on."

Greg looked at his coffee, and then back to her. How much did she know? She'd know everything, as others would be more than happy to fill her in on anything that smelled of scandal. Not to give her information on a friendly basis but to shake her confidence and let her know life may get tenuous in the near future. It seemed like a group schadenfreude. It came from the position of power that Ms. McCormick enjoyed as assistant to the CEO and how that power provided a source of jealousy in others. Greg wouldn't feel too surprised to hear that Ralph had given Bella some information under the guise that she should know for her own good. Finally, he spoke, which caused Ms. McCormick to sigh in relief, "Show them in, Bella. Thank you."

Jack and Robert entered the office and took a seat at the conference table. Greg moved from his desk. "You guys want coffee?" Both shook their heads, no, and Ms. McCormick made an exit.

"What do you have today?" After asking the question, Greg saw the quick look each gave the other and knew the news couldn't be good.

Jack cleared his throat. "Robert has tracked the hacker to the source. He now has the IP address of the computer that the hacker used to get into the system."

"That's great news. Why so glum?"

"It happened via your computer. The one sitting on your desk over there." Jack pointed like a third grader fingering the source of a spitball.

"My computer? You've got to have made a mistake."

Robert stiffened at the insinuation that he would make such an error. "No mistake, sir. I can show you the transactions still on the hard drive. Whoever did it never bothered to erase the evidence."

"What does this mean?"

Jack held up his hand to stop Robert from answering. "It means either you actually did the trades and the hack or someone gained access and then, somehow, put the information on your computer, using your IP address."

"I can assure you; I didn't hack anything. I can barely operate a PC let alone pull off something this sophisticated."

"I believe you, Greg. Our . . . em, Robert, could you excuse us. I need to talk to Greg privately."

Robert nodded and rose. "I shall keep working on this. It could be that I can find some residual data that will give me a lead. I would like to take your computer and give it a thorough inspection."

Jack thought for a second. "Can you make a backup without compromising any of the information?"

"Yes."

"Okay, you can have it. I want the backup delivered to me before you start any exploration." Jack frowned slightly at Robert so that he would get the message and follow through.

"I understand. You'll have the backup this morning."

Satisfied, Jack waved Robert toward the computer. Robert detached the monitor and keyboard and took the computer with him when he left. While he set to work, Greg and Jack didn't talk. Once he went out of the door, Greg said, "Who cares if Robert blows up the computer?"

"The DA will care if something happens to a key piece of evidence. We need to be real careful, Greg. If it looked like we'd tampered with evidence, the DA has severe penalties he can ask for."

"Okay, I understand. I swear, I didn't do anything around those trades."

"I was going to say with Robert here that I believe you. I do believe you, but this is getting sticky. Whoever did this knew they were setting you up for the fall."

"I can't imagine who that could be. To my knowledge, I haven't pissed anyone off to the point where they would want to see me go to jail."

"How about someone who would like your job? Anyone like that around?"

"Besides Ralph Torrence, you mean?"

"I've known Ralph for a while, and he doesn't seem like the type."

"You may be right. I have a meeting with him next. Could you hang around for that?"

"Sure. Be happy to."

"Damn. What the hell will we do now?"

"Like before, we need to remain committed to taking care of business and not worrying about this until we have a real cause."

"You going to alert the DA about the hacking?"

"Now that the end of the road is on your computer, no. I think we should give Robert some time to see what he can come up with."

"Okay. That puts the worry off a little."

Ms. McCormick opened the door and announced that Ralph sat in the reception, waiting. Greg told her to let him in. She stepped aside, and Ralph passed by her.

"Come in, Ralph. I hope you don't mind, but Jack needs to be here. Legal stuff."

Ralph took a seat. "I understand. How you been, Jack?"

"Fine, thank you, Ralph, and you?"

"Just swell. Thanks for asking. I'm glad you're here. I wanted to report that the DA has asked me to come to his office."

Jack's eyebrows resembled railroad crossing gates going up. "What a surprise. Did he mention what they wanted to discuss?"

"No. They did say I wasn't to discuss the conversation with anyone."

Jack leaned forward. "What conversation?"

"Oh, the one we will have in the DA's office."

"So, you haven't talked to them yet?"

"No. I have a meeting this afternoon at two o'clock."

Greg folded his hands on the table. "Thanks for letting us know. You go ahead to the meeting. We will honor the DA's request and not ask you about the meeting."

Ralph looked down and didn't say anything for a few seconds. "I hope you know I didn't have anything to do with the DA asking me in."

"Sure, Ralph," Jack said. "We know that. The DA is fishing, and somehow he believes you have information that will prove useful to him."

"Can I refuse to talk to him?"

"You can if you want him to believe you have something to hide. You don't have anything to hide, do you?"

"Of course not. Sometimes, I wonder why I tell you anything. You come across as the prosecutor the way you ask a question."

"My apologies. I didn't mean to imply anything. I just wanted to check."

Greg unfolded his hands. "Let's all cool down. Ralph, Jack didn't mean anything."

Ralph smiled slightly. "Thanks, Greg. I just don't like getting put in the role of providing information that may cause you trouble."

Jack couldn't keep quiet, "What information would that be?"

"Well, I'm not sure, exactly. Anytime the DA wants to talk, he's the one holding the agenda."

"Do you know of anything specific that would lead you to believe Greg has done anything wrong?"

"No, I don't. I know as much as you and maybe even less."

Greg looked at his watch and grew a little worried about the analysts coming in for lunch. He hadn't had a chance to look at the morning briefing yet. He didn't need to have a simple question muffed because he hadn't seen updated information. "Can we take a break and get the briefing documents for the lunch today?"

Ralph sighed in relief. He felt glad to get out from under Jack's questions. "I have them right here." He opened his portfolio and passed Greg and Jack a copy of the briefing document.

"Let me read this for a minute," Greg said.

The three sat and went through the document. Greg frowned at a couple of the statements and made some notes. Jack used a highlighter to pull out pieces of information. Ralph sat without looking at the document since his team had responsibility and he was aware of its content.

Greg looked up. "Okay, Ralph, anything in here that's a gotcha?"

"No, sir. It's pretty straightforward. The fund is delivering about twenty-one percent growth, as compared to the ten percent Dow. It does show that your strategy of moving to Large Cap stock when everyone else ran for bonds was the right thing to do. The excellent management of the fund is the walk-away message for the analysts. You can point to a stable mix of stocks and bonds and the capability of moving out of any position when conditions warrant. The only question that could come out is the rumor of you selling the fund to a bigger firm. The rumor has been talked about almost constantly for the last year."

"I know. I get a question every time I go to any meeting when I'm about to sell. My answer has always been the same. Never."

"I think with the kinds of returns you can produce, the assumption is that the value of the fund and its management go up. There will be a point where the offers will become more difficult to ignore."

"I understand, but I founded this fund, and it is my life now. I just don't see myself putting in the same kind of blood and sweat for someone else."

"I would expect the question, though."

"Yes, thank you. You see anything, Jack?"

"No. The report all looks good. I think the analysts will go home and post their five-star ratings. I know I feel that way."

"Yeah, but you are almost forced to think that way." Greg smiled in appreciation of Jack's little vote of confidence. "I think we're done here. What time do they arrive?"

"About fifteen minutes. We're putting them in the board room."

"Yes. Lunch will be brought in. Who will handle the presentation before the Q&A?"

Ralph looked at Jack to make sure he didn't speak out of turn. Jack nodded for him to proceed. "I'll do the presentation. It's our standard. I also have handouts."

"Good, I like the way you talk to these guys. They trust you."

Ralph smiled at the compliment. "I do my best."

"I feel good about the meeting. Why don't you guys give me a minute, and I'll join you in the board room."

Jack and Ralph nodded and pushed back from the table. They left, and Ms. McCormick came in. "Anything you need before the meeting?"

"Yes. Did you get hold of Terry's assistant?"

"Yes, we made arrangements for a car to take Mrs. Petros to her meeting and then come for you. The driver will meet you at the house. These arrangements will give you time to freshen up before the event."

"Great, Bella. I feel better about going now."

"Good, you should enjoy yourself. You okay on the analysts meeting?"

"Yes. In fact, Ralph has put together a nice story. It should be a no-brainer." Ms. McCormick smiled and left Greg sitting at the table. He sat thinking of something else that he'd wanted to ask Ms. McCormick, but it had slipped his mind. He turned to the prospect of selling the firm. If word got out about the trades, proof of hack or no, the value of the fund would probably dive with clients jumping ship. The more who left, the lower the values would go. Maybe he should start the process of courting a buyer. The problem was the wheels for the firm's demise had set in motion already. He felt sure that the Grand Jury had already made its decision. Why else would Ralph get a call from the DA? Greg didn't think the DA would go on a fishing expedition with the intent of turning up something. No, he already knew where he wanted to go and would want to line up witnesses. Probably, he would threaten Ralph just as Jack had said. Ralph would find himself in the uncomfortable position of trading what he knew for immunity from prosecution, even though he hadn't done anything wrong. Or, so Greg hoped.

Time to go to the meeting. Greg rose and left his office. He smiled at Ms. McCormick, who had her thumb up, for luck, he guessed. He appreciated the gesture. The board room lay a short walk down the expensively-carpeted hallway. He reached the door, took a breath, and went in.

"Ladies and gentlemen, welcome." Greg used his jolly voice and made a point of going around the table and shaking each of the attendee's hands. It pleased him to see some of the analysts sitting there, all smiles. They would be the ones who would support a good rating. The others would need convincing, which he thought wouldn't prove difficult.

"Why don't we all take a seat. I propose we start with a brief presentation by Ralph Torrence, our CFO, and then have an informal question and answer period over lunch. How does that sound?"

Everyone around the table nodded agreement. Greg smiled at the reception, and then introduced Ralph, who did the usual drama of lowering the screen and lights from his laptop. He ran his own slides, and the show seemed professional. The analysts took notes and appeared to receive the information in a positive way. Once Ralph had finished, the lights came up, and Greg announced the arrival of lunch.

The servers went about their job efficiently. They delivered the salads, took and delivered drink orders, and went back out through the doors. "If you don't mind talking with your mouth full, I'm open to questions." Greg's comment received a good-natured laugh and some ribbing from the group. Greg took this as a good sign that the rest of the meeting would go well.

Greg hadn't called it wrong. The meeting turned out way better than he could have hoped. The questions all stayed around the excellent performance of the fund. They wanted to know the secrets of such good results. Greg said that, in a number of ways, the secret was damn hard work and excellent research. The meeting came to a close, and Greg thanked each for attending. He provided a well-prepared summary handout of the meeting and prospectus. Some thanked him for the lunch and especially for the information as well as the delicious cake for dessert. Greg laughed and said it was an old family recipe, courtesy of catering.

Greg made it a point to shake each hand as they left. The last person, a young-looking woman, extended her hand to Greg. "My name is Felicia Dingwell from Commonwealth."

"Ah, yes, Felicia. Nice meeting you. How is my old friend Duckworth doing?" He referred to the chairman of Commonwealth.

"He sends his regards and is quite well, thank you. I do have a question that I didn't want to raise in front of the others."

Greg let go of her hand and wondered what was coming. He disguised his concern perfectly. "Yes, what is it?" Jack had stood watching the interchange and moved a little closer so that he could hear better.

"We have heard some rumors that the SEC has an investigation underway, and some of the findings are getting followed up by the District Attorney."

"My, my. That is some rumor."

"So, it's not true?"

Jack stepped closer and held out his hand. "I'm Jack Mathews, the corporate counsel."

Felicia offered her hand. "Nice meeting you, Jack."

"I heard your question. Excuse me for butting in, but our firm has not received any information from the SEC or the District Attorney, so it would be quite inappropriate for us to comment on a rumor."

"You've had no communication between you and the DA's office?"

"About what?"

"Any findings by the SEC."

"No. No communication regarding SEC findings."

"Well, okay then. I guess the rumors are just that at this time."

"I guess they are. I have never seen a day when there are not rumors."

Felicia smiled at Jack's comment and started to leave. "It was nice meeting both of you. I hope I can call for any follow-up questions that come up."

Greg gave her a big smile and assured her that she should call anytime. She smiled back and left the room. Greg sat in a chair. "What the hell?"

Chapter Fourteen

"Shush," Jack said. He walked over to the doors and opened them. He stepped into the hall and looked in both directions. "Let's go to your office. Shit, here comes Ralph. We should leave him out of the discussion."

"Okay, but he'll want to know how it went from our point of view."

"Yeah. We'll stay here and debrief him on the meeting, then we need to talk in your office."

Ralph passed Jack and came into the room, looking like he'd just finished kicking the winning field goal in the Super Bowl. He sat and looked at Greg. "So, I think it went pretty well, don't you?"

Jack said, "It couldn't have gone any better. What a piece of art. They loved the presentation, and the questions all stayed upbeat. You should feel proud."

"Thank you. My team deserves the credit. They worked hard on the material."

"It showed," Jack said.

"Yes, it showed. You've stepped up and hit a home run." Greg rose, and Ralph did the same. "I would use this format at all the analyst meetings for the rest of the year. It's a winner."

Ralph felt a rush of pride, and his face turned red. "I appreciate your compliments. Thank you." Ralph followed Greg and Jack out of the door. "I'll give my team congratulations."

"Yes, please do. Jack and I have some business to discuss, so if you will excuse us." The smile on Ralph's face dimmed slightly. Greg imagined that Ralph thought his win would get him into the inner circle. Greg tried to soften the blow, "We'll talk later."

The words had their effect. Ralph's smile widened. "Yes, thank you." Ralph went toward the elevator while Greg and Jack headed for Greg's office. Ms. McCormick asked how everything had gone, and Greg told her all had run to perfection. The information brought a pleased smile to her lips.

Once through the door, Greg sat at his desk, and Jack took a side chair. Greg couldn't keep quiet any longer, "How the hell did anyone find out about the DA's involvement in our business?"

Jack sat a moment. "I have to believe someone in the DA's office has discussed the case with someone outside the office." Jack put his fingers to his lips and plucked at his lower lip while thinking. "I need to call the DA right now."

"Here, use my phone." Greg handed Jack the receiver. "What's the number?"

Jack looked at his phone. "No, I'll call him on my cell. I don't want him to avoid the call because he doesn't recognize the number, or worse, thinks you're calling him." Jack hit speed dial.

The DA answered on the first ring. "This is Thompson."

"Yes, Peter, this is Jack Mathews." Jack lifted his brows while looking at Greg. Greg got the message that Jack had scored a contact with the DA.

"Yes, Jack. This is a surprise. What can I do for you?"

"I just wanted to check in with you to see if you'd had any developments?"

"We haven't received an indictment if that's what you're asking?"

"That's good information but not the reason for my call."

"Why're you calling, then?" Impatience laced Thompson's voice.

"We just had a meeting with Wall Street analysts and one of them raised a question about the SEC going to the justice department."

"Who raised the question?"

"It's not important who but why. Do you have a leak in your office?"

"Now, Jack, if we had a leak, do you think I would know about it? 'Coz if I did, I would plug it. You understand."

"Yeah, no offense. I needed to ask, is all. It seems strange that word has hit the Street about trouble with the fund."

"Well, go fishing somewhere else. My office didn't leak anything. I would be a little more careful before you accuse my office of improper behavior."

"Okay, Peter. Again, no offense. I apologize. You *will* let me know if you hear anything, won't you?"

"Damn right, I will. One thing you should know. I've asked Ralph Torrence to come in and answer a few questions."

"Should I go there with him?"

"That might be a good idea. It will keep everything on the up and up."

"Okay, I'll go with him. Thanks for letting me know. When is the meeting?"

"No problem. My office at two o'clock."

"That's half an hour from now."

"How far away are you?"

"I can make it, but what would have happened had I not called?"

"I would have met with Ralph and apologized later."

"Okay, I need to leave now. See you in a bit."

"Bye, Jack."

Jack dropped his phone into his suit pocket. "I got an invite to the meeting with Ralph. The son of a bitch made it at two o'clock."

"Yeah, I figured as much. You need to go now."

"Okay, but we still need to talk later. I'll come back and brief you on the meeting as well as try to give you advice on how to proceed." Jack moved toward the door, and then turned around. "Don't talk to anyone about this case."

Greg nodded his agreement, and Jack left. He went to his desk and sat heavily in his chair. He thought about the fact that someone had managed to steal his IP address and then hack into the trading program. He shook his head to clear it. The thought seemed almost too complicated to continue. With it happening on his machine, the possibility of going to jail and getting bankrupted moved to the front burner. Someone must have wanted him to get humiliated and destroyed. Who would feel that pissed off at him to do such a thing? He thought deeply about all the people with which he had done business, and none came to mind. He promised himself that he would sit down with his contacts list and try to isolate anyone he may have taken advantage of or otherwise caused such trouble that they now looked for revenge.

Ms. McCormick broke into his thoughts, "Your two o'clock is here. Do you want me to stall, or can you see them?" Greg told her to send them in and, for the life of him, couldn't remember who it was. His schedule sat under his elbow, but he didn't give a shit enough to look. Ms. McCormick brought in his visitors and sat them at the conference table. "When Mr. Mathews comes back, please show him in."

The next three hours got taken up with presentations on capital expenditures, and Greg mostly paid attention. He approved submitting the proposal to the capital committee. The meeting ended with all parties pleased and smiling. As they left, Jack Mathews made his way into Greg's office. He signaled Greg that he'd take a chair by the desk. Greg showed the rest out and joined Jack.

"So, what's going on with the DA?"

Jack looked down at his hands and tried to sort out what he wanted to say. "It doesn't look good. The questions the DA had for Ralph all lay in the category of what did he know and when did he know it. Thompson tried to put words in his mouth, and I had to remind him that there have been no laws broken and that Ralph had attended as a favor to the DA. He backed down, but I'm glad I went there. Long story short, they'll come after you for securities fraud."

"He came out and said that?"

"No, of course not, but having spent time as a prosecutor, I can tell you what's on his mind. By talking with Ralph, he wanted to find out if he made part of the problem or the solution."

"Which is it?"

"I'm not sure he knows. He did tell Ralph not to leave town, so I think he's on the block for an indictment as well. The DA can then trade that for testimony."

"Good Lord. Ralph and I getting indicted is messy."

"I think it'll take a week before anything happens, so at least we have some time to, maybe, allow Robert to find something that will prove helpful."

"I'm not sure I want all my eggs in one basket. Can we do anything else?"

"I guess we could hire someone to check through the company emails and see if there's a pattern of communications with an outsider."

"That could take forever."

"We also have to stop anyone from talking to an analyst. If Commonwealth heard of any irregularity, then we may end up with a whole slew of phone calls. I think you ought to call a meeting for tomorrow and set your team straight on discussing any company business with outsiders."

"You don't mean to let them in on the problem, do you?"

"Hell, no. We just want to make certain all communications to the analysis community goes through me."

"Well, that's a relief. I don't want any more people involved in this mess than necessary."

"Okay, so we agree. I'll go check with Robert and see if he's come up with anything."

"Okay, I have to go to a function tonight, so I'll check with you tomorrow."

"Good. No talking to anyone. Right?"

"God, Jack, how many times you going to say that?"

"Maybe a hundred." Jack got up and walked through the doorway, laughing.

Ms. McCormack poked in her head. "Constance called. She'd like you to call her back when you have a chance."

"Okay, Bella. Thanks."

Greg sat at his desk and picked up the phone. Before dialing his daughter's number, he wondered what she wanted. It wasn't like Constance to call him during business hours. He punched the speed dial, and her phone rang.

"Hello, Daddy."

"Hi, sweetheart. What's up?"

"I just wanted to call and tell you I got a raise today."

"Wow, that's wonderful. Was it a million bucks?"

Constance laughed. "No, Daddy, but it was a twenty percent increase."

"Twenty percent? That's pretty good considering the minimal inflation rate."

"I know, right? You proud of me?"

"I sure am, sweetheart. I guess the job is going well, then."

"Yes, I stopped some fraudulent activity and saved the company about three million in losses."

"Sounds wonderful. What's your title again?"

"Geeze, Dad. How many Risk Analyst daughters do you have?"

"Well, just chalk it up to my declining years. Risk Analyst, huh. Do you want to come work for me? I'm sure I have risks that need analysis."

"Very funny, Father. You know my opinion of nepotism. I want to make it on my own."

"Yes, and I respect that."

"Thank you. Nice to hear. Well, I gotta go. I have more data searches I have to do, and the day is getting short."

"Okay, honey. By the way, have you called your mother recently?"

"I talked to her this morning, why?"

"Oh, nothing. Just curious."

"Anything wrong?"

"Why do you ask?"

"Oh, I don't know. Mom seemed preoccupied. Normally, she likes to chat longer than I want to, but today, she sounded anxious to get off the phone."

"She has a big event tonight at the opera, so maybe that's playing on her mind."

"You're probably right. You okay?"

"Yes, dear, fine."

"Okay, then, Daddy. Talk to you later."

"Bye, darling." As he hung up, Greg thought about Constance asking if everything was okay. It wasn't like her to pay attention to how her parents acted. She'd never been the kind of child to ask if things were okay. She must be growing up.

When he looked at his watch, he realized it had gone past time to go home and get ready for the event tonight. He picked up his briefcase and said goodnight to Bella. She reminded him that the car would arrive at his house at a quarter to seven. He thanked her and went to the elevator.

On the drive home, Greg sat deep in thought about Constance's comment about Terry's preoccupation. Did the news about the investigation weigh on her more heavily than he'd thought? He would have to pay attention to how Terry behaved. The last thing he wanted to have happen was that she became worried and upset about the goings on. It did look as if things would get real messy. If Jack had it right, and an indictment came down, he imagined the financial hit alone might prove enough to cause Terry to feel insecure. She'd never had to worry about money from the first day of their marriage, and it might become too much for her to handle.

Greg turned on the radio and touched the classical station. He needed a little soothing right then, and a round of symphonic music seemed just what the doctor ordered. Before long, he reached home and drove into the garage.

Greg skipped a shower and put on his tux in a leisurely fashion. He had about fifteen minutes before the car arrived. Since he didn't have to drive, he poured himself a gin over ice and sat in the living room where he could see the driver pull up. The cold gin felt good in his mouth, and the soothing effects of the alcohol allowed him to relax for the first time that day. He stretched a bit in the large leather chair and thought about what he should do to protect his money. He couldn't sell major positions in the fund, as that would trigger panic with the clients, and the fund would go bust. He might manage to borrow against his fund holdings, but once the news got out about the investigation, he felt sure the bank would call the loan. Greg felt pretty much in a trap. He took a bigger drink of his gin just as headlights flashed in the front windows, giving a signal that the driver had arrived.

Greg put on his coat and drained the last of the gin. No use in worrying any more tonight; he'd let the gin help fortify him.

The ride to the opera house passed pleasantly. The car had a bar, but Greg decided he need not drown his troubles, thereby causing new ones, so he refrained from having another drink. The driver let him out at the main entrance of the opera house, and Greg went straight inside. He checked his coat and stood looking for Terry. A few people had arrived already, and waiters passed among them with appetizers and took orders for cocktails. Greg felt okay to have one more gin and gave his order to the waiter just as he spotted Terry. She stood talking to a group of people that Greg didn't recognize, so he waited until his drink arrived before he went over there. "Well, hello, Greg," a voice said from behind. Greg turned around. Cynthia stood there, the woman who had left early from the library board meeting, causing Terry to get a lift home from Baron Joseph.

"How are you, Cynthia?"

"Just great. It's so nice to see so many people turn out for this event, yourself included."

"I wouldn't have missed it for the world. Gives me an excuse to take a shower."

"Greg, you bad boy. I must say, you look terrific."

Greg blushed in spite of not wanting to show his embarrassment. "Thank you. By the way, I heard you had to leave the library board meeting early last night. Everything okay?"

"Early? Um, I think you may have me confused with someone else. I didn't even go to the meeting."

"Oh, sorry." Greg grew confused. He felt sure that Terry had said Cynthia needed to go home early, and that's why Joseph had driven her home. "Here's my drink. Would you like the waiter to bring you something?" Cynthia declined, declaring she was on a cleanse and alcohol hadn't made it on the approved list.

147

She spotted someone across the room and bade Greg goodbye with an air kiss.

Greg took a sip of his drink and strolled toward Terry. When he'd come in, people had surrounded her. Now she stood talking to one lone male. The famous Baron de La Rossis, possibly? Terry looked up and made eye contact with Greg. She smiled and waved him over.

"I want you to meet Joseph de La Rossis. Joseph, this is my husband, Greg."

Joseph offered his hand and said, "I'm so pleased to meet you. I am a fan and loved how you played football." Greg and Joseph shook hands, and then moved back a bit from each other.

"Thank you, Joseph. It was a lot of fun, and I enjoyed it. Terry tells me you're on the library board."

"Yes, I just became a member. I feel excited about serving."

"Yes," Terry said. "We need some energetic new members like you. I think most of the members have become quite stale."

Greg said, "I know what you mean. Cynthia over there just told me she didn't attend the meeting yesterday. What kind of behavior is that?" Greg looked at Terry, who made the connection, but he played it as if he'd either forgotten about her statement or hadn't made the connection himself.

"So, Joseph, my wife also tells me you're in the import business." Greg took a drink of his gin. He felt quite good and needed to stay a little careful that he didn't overstep a boundary. And asking about Joseph's employment seemed real close to the line.

Terry spoke up, "We don't need to interrogate Joseph regarding his business."

Joseph shook his head and said, "I don't mind talking about it. We import rare wines and art from all over the world."

"That sounds like a fun job." Greg didn't like the look on Terry's face and figured he'd better drop the inquisition now.

"It is most interesting. The logistical factors can prove quite challenging."

"Like what?"

"If you think of how delicate some wines are, and how far they have to come to the US, you can imagine how hard it is to maintain a safe environment for them. The temperature and movement must get controlled with great care."

"I never thought of that. You must have your share of headaches."

Terry smiled, and it looked like Greg had cleared the danger zone for now. He and Joseph chatted about wine and art for several minutes. Then soft chimes announced that the time to sit had arrived. Greg asked Joseph if he wanted to join them, and Joseph agreed. Since the tables held preset name cards, Greg found someone who could make the switch and seated Joseph next to Terry. The person supposed to sit there had not yet arrived, so probably, there would be no harm done.

The meal and the event went well. Terry received an honor for her contribution to the opera. Greg beamed as she went up to accept the plaque. She said some sweet things about her committee and thanked Greg for his support. Greg felt happy to wave briefly when she called his name. Quite a round of applause followed, and Greg bowed his head in recognition of the attention.

Once the ceremonies had completed, the music began for dancing. The waiters served dessert and after-dinner drinks to those who wanted them. Both Greg and Terry begged everyone's indulgence and, under the guise of an early morning tomorrow, said their goodbyes and left.

The driver waited, ready for them, and shut the door after Terry got inside the car. Greg went around to the other side and slid in, and the driver closed his door as well.

"What was that about Cynthia?" Terry sounded upset.

Greg decided to try the innocent card for a minute, "What's what about Cynthia?"

"You know damn well what about. You made a point of informing me Cynthia didn't attend the meeting when I told you she had to leave early."

"Yeah, so why did you lie?"

"I didn't lie. She dropped me off, and then left the meeting. I didn't feel I had to explain all of that. Yes, she skipped out on the meeting. She had something else to do, but she was nice enough to give me a ride. I would have preferred she told me before picking me up, and then I could have taken my car. So, what are you trying to insinuate?"

"Nothing. I just found it odd that Cynthia wasn't at a meeting where you needed a ride home from someone else, is all."

"So, you think I made up the story to do what? Take a ride with Joseph? I must say, darling, you are acting a little weird."

"I suppose I am. I have a little on my mind right now and have become suspicious of everyone."

"Please, take me off your list. I don't deserve to get embarrassed in front of others."

"Embarrassed? How did I embarrass you?"

"No one else knew what you were trying to intimate with your comment except me. It embarrassed me that my husband needed to poke me about a simple misunderstanding. Didn't you see my face get red?"

"No. I'm sorry, I didn't."

"Well, it must have gone the color of a tomato, and that's hard to explain."

"You're right. I apologize. Sorry I played that game."

"I accept, and we can forget it now. We're home."

Greg and Terry got out of the car and entered the house. No more got said about the so-called misunderstanding. Greg still thought there was something to the situation but, considering Terry's reaction, felt he should drop it. After getting ready for bed, he laid there looking at the shadows on the ceiling and hoped the feeling of betrayal would go away. Terry fell sound asleep after the lights went out. Greg could hear her breathing softly. Maybe, with tomorrow being another new day, all his paranoia would seem silly. Keeping that thought, he rolled over and closed his eyes, trying hard to clear his mind.

Chapter Fifteen

Greg's hope of a new day bringing some relief dashed to pieces when his lawyer came into his office.

Jack said, "The Grand Jury handed down an indictment. They've charged you with ten counts of security fraud, eight counts of money laundering, three counts of bank fraud, and two counts of attempting to conceal assets."

"Concealing assets? What the hell?"

"You need to focus. All told, you're looking at a most optimistic case of thirty years in prison and about twenty million in restitution. You won't like this." Jack hit the remote, which brought the Today show to life on the set. Front and center sat a large photo of Greg, and the reporter detailed the charges.

Greg sat transfixed, watching the show. The color drained from his face. He had difficulty breathing and tried to speak.

Jack held up his hand and advised him, "You need to call your attorney and figure out the next steps. Greg, you okay?"

"I'm—"

"Hold on. Let me get you some water." Jack rushed to the sideboard, poured a glass of water, and came back to Greg.

Greg breathed hard. Jack held out the glass to him.

"Thanks." Greg raised the shaking glass to his mouth and took a deep drink. Some of the water went down either side of his mouth. He wiped his chin, and the color came back into his cheeks.

"Do you want me to stay while you call your lawyer?"

"N-no. I feel okay now. You go ahead. I'm sure you have things to do."

"Okay, then. Please, take it easy. I'll send in Ms. McCormick with coffee. Give the lawyer a call, and I'll check back."

"Thanks, Jack." Greg paused over the phone, and then placed the call. The lawyer told him that he needed to surrender to the US Marshalls so that he could avoid the public humiliation of getting hauled out of his office in handcuffs. The law firm had made a deal with the DA, personally, to guarantee his appearance in court for a bail hearing and the reading of the indictment.

The next day, Greg went with the lawyers and got fingerprinted and photographed prior to the hearing before the Federal District Court. In the meantime, the media went berserk. The story aired on all the national and international wires. The headlines, all of the same type, shouted to the effect that Greg was a football star and indicted by the feds as a con man. Over the next few days, the clients pulled out big blocks of money, and those not fast enough lost their funds when Ralph asked for bankruptcy relief.

The relief came but only after the firm became worth about ten cents on the dollar. The funds established by Greg all tanked when investors panicked and dumped the shares at any price. Within days, no buyers remained for the distressed investments, and so trading came to a standstill.

Ralph took it upon himself to buy out some of the last remaining funds. His rationale was to continue the funds under his name and get rid of Greg and Jack once and for all. It proved quite convenient having had a discussion with the DA before all this happened. Listed in the indictment, Ralph stood in a good position and would make a solid witness for the prosecution. He didn't see how he could lose by buying the funds at such a low price. Once the trial finished, he would open shop and, finally, reach a position to become an extremely rich man.

At the hearing, Greg pled not guilty, and Franklin Bronson, his lawyer, argued that Greg didn't prove a flight risk. He convinced the Judge that the ankle monitor would suffice. The Judge set bail at one-million dollars. The law firm stood behind Greg and presented the money drawn from the five million on deposit with them to the court. The court released Greg and ordered him to wear an ankle monitor to prevent trying to flee to avoid prosecution. The trial got scheduled for a few weeks later, and Greg and his lawyers met almost each day to work on a defense.

In the meantime, Robert the computer guy, continued to investigate to search for any way to prove Greg's computer had gotten used as a front for someone else. Jack, he, and Greg met a few times but had no breakthrough. Greg's lawyers felt fairly confident in the fact that his system getting hacked would go a long way in giving his team some bargaining room should the DA want to avoid a trial. They told Greg that to win in front of a jury, the DA would have to prove beyond a doubt that Greg was the one who'd taken the money. Greg reminded them that his computer lay at the bottom of the withdrawal and that it didn't make it any easier. They assured Greg that he still had room for optimism.

Another development loomed that Greg hadn't anticipated. Constance, who lived in New York with her husband, decided to move to Boston to be near her father while all this went on. She obtained a small apartment and became totally committed to helping in any way she could, providing support during the trial phase of the case. Repeatedly, Greg told her to go home to her husband, but she refused. Her firm allowed her to work from home so that she could stay in Boston indefinitely.

Greg's son kept in touch on the phone. He had started a new job and wanted to be there, too, but hoped Greg would understand his inability to get away. His father assured him it was no problem and that he should stay where he was and take care of his business. It gave the assurance his son had hoped for. A father in trouble wasn't something he wanted to have to handle right now.

Jack Mathews resigned from the firm and came onboard at Bronson and Bronson as a full partner. He got assigned straight to Greg's case, as he had been involved from the beginning. He brought Robert with him as a consultant and continued to press him to find the real hacker.

The team met to discuss the indictment and the obvious way the DA had stacked the deck in the charges. Clearly, he wouldn't allow major reductions in the charges to a point where Greg could avoid prison. The DA had loaded the file and would, in all probability, have a difficult time supporting each of the charges with evidence but still have enough to put Greg away.

Jack and Robert spent a lot of time going over the physical evidence of the hacking. Robert did have an opinion that whoever had cloned Greg's IP address had done it without physically entering Greg's computer.

"How do you know this?" Jack gave him a piercing stare.

"When you use keystrokes on a computer, it leaves a register on the hard drive. Several places can get checked, like the last log-on. Which brings to mind a question I need to ask Greg."

Greg sat preoccupied with thinking about going from being a millionaire to almost broke. The only things left were the houses, as well as the money he'd deposited with Bronson and Bronson. Robert brought him out of his reverie. "What's the question?"

"Did you routinely log-off your computer each night?"

"Yeah, I did. The IT guys told me to do it each night for security reasons."

"Was there a night that you forgot?"

"Sure, there could be, but I would never remember."

"You don't have to. I have a copy of the hard drive and can find those times. I think I might manage to pinpoint the time of the clone of your address as well."

Jack asked, "What does all that mean?"

Robert smiled. "It means we can prove Greg's physical computer wasn't the source of the hack. The hack came from somewhere else, but the hacker cloned Greg's IP address to make it look like it came from his workstation."

Jack's eyes widened. "So, if I understand, you can prove that someone hacked the accounts and also that the hack didn't come from Greg's computer. Right?"

"Right. All I have to do is verify activity on the IP address but no log-on or keystroke activity at the same time."

Greg leaned forward. "You can prove I'm innocent?"

Robert nodded. "It looks that way. I feel confident."

"Do you know what this means?" Jack got up and paced around the room. "It means we will go to court and enter a plea of innocent. There will be a big ole trial, and you'll get found not guilty, and the DA will have to eat crow along with all the sons of bitches who doubted you."

Greg looked down at the table. "I get that. The problem is, I've almost gone broke. I doubt I'll have much left of the retainer once the trial is over. I don't know how I can ever make a comeback on the street. Don't forget, the hacker is still out there."

"I don't know about you, Greg, but I think I would take one step at a time. You won't go to jail, which I see as a big positive. We can always figure out a way to get you back on your feet after we solve this problem. I need you to stay positive, though. You think you can help me with that?"

Greg looked up and made eye contact with Jack. "I'm sorry. You're right. I need to stay positive. All my years playing ball, I should know a positive attitude can make the difference between winning and losing."

"Atta boy." Jack gave Greg a big smack on his back. Greg smiled weakly and got up, stretched, and shook off the negative thoughts. "Let's have coffee."

***

A couple of weeks later, Greg and the lawyers attended the pre-trial hearing where Greg listened to the charges against him, and the judge asked him if he understood them and would he like to enter a plea? Greg answered that he understood the charges and entered a plea of not guilty.

In the meantime, Ralph met with the District Attorney several times. The DA asked him if he had any direct knowledge of the trades that had appeared on Greg's account. Ralph assured the DA that he didn't have direct knowledge, and if he did, he would have reported the violation to the SEC. He did make a few insinuations about the facts when he discovered other irregularities. He related how he'd brought them to Greg's attention and, at the time, Ralph felt Greg too slow to take action and that he didn't seem to want to punish any of his employees.

The DA jumped on this and wanted Ralph to testify that other situations when illegal activities took place had occurred and Greg had done nothing. Ralph tried to explain that action did get taken, just not that fast. The DA reminded Ralph that, as the chief financial officer, he remained legally responsible for the proper fiduciary function of the firm.

"I understand that, but I don't think there was any unreported activity. It just seemed like Greg took his sweet time."

"Did you warn him of the consequences?"

"Sure, I did. As I said, nothing illegal happened."

"Do I need to reopen the case?"

"What do you mean?"

"You may be hiding something and trying to protect either yourself or Mr. Petros. In any case, I thought we had a deal that you would testify against Mr. Petros for immunity."

"Yes, I still agree to that. I don't want to lie, though." Ralph sat squirming in his chair. He now realized the DA wanted negative testimony that he didn't have and threatened to come after him.

"But you can testify he was slow to take action on other irregularities."

"Yes, I can."

"Good, then I think we understand each other. We need to have the particulars of those conversations. Can you supply those?"

"I kept a log of all the conversations with Greg."

"Perfect. I think we will get along fine, then."

So, Ralph became an ally of the District Attorney to save his butt. He also made for the kind of person to turn on a friend if the situation had something in it for him. To say Ralph would not be someone you would want for a friend made quite an understatement.

***

The prosecution and defense readied their arguments and, finally, the day came to appear in court. The District Attorney did not approach Greg's team with a plea bargain. He must have felt he had an ironclad case, and the trial would be such a high-profile event that he didn't want to move off center stage too quickly. He would always have the opportunity to offer a deal if it looked as if Greg might have a chance. The evidence seemed clear. Trades had occurred in Greg's accounts with Greg's computer. The only thing in question was the whereabouts of the money. After a thorough investigation, they had found no trace of the twenty million estimated to be the profits of the sale of one company holding in the fund. Those funds would have vanished the next day, as the company in the fund announced a fifty percent drop in quarterly profits, and their stock tanked. The DA figured that Greg had known about the profit problem in advance and gotten out of that stock before the news hit. After checking the books and cash flow, he found no record of the twenty million getting booked into one of Greg's companies or private accounts. The DA believed Greg still had the money and had, somehow, converted it to other assets or currency, and so he charged him with money laundering. The fraud counts looked clear and gave the best case for a guilty verdict. The money laundering might prove iffy since no evidence had, as yet, gotten uncovered. He had hoped that Ralph Torrence would shed some light on where the money went.

After a series of meetings, it became clear that Torrence either didn't know or hid where the money had gone. The DA requested and received authorization to monitor all of Ralph's communications in hopes of turning up something. The DA thought it suspicious that Ralph had bought all of the remaining assets of Greg's company and checked out all his finances. He discovered no evidence of a windfall, so he couldn't file charges. If he were a betting man, he would bet that Greg and Ralph had figured out a plan that had netted them twenty million. The DA took comfort in the fact that Greg would go to prison and not get his hands on the money. He also hoped that Ralph would somehow double cross Greg and go for the total stash. If so, the DA would have him as well.

They monitored all of Greg's communications. The DA knew better than to bug anything other than Greg's car, office, and home. He hoped none of the lawyers would have any conversations with Greg in those places. The recording of such a conversation would violate client privilege and render the evidence useless in court. The two counts of attempting to conceal assets rose out of the discovery that Greg had given his lawyers a five-million-dollar retainer, and the attempt to buy a watch for his wife. Ralph and Ms. McCormick already sat on the list of witnesses. The DA didn't think the charges would stick but kept them in the mix as possible bargaining chips.

The first few days in court they spent getting a jury seated. The DA, wisely, did not exclude potential jurors simply because they were fans of Greg. If so, the process would have taken a year. His only real question on which he based his request to excuse was, "Do you think you can be impartial in the case?"

After seating the jury, and when both sides had given their opening arguments, the trial fell into a daily routine of witness testimony and cross-examination. For some reason unknown to the defense, the DA chose to introduce evidence on the concealing assets charge. He called Ralph Torrence to the stand, and after establishing his position as Chief Financial Officer, the questions led to the point that he had to sign off on the five million sent to Bronson and Bronson. The implication was that Greg had tried to steal five million in company funds.

After the DA had no more questions, Jack rose and walked to face Ralph on the witness stand.

"Mr. Torrence," Jack said. "Is it fair to say the five-million dollars was the personal property of Mr. Petros?"

Ralph looked down, and then at the District Attorney, who raised an eyebrow. "Yes, it is fair to say the five million belonged to Mr. Petros."

"Can you tell the court why you, the CFO of the company, had access to Mr. Petros' money?"

"He loaned the company over one-hundred-million dollars, and the fund was the interest deposit fund. I oversaw it until it moved to other locations."

"What locations?"

"Like Mr. Petros' bank or financial planner."

"So, the movement of the money was an everyday occurrence?"

"Well. Not every day but frequent."

"And isn't it fair to say you were asked to remove the five million from Mr. Petros' account and send it to Bronson and Bronson?"

"Yes." Ralph became more nervous, as he knew he'd misled the jury with the answers to the DA's questions. He didn't lie but left the impression the money was company property.

"Were you told why the money got sent?"

"Yes."

"Tell the jury why five-million dollars got sent from Mr. Petros' private account."

"It was a retainer for legal services."

"No more questions."

The DA jumped out of his seat before the judge had a chance to ask for any redirect and answered the question that the judge didn't ask. "Yes, Your Honor, I have one more question for Mr. Torrence." He walked over to the witness stand and leaned in close to Ralph. "Mr. Torrence. Did you think it was outside ethical boundaries to send money to a law firm?"

Jack left his chair. "Objection, Your Honor. Conjecture by the witness, who has not been sworn in as an expert on the appropriate handling of legal retainer payments."

"Sustained. Does the prosecution have more questions for this witness?"

"No, Your Honor."

"The witness is excused. Please, call the next witness."

"The state calls Bella McCormick."

Bella came through the back doors of the court and walked to the witness stand with every eye in the courtroom on her. She sat in the witness chair and gave Greg a look of regret. Greg smiled to give her assurance that he knew she wasn't there because she wanted to be. She smiled a thank you in return. The bailiff swore her in, and the District Attorney came close.

"Please, state your name."

"Bella McCormick."

"What is your occupation?"

"Special assistant to the CEO of Petros fund."

"And you work for the defendant, is that correct?"

"Yes, and I hope I still do."

"Please just answer the questions, Ms. McCormick. How long have you worked for the defendant?"

"Five years."

"In that time, did the defendant ask you to buy things for him?"

"He asked only once."

"And when was that?"

"Just this month. He felt worried about a gift for his Twenty-fourth anniversary, and so he asked me to buy a gift that he'd picked out for his wife."

"And did you buy the gift?"

"I did."

"The state enters this receipt for a watch as evidence number one, Your Honor, and ladies and gentlemen of the jury." The DA passed it to the judge, and he gave it to the bailiff, who passed it to the jury. After each had looked at it, the bailiff returned it to the DA's hands. "Ms. McCormick, please look at this receipt carefully. Is this the receipt for the watch you purchased?"

"Yes, I believe it is."

"You believe or know it is?"

"I know it is."

"Good, now, would you be kind enough and read the receipt to the court."

Bella cleared her throat and glanced at Greg. He still sat smiling. She started to read the receipt, and the DA asked her to speak up and start over. "Moratti Jewelry, One East Boston Street, Boston, Mass., 02127. Received for one Patek Phillippe ladies diamond and white gold watch, serial number

00077776543A. Thirty-two thousand four hundred and fifty dollars."

"Thank you, Ms. McCormick. Do you know where the watch is right now?"

"I think it went to Mrs. Petros."

Jack got on his feet once more. "Objection. Opinion."

"Sustained. Mr. Peterson, would you like to rephrase the question?"

"Yes, Your Honor. Ms. McCormick, did you give the watch to Mr. Petros?"

"Yes."

"Do you know if he gave it to Mrs. Petros?"

"I do not know."

"Thank you. No more questions. Your witness, Mr. Mathews."

Jack didn't get up and spoke from the defendant's table, "Ms. McCormick, do you have any information or knowledge that the purchase of the watch was for any other purpose than as a gift for Mrs. Petros?"

"No, I do not."

"Thank you. No more questions."

"Mr. Peterson, does the state have any further questions of this witness?"

"No, Your Honor."

"Ms. McCormick, you are excused."

It looked like the State did not prove the two counts attempting to conceal assets. Later in the trial, Peterson tried to say the five million and the watch were attempts by Greg to hide assets from the government. Jack blew the charges out of the water and reminded the jury that out of about one hundred million, which Greg had lost when the firm collapsed, the five million and thirty-some-odd-thousand watch were minuscule.

The DA made a play to intimidate the defense by bringing the concealed asset charges first. The DA hoped having two witnesses close to Greg testify about the minor charges would raise doubt in the mind of the defense team as to what more these witnesses might prove willing to say.

The strategy worked on Greg. Jack had to calm him during the recess and let him know those charges would not stand up, and that Peterson merely played a game. Greg did calm and tried to relax for the rest of the prosecution's presentation of evidence.

The evidence came in the form of a series of forensic experts testifying to the effect that the trades came from Greg's account and got made on Greg's computer. Jack raised enough doubt about the validly of the forensic evidence. He asked each witness if it were possible to have hacked his accounts, and each replied that it was possible. He also asked the expert who'd testified that Greg's computer was the source of the trades if it were possible to clone the computer. The expert was forced to say it would be possible that the computer could have gotten cloned. All in all, Jack set up the defense's position and would drive these points home when it came time for the presentation of the defense's case.

Peterson also paraded a few witnesses who were clients of the Petros Fund, who had lost money. Each had gotten caught unawares upon the plunge in the company stock. Some even told of Greg's sales people trying to convince them to put more money in the fund. Jack jumped on those witnesses and made the point that if the salespeople were trying to sell more shares of the fund, it was doubtful anyone was aware the company stock price would fall.

Peterson did not call any witnesses who could say Greg had any awareness of any inside information prior to the sales of the stock. Every time a witness for the prosecution testified, Jack would ask if they were aware whether or not Greg had any knowledge of the announcement by the company that the profits were off by fifty percent. Not one witness could say they had any knowledge. By the time the prosecution rested, the evidence presented looked light. Jack managed to punch enough holes in all of the DA's case that he felt tempted to tell the court that the defense rested. A better part of not taking such a risk prevailed, and Jack called witnesses for the defense. He did call for a directed verdict of not guilty, which the judge declined. This was normal protocol, and Jack only went through the motions.

He called Ralph back and got him to say, unequivocally, that the money sent to the lawyers came from Greg's personal funds. He also put a member of the state BAR on the stand, who testified that a retainer of five-million dollars was ethical and, under the circumstances, reasonable. He called Bella back and asked her if Greg had ever said anything about wanting to buy a watch to hide the money. She sounded wholly believable when she denied ever hearing anything of the kind.

Jack's star witness was Robert. He testified that not only did Greg's account get compromised but also that someone had hacked the computer from a remote location and cloned its IP address. Jack remained careful to take the questions slowly. He needed the jury to understand the exact technology and how it was possible for someone to use Greg's computer identity just as if they had taken the identity of a person. The testimony took all day, and when Jack finished, he felt certain that the jury now understood Greg as totally innocent. He finished with Robert too late for Peterson to conduct a cross-examination. The Judge called for a recess for the day and reminded the jury not to discuss the case with anyone, including among themselves.

Jack and Greg met to debrief and felt optimistic that Robert's testimony would go a long way in putting the prosecution on its heels. Jack met with Robert and prepared him for the cross-examination. He warned Robert that the DA would try to discredit him and, above all, would try to get him to admit he was either mistaken in his conclusion or lying. Robert assured Jack that neither of those conditions was true and that he felt good about tomorrow's session.

Chapter Sixteen

The sunrise exploded in the profusion of red that sailors used to take as a warning of approaching storms. Greg had a stirring in his stomach upon entering the courtroom. He couldn't put his finger on why he felt so nervous, but the laughing of the prosecution team at an inside joke didn't go a long way in helping him feel that they faced defeat. If anything, it looked like they sat celebrating some small victory.

Constance came into the courtroom. Greg smiled, went over to her, and gave her a hug. He asked how she was, and she said she was good and not to worry about her. Jack came up behind them, and Greg said he would see Constance after the session, and then he and Jack went to the defense table. Once seated, Greg leaned over and whispered to Jack about how happy the prosecution team seemed. His counsel told Greg that they just tried to fake it to throw him off. Greg felt a little calmer.

The jury came into the courtroom and took their seats, and the judge asked Peterson if he wished to cross-examine Robert. Peterson rose from the table and told the Judge that the prosecution would like to recall the witness for a cross-examination at a later time.

"Very well, Mr. Peterson. Mr. Mathews, you may call your next witness."

Jack rose. "The defense calls Greg Petros."

The courtroom hummed like a hive of bees while Greg approached the witness stand. Jack followed him, and when Greg had sworn in, he asked, "Please, tell the court your name and city of residence."

"Samuel Petros. Boston."

"Mr. Petros, you are the CEO of the Petros Fund are you not?"

"Yes, I am."

"How long have you been the CEO?"

"About ten years."

"And before that, you were a sportscaster?"

"Yes. Yes, I was."

"And, a football player before your sportscasting career."

"Yes."

"How many Super Bowls did you win?"

"Three."

Peterson got up. "Your Honor, the prosecution will acknowledge the history of Mr. Petros as one of distinction."

"Mr. Mathews, is there a point to this resume statement?"

"Yes, Your Honor, and I'll get right to it."

"Very well, I will allow you to continue, but please come to your point."

"One more question, Mr. Petros. In all that time, did you manage to save a lot of money?"

"Yes, I did."

"Is it safe to say you were able to save over one-hundred-million dollars?" The audible whoosh of air from the spectators caused Greg to look down in embarrassment.

"Yes, I think that is safe to say."

"And after you retired from broadcasting, what did you do with the one hundred million?"

"I founded the Petros Fund."

"So, you took your money and started a company."

"Yes."

"Did you ever ask for your money back?"

"No. I kept it in the company."

"Where it earned interest?"

"It grew along with the rest of the funds and money that people invested."

"How much do you think it was worth prior to the bankruptcy?"

"About three hundred million."

Another audible wave of comments rose in the room, causing the Judge to rap his gavel and call for order.

"Where is this three hundred million now?"

"I don't know."

"You don't know? Can you tell me why you don't know?"

Greg looked down and became hard to hear. The judge asked him to speak up. "I lost it all when the funds went bankrupt."

"So, you never had a chance to get your money out of the firm?"

"No, it all happened too fast."

"What, in your opinion, caused the collapse of the Petros Fund?"

"The charges of fraud and money laundering caused a rash of sell orders on the fund elements."

"So, if you were guilty of illegally trading twenty million, you would have done that by trading three hundred million for twenty. Does this seem reasonable to you?"

"I did not illegally trade the twenty million, so I never contemplated such a trade."

"Thank you, Mr. Petros. No more questions. Your witness, Mr. Peterson."

"Thank you, Mr. Mathews." Peterson walked over to the stand, paused to look at the jury, and turned toward Greg slightly. "When you traded the twenty million, you didn't think anyone would catch you, did you, Mr. Petros?"

Jack did not get up but said, "Objection, Your Honor."

"Sustained. Mr. Peterson, you and I both know that that kind of question is not allowed. You are leading the witness."

"Yes, Your Honor. I apologize. Let me restate the question. Mr. Petros, you never thought anyone would catch you, did you?"

"Objection."

"Sustained. Mr. Peterson, I am warning you. One more question like this, and I will find you in contempt."

"Yes, Your Honor. No more questions."

Greg stepped down from the stand totally confused as to what had just gone on and unaware that the prosecutor had planted doubt in the juror's minds about the scenario Jack had created. Jack knew the jury would find the trade of twenty million for three hundred illogical. Peterson had now established that such a trade would be feasible if Greg weren't caught. After Greg had stepped down, the Judge cautioned the jury to disregard the questions posed by Peterson. Everyone in the courtroom knew the Judge's instruction would prove impossible to follow. The damage was done.

Jack rose and asked to approach the bench. The Judge waved him forward. Peterson joined.

"Your Honor, I think I would be within my rights to call a mistrial given the bold disregard of the prosecution for the rules of testimony."

"I understand how you feel, Mr. Mathews. I am not about to call a mistrial unless this happens again. I will make a note of the prosecutor's poor judgment for a possible appeal. In the meantime, Mr. Peterson, one more incident, and I will hold you in contempt, and you will serve jail time. Your performance goes beyond my personal ethics, and I will not tolerate any more of it in my court. Do I make myself clear?"

Peterson looked at the floor and said in a whisper, "Yes, sir, Your Honor."

"Now, let's go back and continue this trial."

Jack and Peterson returned to their tables. Greg whispered, asking Jack what went on, and Jack waved him off. The Judge asked Jack if he had any more witnesses. Jack said that the defense rested. A few comments murmured around the room, and Jack took that as a good sign. He believed that most thought Greg innocent, and that he had made his case. The Judge called on the prosecutor for any redirect. Peterson called Robert back to the stand.

Robert walked from the rear of the courtroom and took the stand. He felt a little nervous, as the prosecutor hadn't examined him right away when he'd taken the stand the first time.

Peterson moved from his table to the center of the room. "A reminder that you are under oath. You testified earlier that Mr. Petros' accounts got hacked and his computer IP address cloned and, therefore, he was not the person making the trades. Is that right?"

"Yes, sir, that is right."

"You know this because you did an extensive examination of the accounts and the computer. Is that right?"

"Yes, that is right."

"You also were not able to identify the person doing all this dirty work. Correct?"

"That is correct."

"So, if someone were able to track the person hacking the computer, it would surprise you. Would it not?"

"Yes, I believe it is almost impossible to track that person."

"If it were possible, then your testimony would be flawed, would it not?"

"I don't understand."

"For example, let's say I have an expert who can testify that the information you have given in your testimony is not correct."

"Objection, Your Honor. No such witness was identified to the defense."

"Sustained. Mr. Peterson, do you have an additional witness to present to the court?"

"I do, Your Honor, and I apologize, but we just received a report from an independent consultant. I didn't want to take the court's time if the information didn't bring anything new."

"Please, present what you have to the defense, Mr. Peterson. Until they have had a chance to review the information, you will refrain from any further mention of the potential witness and information this witness may present. The jury will disregard the previous questions."

"Yes, Your Honor. No more questions."

Robert got down from the stand and looked at Jack. Robert had the palms of his hands turned out in a classic "what the hell?" gesture. Jack raised an eyebrow and gave Robert a sign that said, "we'll talk later." Robert walked to the back of the courtroom and sat heavily on the chair. Peterson had, once again, presented damaging information without even having the evidence available. The assistant DA walked across the courtroom and laid a large but thin manila envelope on the defense table. Jack did not pick it up.

"Any more redirect, Mr. Peterson?"

"No, Your Honor, but the state would like to call an additional witness."

"Objection, Your Honor. The defense has not been privy to the existence of an additional witness."

"Yes, Mr. Mathews, I think Mr. Peterson explained the reason. I have to overrule your objection."

"May I approach the bench?"

"Mr. Peterson and Mathews, please approach."

"Your Honor," Jack said. "This is an outrage. The prosecution is not even following proper protocol."

"Your Honor, if I may," Peterson said. "We hired an expert, and I waited to see the report before knowing if it held any relevance. I believe it will shed some light on the case and believe it proper to allow."

"I will allow the witness and the inclusion of the report as evidence, but let me warn you, Mr. Peterson, you have jeopardized this trial already. If this is some rabbit trail and the evidence becomes more circumstantial than fact, you will be in a large amount of trouble."

"I understand, Your Honor. If it were not important, I would not have bothered."

"Okay, then. Mr. Mathews, I will allow the evidence."

"I would like a recess in order to review the information."

"Any objection, Mr. Peterson?"

"No, sir." Peterson wouldn't risk getting tossed in jail, even though he didn't want the recess.

"Okay, gentlemen. Return to your tables."

Jack and Peterson returned to their teams. The Judge rapped his gavel and announced a recess until tomorrow. He looked at Jack to see if he understood the generous nature of the recess. Jack stood and nodded his recognition of the favor.

When the court cleared, Jack went to the back and told Robert to meet him at the law firm. Robert understood, and they agreed to meet after lunch. Jack had invited Robert to lunch, but he declined. He had a prior lunch appointment. Jack felt reluctant to let Robert out of his sight but had no choice. He couldn't very well order Robert to do his bidding. He sighed as Robert left through the front door.

Constance declined an invitation to lunch with the excuse of having work to do. Greg and Jack went back to the law firm and for food. Greg asked what was in the envelope. Jack told him he didn't want to look at it until Robert could check it over. They ate in silence while Greg worried about what the testimony from the expert would entail. He wished Jack would just open the damned envelope and let him see what lay inside.

"Greg," Jack said. "You can bet whatever is in the envelope is not the full story. This prosecutor is out for bear and not giving up easily. I'm at the point, now, where even if you get found guilty, I have enough evidence of an unfair trial at the hands of the prosecution. The appeal process will take years. As long as your five million holds out, I don't think you should worry."

"Well, five million isn't what it used to be. Don't forget, besides that, I have very little."

"I understand, my friend. I still think we will get you off, and then can start to figure out how to rebuild a life for you."

"Can I sue these sons of bitches if they lose?"

"I don't think you would win a suit like that. They had probable cause to believe you had broken the law."

"What about destroying my firm?"

"They could argue that they had no control over the investors, and I think they would be right. No, we need to work out a plan to get you back in the public eye. If you win this, you will become a hero again. You know, the old press conference on the steps of the courthouse where I declare justice is served, and an innocent man has gone free."

Jack and Greg finished as Jack's assistant announced Robert's arrival, and then escorted him into Jack's office. Robert took a chair at the table where Greg and Jack had eaten lunch.

"So, what was in the envelope?" Robert said.

"I don't know. I haven't opened it yet. Here, you do it."

Jack slid it across the table. Robert picked it up and tore it open. He started reading what looked to Jack like a two or three-page document. "Aw, bullshit," Robert said.

"Bullshit?" Jack said. "What does it say, Robert?"

"Let me read the whole thing. So far, it looks like a pack of lies."

"Hmmm," Jack said. "Doesn't sound like something Peterson would put forward if untrue."

"It could be a matter of point of view. Okay, maybe it's not lies, but I wouldn't make these conclusions from the evidence that I saw."

"How do we break this down so that I can understand what it says?" Jack asked.

"I'll just have to lay this out one part at a time. That might make for the best way."

"What can I do?" Greg glanced from man to man.

"Remain calm." Jack gave him a smile. "So, Robert, go over this one point at a time."

"This report says there is evidence on Greg's computer that shows use for the trades. The opinion of this consultant is that log items show log-in times and active keystrokes that happened at the same time as the trades."

"How can this information be so different from what you presented?"

"There can only be one answer. This guy is not telling the truth."

"You sure? Calling a witness a liar would be a damaging charge to levy in a court of law."

"He may not know he's lying. I see where he looked at the same evidence as me but came up with a different conclusion."

"Could it be this guy isn't as good as you?"

"Thanks for the compliment, but it might be that he didn't go the additional step of following each of the indicators to find the ghost entry deep into the program."

"So, we might be dealing with someone unqualified to testify?"

"I think that's it."

"Who is this guy?"

"Uh, his name is Perry Goshman, an independent consultant."

"Can you find out everything about him before tomorrow?"

"I'll get right on it."

Robert handed the report to Jack, who looked it over.

"I see the point where Goshman made his conclusions. I note that Goshman agreed with Robert about the account hacking. The only contention is the question of whether or not the IP address on Greg's computer got cloned, or the computer was used to hack the accounts. If cloned, Greg would go free. If it was his computer, then Greg won't look so good. Of course, the DA will have to establish proof that Greg acted as the operator of the computer. To place Greg at the computer at the exact time of the trades might prove a tall order. Tomorrow will be interesting."

Greg sat up, "So, even if someone believes this guy, it would still be hard to say I'm guilty?"

"That's exactly what I'm saying. You need to go home and get some rest. I believe all will be well in the end."

Chapter Seventeen

Greg drove home without the same optimism as Jack. He couldn't shake the feeling the trial would put a nail in his coffin. Perturbed, he thought back over the last few weeks. His money had disappeared. He and Terry had not spoken for a few days. She seemed angry all the time, and there never came a good time to start any discussion. The last time he'd tried, he mentioned the weather to try and break the ice. All he got was a statement that she wasn't interested in something as stupid as the weather when getting enough money to get her hair done was the biggest priority of the day. Greg recognized passive-aggressive behavior when he saw it and decided not to enable more of the same. Instead, he would speak when spoken to and nothing else. He tried to think of the last time they'd had a discussion and couldn't remember.

Upon pulling into the garage, he noticed the absence of her car. Did she have a meeting to attend? Unlikely, as most of the organizations had asked her to step down from her board memberships once the news had broken. He felt sorry for the pain Terry went through right at that time. She had gone from a queen to a commoner. And Terry didn't have the capability of sustaining the life of a normal person. She thrived on being the center of attention. Loved getting fawned over and having others seek her favor. How quickly those folks turned on her when they found out their money was no longer there. It seemed almost as if the money had made the only reason for the friendships. Greg had never thought that the case until he tried to reach any one of his old golf partners and found them perpetually unavailable. At that point, he came to the realization that Jack remained his only friend.

Greg found the house empty. He didn't call out for Terry. Since she usually greeted him when he came home, he grew worried. He'd arrived a little early, but still, she should be here. He stopped at the refrigerator and pulled out a bottle of water. The cold bottle on his forehead felt refreshing. While he took a drink, he saw a stack of papers on the island. They looked legal sized. His knees went weak, and he edged his way to the island. The papers came from an unfamiliar law firm. A handwritten note from Terry lay on top of the pile, which Greg picked up and read.

Dear Greg,

I know this will hurt you, so I don't want to say it in person. As you know, I've loved you with all my heart. It is a sad thing, but I can no longer face the humiliation of being part of your life. I'm not sure if you are guilty or not. I do know you've changed, and I need to move on. I want a divorce, and here are the papers that I hope you will simply sign and let me go.

I'm sorry our life has come to this.

Love.

T

Greg sat on a barstool and reread the note. He didn't believe that after a wonderful life of twenty-four years Terry would abandon him just because someone wanted to put him out of business. Where was she right now? His self-pity morphed into concern for her welfare. With the note in one hand, he pushed her direct dial number.

"Hello," Terry said. "Did you get my note?"

"Yes. What's this all about?"

"Greg, I just can't stand to be poor. I feel scared to death and cannot sit and watch what we had destroyed."

"And you think a divorce will help all of that?" Greg realized he needed to tone it down. "I mean, how will a divorce help?"

"The truth of the matter." Terry started crying. "I have found someone else who can take care of me and make me happy. You and I haven't been happy for a long time."

"I don't understand. The loss of money is a short-term problem. We can work out of it. We've been happy until this came up."

"You may have been." She paused, and Greg heard her sobbing anew. She composed herself and continued, "I've felt miserable, and you haven't even bothered to notice. I haven't laughed in years."

"Laughed? What do you mean?"

"We have no passion. Life just runs from one day to the next. This last problem makes for one of a string. I kidded myself that I should give up my happiness for your sake since you were such an important public figure. That's over now, and I don't feel I need to support you anymore."

"Wow, Terry. I don't know what to say. Who is it that makes you so happy?"

"Not important. It's not you, and that's all you need to know now." A change entered Terry's voice. She had begun in a mess and now sounded clear and hard.

"Terry, I—"

Terry spoke over Greg, "If you love me, you'll just accept my decision and not put me through any more agony over this. I have suffered enough and need to move on. Let's get off the phone. Please, don't call me again. If you want to discuss anything, please call my lawyer. Goodbye, Greg."

Greg wanted to say more, but the phone went dead on the other end. Before he could set the phone down, it rang. Constance flashed up on the caller ID. "Yes, dear?"

"Hi, Daddy." Constance sounded like she had a cold.

"You okay?"

"I talked to Mom a half hour ago. I've been crying."

"I'm sorry, honey. Why are you crying?"

"Oh, Daddy. It's so fucking complicated, I can't even start. Let's just say that I'm so sorry for everything."

"For everything? What do you mean?"

"You losing everything and now your wife leaves you."

"Oh, that. Yeah, I guess I'm pretty sorry for that as well."

Constance sobbed again. Greg didn't know what to say, so he remained quiet. He couldn't stop the lump from forming in his throat. Finally, he croaked, "Why don't you come over? We'll have some meat and a few drinks. Hell, maybe we'll even get drunk. I don't know. I feel like the floor has dropped out. I don't understand why your mom decided to leave. I suspect her desire to go started long before this bullshit blew up. What about it? Come on over."

"Sounds real good, Dad, but I just can't leave the apartment in this condition. I know I should come over, if nothing else but to comfort you. I need some time to think about this whole thing. I want to talk to Mom one more time and try to understand her decision. Don't forget that I'm now the product of a broken home."

Greg couldn't help chuckling at her comment. "Okay, darling. Take all the time you need. I understand."

"I wish you could *really* understand, Daddy. Also, I think I should go back to New York. Your trial will go fine, and I need my husband right now. I wish I could talk to you, but right now, it feels impossible. I'm not making any sense at all, Daddy, and I'm so sorry."

Constance stopped talking, and Greg heard her sobs. It broke his heart that she had a problem that she couldn't tell him about. He surmised that it came down to more than Terry leaving him. "Honey?" Greg wanted her to stop crying.

"Yes, Daddy." She tried to catch her breath.

"I understand. Go back to New York. It will do you good to see your husband. I'll be fine. When you can talk, I'm here for you. Okay?"

"Thank you, Daddy. I'll catch a flight tomorrow and will text you when I get back to New York."

"Yes, darling. Thank you. I love you."

"I love you, Daddy. Goodbye."

"Goodbye, kitten." The phone went dead once more. Greg stared at the screen with Constance's name and the selfie she'd put on his phone. He whispered, "I love you, baby." Then, reluctantly, he put the phone on the island next to Terry's note and grabbed a kitchen towel. He buried his face and screamed into it, crying large tears for what seemed like twenty minutes. He cried for Terry, Constance, and mostly himself. He tried several times but couldn't stop. Finally, he sat on the barstool, put his head down on his arms, and continued to sob. After a time, he'd cried out. He no longer had any tears to shed. In a strange way, Greg felt better. Though bone tired, he felt relieved. His stomach no longer turned over, and his nerves had calmed. He walked over to the refrigerator and pulled out a bottle of gin, grabbed a glass, and poured a measure. The cold gin felt like a soothing potion all the way to his stomach. The effect made him believe he would make it through this trauma and feel happy again. He put ice cubes in the glass and poured a larger portion.

Greg needed to get drunk, and nothing in the world could stop him. He had no plans to go out, and no one would come in. The gin made for his only friend right now, and his pal needed to get entertained. Greg went to the living room and dropped into a big comfortable chair. He placed the bottle of gin on the side table and picked up the remote. The TV came to life in time for the news. His picture hung behind the newscaster. Greg took another sip of his drink and kicked off his shoes. Then, turning up the volume, he paid attention as the broadcaster described the day in court. In the opinion of this guy, the trial had gone well for Greg's side.

Greg clicked around to all the local channels and met with a consensus that he would win the case. One of the broadcasters described Jack as the "brilliant defense attorney." Greg turned off the TV and rotated the kinks out of his neck. He finished his glass of gin and poured another. Maybe he should get something to eat. The idea of steak popped into his head. He got up and felt the effects of the alcohol. His appetite for steak gave way to the desire to get something in his stomach without a lot of fuss. Instead, he went to the refrigerator where he saw some ham and cheese in the meat keeper. Then he found the bread and settled on a sandwich. As he sat in the kitchen eating, he thought that it was a long trip up to power and money and an extremely quick trip down to eating a ham sandwich, alone, half drunk in a kitchen.

The food gave him a little strength. He poured one more glass of gin and dumped the dish in the sink. "Time for bed," Greg said. He realized that he had spoken to himself and added that trait to someone who'd hit bottom. He went to the bedroom. Terry's closet stood empty. She must have had help pulling all her stuff out of her walk in. The closet took about the same space as a normal room and held enough clothes and shoes to stock a store. Of course, everything was one size, but there would be plenty of inventory. Greg felt quite entertained at his store analogy and thankful his buddy gin had helped raise his mood. He also realized that another glass of his friend and the mood would change. He would become depressed and probably end up with a crying jag as a result. He drained his glass and remembered that he'd left the bottle in the kitchen. "Time to stop now," Greg said. The talking out loud didn't bother him since he'd embraced the effects of the gin and looked forward to blessed sleep.

Greg pulled off his clothes and left them on the floor. He'd grown numb enough not to miss the fact that Terry didn't lay beside him in the bed. He got down to the basic anesthesia effects of the gin. Greg passed out and slept the sleep of the drugged. Not deep and restful, but not half awake and restless either.

***

The morning brought the usual pain in the head along with the flip-flop of a queasy stomach. Greg sat on the edge of the bed and realized his good friend from last night had a payback period. "God," Greg said. He now remembered why he hated to get drunk. His mouth felt filled with feathers. He half expected to spit one out, but managed to get to his feet while trying to work up some moisture around his tongue. Then he lurched to the sink and filled his hands with water. When he sucked down the cold liquid, his stomach told him it was too soon for major intake. One or two heaves brought all the water back to the sink. "Shit." Greg seldom swore, but the prospect of cleaning up the mess caused him to vocalize what he felt. He ran the water and tried his best to wash away the mess, glad for one point: No one was here to know what he had done.

His hands shaking, and stomach gurgling, made getting dressed a little more difficult for Greg. He didn't have time for a shower since he'd overslept. His best use of time would be to get coffee ready. Greg went to the kitchen and winced at the half-empty bottle of gin. Though he couldn't remember drinking that much, he did understand why he felt like hell. Terry's letter and the divorce papers lay where he'd left them. He made a mental note to take them to court today. Maybe Jack could represent him in the divorce as well. The coffee only required a push of the button, merciful this morning. Should he try to eat something?

His stomach gave a warning flip to let him know he could try it but would feel sorry.

Coffee and divorce papers in hand, Greg went into the garage and climbed into his car. He hit the garage opener and grabbed his sunglasses, as he felt half-blind in the bright morning sun. Then, backing out of the garage, he swung out and onto the private drive to his house. He drove up to the gate that covered the entrance to his property. Half a dozen reporters and several TV vans waited on the other side. He stopped and got out of the car. The reporters shouted questions through the gate. Greg held up his hands. He thanked all of them for their interest in the case and told them that he couldn't comment by orders of his lawyer. He also asked them to move out of the way, or he would arrive late for court. The strategy worked, and the reporters made way. He also said he would have a press conference where he would be free to talk, which helped ease the situation. Some of the reporters even hollered, "Good luck."

Greg drove to the courthouse and noticed a pack of reporters lurked there as well. He gave the same spiel and made it into the courthouse.

"Jesus, Greg," Jack said. "You look like something the dog dragged in."

"Had to fight my way through a bunch of reporters. Wish you were there."

"You say anything?"

"No. Just we would have a press conference when we could talk."

"Good job. You don't smell so good. Have a few cocktails last night?"

"Got drunk. Terry's asking me for a divorce."

"Oh, man. You need that like a hole in the head."

"Tell me something I don't know. Here are the papers."

"Let's talk about this later. I must say, I wish she had waited if she was hell bent on doing it."

"Why? What's the difference?"

"Well, for one, she and the government will have a fight over your assets if we lose the case."

"But we won't lose."

"That's right. Thanks for reminding me. It's my job to worry about everything."

"What about this expert witness today?"

"I think we can handle him. I want to see what he says, but I have a couple of questions for him that I don't think he will be able to answer. Robert worked half the night looking into this guy's credentials. He has a few questionable areas that I hope to exploit."

"So, I don't have to shake myself apart with worry?"

"You may shake yourself apart with a hangover, but leave the worry to me. Here comes the judge."

The bailiff called for all to rise, and the Judge gaveled the room to silence. "Mr. Peterson, you may call your witness."

"Thank you, Your Honor. The state calls Mr. Perry Goshman."

The room watched a young, well-dressed man walk from the rear and take the stand. He got sworn in, and Peterson took him through his identity and credential questions. He then asked, "You have had a chance to examine the evidence?"

"Yes, I have looked at the computer and the account software for traces of unauthorized entry."

"And did you find any?"

"I found the accounts had, indeed, been hacked."

The Judge gaveled the room to silence.

"Did you find evidence that the computer belonging to Mr. Petros got accessed remotely?"

"I did not."

The Judge warned the room that it would get cleared if order was not maintained.

"So, Mr. Goshman, is it your expert opinion that Mr. Petros used his computer to hack his accounts?"

Jack jumped to his feet. "Objection. Conjecture by the witness. There is no evidence Mr. Petros used his computer for the purpose of hacking his accounts."

"Sustained. Mr. Peterson, such a short-cut is not proper."

"Yes, Your Honor. Mr. Goshman, is it fair to say the computer owned by Mr. Petros was not remotely used to hack into the accounts?"

"Yes."

"Would you, please, share with the court your reason for coming to this conclusion?"

"I checked all the drives and found evidence of keystrokes."

"What kind of evidence?"

"It was hard to find, but when I went to the second registry, I found strokes around the same time as the hack on the accounts."

"You are sure of this?"

"No doubt about it."

"And your conclusion as an expert?"

"The computer in question was the source of the hack."

A low rumble of conversation grew. The Judge raised his gavel, and the noise ceased.

"For the record, Your Honor, Mr. Goshman refers to State's Exhibit Two, the computer taken from the defendant's office." Then, after a glance at the courtroom, he said, "No more questions for this witness, Your Honor."

"Mr. Mathews, your witness."

"Thank you, Your Honor." Jack walked over to the witness stand. He looked at a set of notes given him by Robert. Jack made a show of looking closely at the papers in his hand. "Mr. Goshman, according to your biography, you graduated from MIT. Is that correct?"

"Objection, Your Honor. Mr. Goshman has already testified to that fact."

"Sustained. Mr. Mathews, please spare the court a replay of evidence already given."

"Yes, Your Honor. May I have the testimony read back for the jury?"

Peterson rose. "Your Honor, the state has already established Mr. Goshman is a graduate of MIT."

"Mr. Mathews. Although this seems like a small issue, are you trying to make a point here?"

"Yes, Your Honor."

"Would you please enlighten all of us as to the point you are trying to make."

"Your Honor, I have information from the Provost of MIT that Mr. Goshman did not graduate from MIT."

"Objection, Your Honor."

"Overruled. Mr. Mathews, Mr. Peterson, please approach the bench."

Jack and Peterson walked to the Judge's stand. "Let me look at your evidence, Mr. Mathews." Jack handed the Judge a copy of an email from the Provost's office. The Judge looked at the email. "Can you get the Provost to submit a sworn statement?"

"Yes, Your Honor. We have a recording received this morning where the Provost is sworn in. I can show it to the court."

"Very well. I will allow the questions around the degree to proceed. Mr. Peterson, if your witness has lied under oath, I'm going to ask for an arrest since I will declare him in contempt. You understand?"

"Yes, Your Honor. Believe me; I'm as surprised as you."

"Okay then, let's get back to the trial."

Jack and Peterson left the Judge. Jack returned to the witness stand. "Now, Mr. Goshman, I again ask you if you are a graduate of MIT?"

"I have completed all the required coursework."

"Do you have a diploma?"

"No."

"Why did you testify that you had a diploma, then?"

"I have been battling the university to release it. I believe I have earned it, and their administrative process is ridiculous."

Peterson slumped in his chair. He didn't like where this line of questioning was going.

"Is it not true that you were accused of cheating on your final exam in the computer technology course and your diploma got withheld?"

"There is no evidence I cheated."

"That is not the question, Mr. Goshman. Did the university withhold your diploma and accuse you of cheating?"

"Yes."

"Now, you testified that you found evidence of keystrokes in the second register of the computer."

"Yes, I did."

"And who told you to say that?"

"Objection, Your Honor."

"Sustained. Mr. Mathews, please."

"Yes, Your Honor. Mr. Goshman, you did not tell the truth under oath about your diploma. I want you to state under penalty of perjury that you found evidence on the second register."

"Well, I could be mistaken. I didn't inspect the computer but had an employee do it."

"But you testified that you personally looked at the computer."

"I lied."

"Under oath."

"Yes."

"Can you tell the court why?"

"I felt afraid that if I didn't find evidence, Mr. Peterson would carry out his threat to turn my tax returns over to the IRS."

Peterson jumped out of his chair. "Objection, Your Honor. Mere hearsay."

"Overruled, Mr. Peterson. Mr. Mathews, you have established that this is not a credible witness. Is there anything else?"

"I guess not, Your Honor. The defense requests a directed acquittal of my client."

"I quite agree, Mr. Mathews. I want to thank the jury for their service and let you know you are excused."

The courtroom erupted in shouts and cheers. The Judge rapped his gavel and threatened to clear the room. The jury filed out, and order restored.

"Mr. Goshman, you are in contempt of court. Bailiff, please take Mr. Goshman into custody. Mr. Mathews and Mr. Petros, please approach the bench."

Jack and Greg rose and stood in front of the Judge.

"Mr. Petros, the judgment of this court is that you are found innocent of all charges." The Judge rapped for quiet once more. "Mr. Peterson, please approach the bench." Peterson rose slowly and knew he was in for a beating and didn't feel anxious to get it started. "Mr. Peterson, I want to admonish you for your preparation and conduct in this case. If the state plans to appeal my decision, the official record will show my concern. The justice system in this country is not built upon coercion and threats. Your evidence and witness stream fell so far below the standard that you could rightfully be accused of malfeasance."

The Judge, again, rapped his gavel. "Court dismissed. Mr. Petros, you are free to go."

Greg grabbed Jack and gave him a bear hug. Several spectators rose to their feet, clapping. The reporters yelled questions, and the Judge stepped down. He came around and told Greg and Jack that they could leave through the back. Jack shook the Judge's hand, and the Judge shook Greg's as well. Greg thanked him, and the Judge told Greg he felt sorry that the state had brought the charges in the first place.

Jack took the lead, and Greg followed him out. "Let's go to the law firm," Jack said.

"I promised the press a conference."

"Okay, let's set it up on the steps. I want you to smile and thank the judge, the court, the President, and every federal official on the planet. We don't want to start another war where one of these Jackasses will want to prosecute you again for anything."

Chapter Eighteen

Jack and Greg went around to the front door of the courthouse. A large crowd of reporters waited. One of the TV stations had set up a podium, which had at least ten microphones attached to it. Jack made some opening comments, and then Greg did as Jack suggested. He thanked everyone he could think of thanking. The questions proved easy for Greg to answer all except for one. He could not respond when asked who had hacked into his accounts. He could only say that he had no idea. The press conference lasted about half an hour. In the end, Jack once again thanked the judge and jury. A final question came out of the crowd and asked Greg what he would do now that his firm had closed. He wanted to say that he planned to go to Disneyland but thought better than to make a joke. "I shall start over." The crowd burst into applause, and Greg thanked them for their support.

Jack and Greg went back through the courthouse so that they could make a nice exit. Once again, Jack suggested that they go to the law office. Greg told Jack he would meet him there and went to his car. Once inside, he placed a call to Constance. She answered after a couple of rings.

"Tell me all is good."

"Yes, darling. The judge directed an acquittal. I'm a free man."

"Oh, that is so wonderful, Daddy. I'm happy it came out the way it should have."

"So, you figured your old man was innocent."

"I know you are."

"How's that?"

"Daddy, I need to talk to you. I'll catch a flight tomorrow and come see you. We need to talk."

"What about?"

"We need to wait until tomorrow. I have some things that need to get explained. I can't do it over the phone and will need to meet you face-to-face. Please, don't ask anymore. I love you, Dad. Goodbye for now. I have a meeting and got to run."

"Okay, sweetheart, I'll let you go. Sounds mysterious, though. Take care. Text me your flight, and I'll pick you up."

"Okay, Daddy. Bye."

Greg looked at his phone. The call seemed strange, and he couldn't imagine what Constance thought so important she would fly here. He hoped nothing had gone wrong with her marriage. Her husband came across as a little strange but an okay guy. He would just have to wait until tomorrow.

Greg reached the law firm and met Jack in his office.

"Well, I guess we took care of that one," Jack said.

"Thank you. You guys were terrific."

"I think Robert deserves most of the credit. He uncovered all that crap on the so-called expert. I can't believe the DA didn't do a check on him."

"He seemed a little too anxious, don't you think?"

"For sure. We also had information that the so-called expert had come under investigation for running an internet scam while in college. The charges didn't go forward, but it gave us something we could have used to put a crack in his credibility if necessary."

"Sure wasn't needed, though."

"Now, what about the divorce? We have a good family practice. I'll refer you to a partner. He will take care of you. I had a chance to look at the papers, and Terry is asking for spousal support in addition to half of everything."

"I don't know how I will pay for spousal support without a job."

"That's why we need to get you over to our family practice. Did you know Terry has gone to stay with a guy named Joe de La Rossis?"

"Son of a bitch. Now it makes sense why they hung out together. I didn't know much but could never understand the reason this guy volunteered on some of the same boards as Terry. Also, I never heard his name until all this shit hit the fan."

"Looks like this guy has a lot of dough as well."

"Yeah, I'm not surprised. He's an Italian Baron."

"Baron? Do they still have those titles?"

"How do I know? Terry left me a note saying she had changed in her feelings, and it wasn't just the fact I'd gone broke. Now I know it had more to do with her finding a new boyfriend. I can't believe I didn't have a clue."

"Greg, I've been married three times, and I never have a clue about anything. You should take some time and figure out what you'll do now that this crap is out of the way."

"I know. I need to find out how much money I have in my retainer account."

"That's no problem. I'll get that for you."

"Once I know what I have, I can make plans."

"Your houses are all paid for, right?"

"Yeah."

"I think you have enough to give you time to figure things out."

"Okay then, I'll head home if you don't mind."

"Wise. You should take it easy for a while. I'm no doctor, but you've come through a lot and should try and unwind before you come down with something."

"Yeah. I reckon I'll go out and have a burger tonight and get to bed early."

"I would come with you, but I have plans tonight."

193

"That's okay. I have this little pub where no one seems to recognize me, and to sit alone is something I can do there. Constance plans to come tomorrow, so I'll need to get some rest." Greg got up, and Jack walked with him to the elevator. They shook hands, and Jack saw that Greg didn't look well. His eyes seemed puffy and his skin paler than he'd realized. All of Greg's tan had faded, and the age lines appeared more pronounced. Greg looked like a man in need of a two-week resort stay. Rest could do wonders. Jack mentioned a vacation to Greg as the door to the elevator closed, and Greg disappeared. Jack didn't hear Greg's response, but he bet it was no.

***

Right here, I need to interrupt. It's Keith again. If you will recall, Greg went to the bar and put his head on his hands and looked about to leave this Earth. I have to tell you that, indeed, that did happen. Though unaware, he'd had a massive stroke and felt more than glad to give in to its final solution. Since I knew Greg's time had not come, the only thing I could think to do was pray that I could do something to help him. I asked The Leader for the power to get seen and heard, as well as a way to stop the stroke. An answer to my prayer arrived. The Leader gave me permission for people to see and hear me. He told me he would take care of the stroke. These kinds of things require faith, so I bent down close to Greg's head.

***

"Greg. It's me, Keith. Wake up."

I move slightly and do not raise my head. I open my eyes. "Keith? I must be dreaming."

"Greg, this is no dream. I'm here with you. Raise your head."

"Keith, it can't be you. I've missed you for almost my whole life, and you're dead. I think I died as well."

"You didn't die. Listen to me. I've been hanging around for years, making sure you stayed okay. I'll have to leave pretty soon, and you need to talk to me. Get up and look at me."

I lift my head slowly. Drool pools on my cheek, which I wipe away. I look at Keith and blink several times. "You're still here."

"I told you so."

"Come on, Keith. Seeing you is just a little weird, you know."

"I know. You and I need to get out of here so that we can talk."

"Hey, Greg," says Jerry. "I just called 911. The EMT will get here in a minute. I thought you were a goner."

"I'm fine, Jerry. I need to go home, though."

"I don't think you ought to leave until someone looks you over."

"Seriously, I'm fine. Sorry to bother you." I get off the stool, and Keith follows me out of the bar. The crowd parts as I move to the door. Some seem to recognize me and get to talking about my case and career. Most sound disappointed that they didn't get a chance to talk to me or ask for an autograph. I smile and raise my hand like I'm walking off a football field after getting shaken up by a play. Keith and I make it to the door and go into the street. It is strange to feel this way, but the previous outrageous condition of Keith being here doesn't seem so outrageous now. For some reason, it feels quite normal. "My car's over here. Can you ride in a car?"

"Yes, sure can." Keith nods. "You'll have to open the door since my hand passes through the handle."

"Can I touch you?"

"I don't know. Give it a try."

I reach out and, carefully, let my hand descend on Keith's shoulder. My hand doesn't stop but continues down through

Keith. "I guess that would be a no. Damn, Keith, how is this happening?"

"I'm not sure myself. I'm pretty new at this stuff."

"You died over twenty years ago."

"I know, but to me, it seems like yesterday."

"Did it hurt?"

"Did what hurt?"

"When you got in the accident."

"I never knew what hit me. So, no, it didn't hurt."

"That's a relief. I worried about that all these years. I felt responsible, you know."

"Yeah, and you need to knock that off. Okay, though this is a nice chat, we need to leave."

"Can anyone else see you?"

"I'm not too sure. Get in the car and turn the rearview mirror toward me."

"If you don't have physical substance, how do you sit on a seat?"

"I sort of hover, Greg. Let's go."

I open the door for Keith and go around to the driver's side. After getting in, I put on the seatbelt and turn the mirror toward Keith.

"Look in the mirror, Greg. Can you see me?"

"N-No, I can't. This is creeping me out."

"Stay with it. I need to help you figure out who put you in the situation of losing your money."

"Do you know who did it?"

"Yes, but I can't tell you. The person needs to let you know."

"Why can't you tell me?"

"I'm not allowed to alter the natural course of things. If I change outcomes, the stability of time itself may get disrupted."

"What does that mean?"

"Damned if I know. It formed part of my instructions when I came over. Now, let's go."

I start the car and pull away from the bar. Behind us, flashing lights pull up to the front door. "Well, I guess Jerry will feel a little pissed."

"He'll be okay."

"Do you know that for a fact?"

"Yes. I feel amazed at the stuff I know."

"Is this like a super power?"

Keith laughs, "No, it's a gift they give you when you cross over to the other side."

"You keep mentioning the other side. Is it Heaven?"

"No. It's another plane. You could call it the fourth dimension."

"So, that's a real dimension?"

"Not exactly right but close enough."

"Is there a god over there?"

"Called The Leader."

"Gold throne and all that?"

Keith laughs. "No, Greg. The Leader is a spirit without form."

"Can you talk to The Leader?"

"Not in a real sense. You feel The Leader."

"Man, Keith. I have a hundred questions."

"I know, and we've almost reached your house. We can talk more, but I have to warn you, my job of picking you up from the bar is complete, and I'm not sure how much time I have. Also, I can't tell you much more about the other side. If you have more information than others, I will have violated my instructions."

"Why did you come back, then?"

"I never left. I've waited for you to give up. They gave me the assignment of watching over you, which I accepted, and that has been my life's work. You gave up in that bar, and now you've come back. You can have a happy life, and it was too soon for you to go."

"I didn't even know I was giving up. How did you?"

"Giving up is not a conscious decision. It happens, and I was there to pull you back. I have to tell you that they promised me a good outcome for staying with you. That's not why I did it, but it is like frosting on the cake."

"Who told you to do all this?"

"The Leader, of course. Let's go in the house."

I turn the car off, and we leave the garage and move into the house.

"You spirits drink anything?"

Keith chuckles. "No, Greg. We gave up food and drink for Lent."

I can't help laughing. "At least you still have your sense of humor. Are you sure I'm not dreaming? Why does this seem so normal?" I take one of the barstools.

"No, you're awake. It's normal because you're in the presence of a spirit, and I have willed for you to feel comfortable. We need to get down to business, as I'm not sure how much time I have here."

"Okay. What do we need to talk about?"

"First of all, Constance has been in some trouble."

"Trouble? What kind of trouble?" I get up.

"Settle, Greg. She got out of the trouble, but she will need to tell you about it, and you can't mention it to her."

"Damn. You have so many rules."

Keith sighs. "I know. I'm sorry. Let's just hope all will come good in the end. Anyway, you will need to keep an open mind and give her the support she needs."

"An open mind? She's my daughter, for Christ's sake. Uh, sorry."

Keith smiles. "It's okay. He says the same thing, sometimes." Keith turns more serious. "You won't understand what I'm saying about an open mind until later. Just promise you will remember this discussion when the time comes."

"I'll try, but this sounds pretty complex."

"Yes, it is, and it will become apparent to you how complex. It will include some nasty guys from the third world."

"Third world? My God, give me more information."

"I can't, Greg. You have all the information that they authorized me to give you. Please, understand that if I could, I would."

I look down at my shaking hands. The thoughts going through my head give me the feeling I've had too much to drink. I look up, and Keith has disappeared. I call out Keith's name. With no answer, I get up. While walking through the house, I come to the realization that Keith is, in fact, not in the house ... if ever he came here. Now, I believe that I hallucinated the whole episode. Sure, I was in Jerry's bar and felt tired. Probably, I just took a nap and dreamed about Keith. Who would ever believe me if I related this story? Keith has been dead for years, and why would I start thinking of him now? Yes, I have been under a lot of pressure, but now that things have improved, why conjure up a spirit? Maybe I have cracked finally. I have lost millions, my wife, and my business. All these circumstances give a perfect excuse to crack.

Then I notice that I ache all over as if I've been beaten with a ball bat, and I think (like I always do) that maybe I'm coming down with the flu. It could be that all my visions are flu-related, and that thought gives me a bit of comfort. After going into the bedroom, I crawl into bed without taking any clothes off except for my shoes. I drop into an immediate deep sleep, hoping the   morning   will   give   me   some   peace

Chapter Nineteen

I hear a small annoying noise in the back of my dream that comes closer. Is it an ambulance or a smoke alarm? I lurch awake and realize it comes from my cell phone, still on my belt, which still wraps around my waist. I fumble for it and pull it out of the stubborn leather case. I say hello and hear in my voice the thick sound of someone who has just woken from sleep. No use in lying to whoever is calling.

"Hello, Dad. I wanted to call and tell you I will arrive at Logan at eleven."

"Hi, sweetie. I must have overslept. What time is it?"

"Seven-thirty. Sorry to call so early, but I wanted to make sure you got the message. I texted you last night but didn't get a reply."

"Oh, I'm sorry, darling. I guess I didn't hear it."

"You okay, Daddy?"

"Yes, honey, I'm fine. A little tired from all the crap but never better."

"Okay, that's good. I'll see you at eleven. I shall come out and meet you at the curb. I don't have luggage, so if I'm not there, just keep circling."

"They have a cell phone lot at Logan. Why don't you call from the plane when you land."

"Great idea, Dad. You're the best. See you then."

"Bye, sweetheart." I end the call and put the phone on the side table. I feel like I went on a week-long bender. Damn, I hate to sleep in my clothes. They get all wound around, and you feel hot and sweaty. I need to get up and face the day, I guess. The conversation with my Keith hallucination has me a little spooked. If Constance is in trouble, I don't know what I can do about it. As far as I can see, I have this house, the place in Telluride, and what's left of the five million. Not much, and for certain, I don't know what will remain mine after Terry gets through with me. I hope that whatever trouble Constance got into, money won't be the answer.

With a groan, I get out of bed. A shower will make a new man of me. I have to say that Keith sure did look good even if it was a dream. His statement about not feeling anything in the accident made me feel better, whether real or not. After turning on the shower, I strip off my clothes. The suit will need to go to the cleaners. It looks like a mass of wrinkles. I toss the bundle onto the floor of Terry's closet. Plenty of room there.

The shower feels wonderful. And standing under the scalding-hot water clears my head and makes the aches a memory. How I wish I could stay in here for the day. I recall when a bunch of us in high school did a fundraiser with a marathon shower. The bad part happened when the hot water ran out, but up until then, it felt like Heaven.

Back to reality, I turn off the water and grab a towel. As I rub my hair, my cell phone rings. I'll never get there in time, and so let it go to voicemail. I continue to dry off and go over and pick up the phone. The missed call came from Jack. I go to voicemail, and Jack asks me to call him. What does he want at this hour? Can't be good, but I hit his callback number.

"Hey, Greg. You sleep okay?"

"Yeah, why?"

"I just wanted you to know several shareholder suits got dropped. I think the lawyers figure they would have a tough time proving you responsible."

"How many left?"

"A couple, but I expect they'll go away as well."

"Great news."

"Yes, especially since you have to go through a divorce and don't need the hassle."

"You get a chance to check on my balance?"

"Yeah. Let me see ... the number's here somewhere. Ah, here it is. You have four million, eight hundred and some change left."

"That is good news. How much do you think a divorce will go in legal fees?"

"Couldn't cost more than twenty thousand, and that's with a lot of bullshit ingredient."

"I won't contest. I just want to make sure the split stays fair."

"Any more than fifty-fifty, you would be right to fight."

"When can I see the divorce guys?"

"I'll set it up. When you free?"

"Constance arrives today and will stay here through Sunday, so I would say any day next week."

"Great. Let me do that for you."

"Off the meter?"

"Greg, you devil."

"Jack, I'm a mere shadow of my former self, money wise."

"Of course, off the meter, you jerk."

"Thank you, Jack."

"I'll be in touch. Bye."

Jack hangs up before I can say goodbye. He is the greatest. I hope I didn't hurt his feelings with that off-the-meter crack. Well, he had a chuckle in his voice, so we're okay. While getting dressed, I get a flash about Keith. I still feel unsure if that whole episode was a dream or not. It felt like a dream but so real. The only way I'll manage to tell is when Constance comes to see me. If she doesn't talk about trouble with a third-world leader, then I'll know I did, indeed, hallucinate.

Keith also told me I couldn't ask her about any of her problems, so I can't lead the question about the third world. Of course, if her trouble is with her husband, then all bets will be off. I will know Keith's visit as a figment. I decide to stop thinking about the situation any further. No good will come from obsessing over it. It will be what it is, and I'll find out no more until eleven o'clock.

I watch the news while eating an English muffin, and the lead story runs the conference on the steps of the courthouse. I would have thought the late news would have exhausted that. I guess the morning folks have to get brought up to speed. Jack looks terrific, and I look like I could use a good night's sleep. Whether it's the camera or lighting, the black circles under my eyes seem terrible. I wish I'd had a make-up person handy before the conference. I mute the volume, as I sound like someone who has never done a broadcast. The uh's in the conversation irritate me. I should have paid attention to my training, but now I look like an average guy stumbling on his words. I hope none of the network guys decide to view this as an audition tape.

The thought of going back to broadcasting came to me a day or so ago. Is it at all possible? I don't even have an agent anymore. When I left the network, I also let my agent go. I should give her a call. The possibility of going back into broadcasting makes this conference bother me right now. The entertainment business is so fickle. If they think I've lost my ability or have no following, I'm as good as dead.

Hopefully, I still have my agent's number. I go to my bedroom and the top drawer of my bureau, where I keep all my old business cards. Grim-faced, I grab the stack and go through them. Sure enough, I come to the card with Sarah Strawberry's name and number. From the time I met her, I thought her name wasn't real but could never get her to admit it. Brighter, I return to the kitchen and pick up my phone and call the number. My watch shows the time as after nine, so she will be in the office. I remember she used to come in early, and sure enough, she picks up after two rings.

"Sarah Strawberry."

"Hi, Sarah, this is Greg Petros."

"Greg. How the hell are you?"

"Just fine. You been following the news?"

"I sure have. Man, you must have some PR rep to get you all that press."

"Pretty funny."

"Yeah, I guess a bad joke."

"No, it *was* funny. It's just, I still need to get over that whole mess."

"I can imagine. What are you doing these days?"

"Well, that's why I called. I was thinking of getting back into broadcasting."

"Whoa, Greg. You kidding me?"

"No, I've given it some serious thought."

"How long has it been, again?"

"About ten years."

"Hmmm. Let me check around and see if I can find any opportunities."

"You're still my agent, aren't you?"

"Well, 'til death or the fifteen percent goes away. Yes, of course, I'm your agent. I made big dough with you. Maybe we can do it again."

"Sounds good. I'll wait for your call."

"Give me your number. You called my office and not my cell."

"Okay, 617-555-5631."

"Got it. Give me a couple of days. I feel real excited, Greg. I love going back to the good times, and they *were* good."

"You doing well?"

"I'm doing great except for getting older."

"I'll bet just as pretty, though."

"Shit, yeah. Bye, Greg."

"See you, Sarah."

I put the phone down and have a rush of excitement of my own. Maybe everything will work out just fine. I don't have the time to build a multi-million-dollar business, but I sure as hell can take a shot at a few million. The thought of managing to get back on my feet seems worth more than ten nights' good sleep.

Upon looking at my watch, I realize I'd better get going. No telling the traffic situation near the airport. The Callahan Tunnel always offers a risk, no matter the time of day. Some yahoo always messes up the traffic with a breakdown or running out of gas. Constance's flight lands a whole hour away, but better safe than sorry. If all goes well, I will get there in twenty minutes and can sit in the cell phone lot until Constance calls. I grab a book and keys and dash out the door. After leaving the garage, it surprises me to see no reporters on the outside of the security fence. I guess they have a better story to chase now.

The cell phone lot seems relatively empty, and as luck would have it, the trip took only the normal twenty minutes. After turning off the car, I open the book and begin the first chapter. I can't remember the last time I read a novel. This one starts out pretty good. Some guy decides to take a leave from his law firm and buys a boat that terrorists already want to use to blow up the Annapolis Midshipmen. Before I know it, I've reached thirty pages in and my cell phone bursts into shrill ringing. Constance. "Hi, darling."

"Hi, Daddy, the plane just landed. We're taxiing to the terminal. I should get out in about five minutes. I'm on the US Air Shuttle, so go to that arrival area."

"Okay, I think I got it." I smile at the thought my daughter thinks I've never been to the airport before. "Bye, sweetheart."

From picking up Terry for a number of years, I know that the call to pick up takes more like ten minutes. I'll pull out of the lot at about seven minutes after eleven. The connection with Constance should be a matter of pulling up to the curb. She might have a one-minute wait if the traffic proves heavy. It doesn't look like it today, though.

I bookmark my place and see that the time to go has come. Upon pulling out of the lot, I confirm the traffic is nice and light. When I cruise up to the terminal, I see Constance just coming out of the door. Perfect. I pop the trunk, and she throws her carry on inside. She opens the door and gives me a smile. "I see you've done this before," she says.

"Yeah, a few times. Get in."

Constance slides into the car, and I give her a big smile and a half-hug. "Good to see you."

"It's good to see you too, Daddy. I'm so glad the jury found you innocent."

"It was a directed verdict, so they didn't have a choice. I'm glad as well. How have you been?"

"Oh, I've felt better, but for the most part, things are good."

"What do you mean, better?"

"Let's wait until we get home. I'm starved and didn't get any breakfast. You have lunch makings?"

"Of course. Lunch is always available. We could go out if you'd rather."

"No, I think home will be just right. Maybe we could go out for dinner."

"You got it. How's Peter?"

"Fine. He's doing well with the firm."

"He's in investment law, right?"

"Yes. He loves it."

"I never get to talk to him to find out what he does."

"Yeah, I wish you lived closer. He helps underdeveloped countries secure investment funds for infrastructure development."

"I'll bet he knows a lot of heavy hitters investment-wise."

"Yes, he does. His main job is to make sure the documents get drawn correctly to protect both parties."

"Sounds important."

"He also has to monitor the performance features to make sure the parties perform according to covenant documents."

"How about you? How is the risk analyst business?"

"Just great. As I said on the phone, I just got a raise. I also just saved the firm about three million in fraud losses."

"Wow. How did you do that?"

"I monitor usage of debit cards and have developed an algorithm that predicts behavior that gives me a warning of possible fraudulent activity."

"Like what kind of activity?"

Constance looks like she feels happy to discuss her job. "Like taking a tax refund and putting it on a debit card, and then passing the card to another user, who makes a deposit in a bank."

"What's wrong with that?"

"Nothing, unless the tax refund is fraudulent. I have found that when a card gets handled by more than one person, there is reason to investigate."

"You developed this system."

"Sure did. What do think about that?"

"Proud as hell. Where did you learn to do this stuff?"

"Remember all those bucks you spent to send me to Harvard? I took four years of math and computer science. There isn't much I can't do with an algorithm and a computer."

"Maybe I should have asked you for help on my case?"

"Looks like you got the best expert, anyway. Oh, look, there's the gate. When's the last time I came home?"

"When you and Peter were here last Christmas."

"Sure seems longer than that. It feels strange not having Mom here. I should have stopped by while I came to town for your trial."

"I haven't had time to process what's going on with your mom. I'm still in shock. She said she got fed up long before my trouble, but I think she saw an opportunity to keep what she has become accustomed to and went for it. She say anything to you?"

"She told me the same thing she told you. I think she's going through some kind of crisis. Maybe she will come to her senses and come back. Especially now that you have no more legal troubles."

"I'm still about three hundred million poorer, though. That can be a big thing to get over." Constance looks away at the mention of the money lost. I want to ask if she has some of the same feelings as her mother, but think that might not be a fair question.

She whispers, and I can barely hear her, "I'm so sorry, Daddy."

We enter the garage, and I help Constance with her suitcase. Once inside, I tell her, "Your room is ready. While you're getting settled, I'll start lunch." I watch her go through the kitchen and then out of sight. Does she ever miss this place? We used to have so much fun running through the house, playing monster. I was the monster, and the kids were the townspeople screaming in abject terror. Those years passed so quickly and were not long enough. I find myself with one hand on the refrigerator and realize I must have stood in this position for some time, deep in thought. I had better get the lunch going and quit the daydreaming.

Still distracted, I fix us a sandwich with chips on the side. Constance comes back, and I ask her if eating at the kitchen island is okay and what she would like to drink.

"I'd love a beer."

"Coming up. I'll join you." I get two frosty bottles from the refrigerator and grab a couple of glasses from the cooler. People think I'm strange to keep glasses in the wine cooler, but I find beer tastes better in a cold glass. While pouring Constance a beer, I ask her about the trip.

"You know the shuttle. Cattle car with wings. It was fine. No bad weather or anything. I need to tell you something." She takes a long drink of her beer. "I'm not sure how to tell you what I have to say, so let me talk and get the important information out."

"Sure, honey. Clearly, you feel troubled by something."

Constance fumbles for a tissue that she has tucked into the sleeve of her blouse. She dabs her eyes. "This is so hard, Dad."

"My poor baby. Please, what is it?"

"Please, don't be nice. You're killing me with your concern. My problem isn't about me but more about you."

"Me?"

"Please, Dad. Let me finish. Peter and I got into some trouble, and I was the one who hacked into your accounts and used your computer to make the trades." Constance starts a full out cry. I get up and go to her. I try to hug her, but she pulls away. "Dad, please. Don't you understand it was your loving daughter who caused you to lose your money, company, and wife?"

"It doesn't matter, honey. You must have had a good reason."

"For God's sake. Your calm and kindness are how Peter said you would react. You should take a ball bat and hit me hard. Instead, you try to comfort me. I don't need comfort. I need to suffer. I need to get shunned and cursed. I need to face punishment."

I can see Constance is losing control and have to help her. I remember Keith, on the day of my dad's funeral, handing me a tissue. I wanted him to leave me alone, and surely my daughter feels the same way. I can't let her go through this alone. "Constance, listen to me. It's okay. I've come out of that mess okay. To use a cliché, it's only money, for God's sake."

Constance continues to cry. "Daddy, I have felt awful since all hell broke loose for you. I thought I could make a quiet transaction and come to you and explain what I was forced to do. I never meant for you to get into trouble."

"I understand, honey. If you will stop crying and eat your lunch, we can figure this out. The problem will seem easier to discuss with a full stomach, and I might add a couple of beers."

Constance laughs through her tears. "Oh, Daddy, you're the best." She dries her eyes, and I think the worst is over. I want her to explain everything, but want her to eat as well. One thing at a time. "Good. Now, eat your sandwich. I spent one hundred percent of my culinary talent on that puppy."

She smiles broadly, which warms my heart. Then, picking up her sandwich and taking a big bite, she talks while chewing, "Peter was helping a small country secure a World Bank loan." She pauses and chews, and then takes a sip of beer. "He secured a loan and had the funds dispersed. The leader of the country got the money somehow and put it in his private account. Peter called him on it, and then before we knew it, this guy threatened to kill both of us if we didn't give him another twenty million."

"Wait a minute. He blackmailed you?"

"Yes. There's more. He also gave us pictures of you taken by an assassin through a scope on a rifle."

"Of me? Why of me?"

"They knew Peter would be reluctant to come up with the money, so they threatened to kill you as well."

"Did you go to the police?"

"No, Dad. He warned us not to do such a thing. He also had his agents everywhere. This guy is the moral equivalent of a pirate."

"Why didn't you come to me?"

"I thought about it but didn't want you to get involved until we had the situation under control."

"But, honey. I could have given you the money, and none of this would have happened."

"I know. In retrospect, not coming to you is why I think I should be shot. This guy told me though that if you found out about what I did, I'd be sorry."

"Well, hindsight is a real good problem solver. You must have felt terrified at the time."

"They decided to hold Peter until I delivered the money."

"You're kidding. They physically held him?"

"Yes, and wouldn't let him go until the money sat in the bastard's account."

"Does this bastard have a name? By the way, keep eating."

Constance takes another bite and chews quickly. "His Royal Highness Adebowale Afua of the tiny West African country Soto."

"Never heard of him."

"I know. He has been under the radar. The country has a small population and almost no literacy. Afua came to power by taking the country in a military coup. He set up relations immediately with the Western world, and that's where Peter came in."

"So, how did everything go sideways?"

"Peter proved instrumental in getting the loan documents in acceptable shape and presented to the World Bank. The bank granted a fifty-million-dollar loan at … I forget the interest rate."

"It doesn't matter. Go on."

"After delivery of the money, Peter needed to go over the covenants and provide the World Bank with a report. That's when he discovered about four million missing."

"Missing? How missing?"

"There's some phony entry in the disbursement, but Peter felt sure the money went to a private account. He asked me to do a search to see if I could find it."

"You searched?"

"Yes, I have a program that can follow the money, provided there is some electronic footprint."

"Man, you are above my head now. What's an electronic footprint?"

"I'll make it easy. Let's say you make a deposit at your local bank. That deposit gets recorded on the books electronically. The record then gets transmitted to a central data depository where it is stored. In this example, we have three electronic markers of the transaction. I can hack into the bank records and look for the transaction. I need to know the account number or another identifier to find it."

"My God, you can hack into bank records?"

"Yes. I learned how when building my algorithm for fraud detection."

"You're scaring me now."

"Anyway, Dad, to the point. I found the four million, and it was deposited in an account under a name that Afua uses as an alias."

"What did Peter do?"

"He wanted to turn in Afua to the World Bank and have them call the loan but thought he would talk to him first. Apparently, Afua had Peter convinced they were friends. When Peter told him what he had learned, Afua became furious. He accused Peter of working for his opposition and claimed he was innocent. Peter didn't want to expose my special talents, so when Afua asked for the evidence, Peter politely asked him to repay the money. He also told him that if he did, there would be no consequences. That's when Afua learned that Peter had told no one about the irregularity. He then had his men grab Peter and throw him in a locked room."

"Damn, Constance, he's lucky they didn't kill him."

"Oh, they threatened him and tried to make him tell where the evidence was stored. Peter told them he had it in his head, and they didn't believe him. That's when they came for me."

"They took you?"

"Yes, they took me to the place where they held Peter. They would have shot me unless Peter gave them the information. It was then they discovered I was your daughter. One of their guys got to playing with Google and stumbled across our relationship when he searched my name."

"I'm so sorry. You must have felt scared out of your mind."

"Tell me. I don't think I've ever felt so afraid. Not for myself but more for Peter. He kept my secret, and I thought they would kill us both. I told them that I was the one who'd hacked into the bank accounts. My confession came as a big revelation for Afua. Highly intelligent, he decided he had found a goose to lay golden eggs. Afua reckoned that he would have a bigger opportunity by forcing me to get money from your accounts. I did convince him that I could pull it off but only for about twenty million. That number seemed to satisfy him, so he told me to get the money without getting discovered and to send it to an offshore account. Once he confirmed the money had arrived, he would release Peter."

"So, after you delivered the money, he let Peter go?"

"Yes, and he told me that if anyone found out about the transaction, he would personally make sure Peter suffered immense pain before dying."

"You believe him?"

"Oh, my God, Dad. This guy has people everywhere. He could pull off any threat he made."

"So, you telling me this story puts Peter at Risk?"

"I would say, unless they have your house bugged, no. If anyone outside of you, Peter, and I finds out, Peter will be a dead man."

"Does Peter know you've come to tell me?"

"Yes. He wants to get this thing off his conscience. He feels guilty because he hasn't reported the four million to the bank and for still being alive, and you broke. He can't do much about the four million, but he hopes you forgive him."

"Of course, I forgive him, and you too."

"Oh, Daddy." Constance gets up and gives me a giant bear hug. I hug her back and now grow angry about this despot putting my family through this nightmare.

"We need to do something."

"I wish I knew what to do. I've lived with this for weeks and don't have an idea."

I release Constance and look at her. She must have gone through hell trying to stay afloat while dealing with this maniac. The worst part is that he will come back and demand more payments. It is just a matter of time until he thinks about having my little girl start emptying accounts all over the place, including those of her employer. This Adebowale Afua must be stopped. The son of a bitch deserves a bullet to the brain for what he's done. I try to think of anyone I know who has any connections with an assassin. I have to admit to myself that my underworld connections are nil. "We need to come up with some kind of plan. We cannot let this guy intimidate us for the rest of our lives."

"I agree. Maybe we should go to the authorities and tell them the story. They might shut him down."

"The authorities will not believe you, Constance, since you have no evidence. They will put you away for the securities fraud they tried to pin on me. It's all too clear that you used my computer for the scheme, and you probably won't be able to tell anyone without putting yourself in jeopardy."

"I do have all the research and tracking codes on the four million. I also have the information on the twenty."

"Wait a minute. Let me think."

Chapter Twenty

Constance and I finish lunch and put the dishes in the dishwasher. We decide to go to my home office, located near the front-door entrance. I ask Constance if she feels okay working on some plan that would give us a chance to get the money back. She looks at me with a frown. "You know that if we take his money, he'll come after us, don't you?"

"I hadn't thought of that possibility, but here's what I think. Somehow, we get the money back, including the four million, and do it so that he won't know it's us."

"I don't know how that's possible. He will know I reversed the process to take money instead of depositing it."

"Okay then, let's broaden our thinking. How can we make sure he doesn't come after us even if he knows we took the money?"

"What you're asking is how we neutralize Afua so he cannot possibly get us."

"Now, that's a good way to look at it. Any ideas? Oh, wait, before you answer, I just thought of another question. Should we get Peter involved?"

"I don't think Peter can add anything. He feels traumatized about the whole affair. I don't believe he could give us any clear thoughts on the matter."

"Okay, I'm good with that, then. How about anyone else?"

"The less who know anything about this, then the better."

"You're probably right. I just wonder if we'll need help in pulling off a stunt that will get rid of Afua for good."

"How about we come up with a plan, and then if we need someone, we can recruit them."

"Good idea, darling. A few minutes ago, I got to thinking that maybe we could embarrass Afua somehow. You know, set up a situation where he looks guilty and then has to resign his office. Is there any way to get his travel schedule?"

"Why do you need that?"

"You and I can't travel to Soto. Not only is it far away, but also, the minute we step into the country, Afua will no doubt know."

"I can look in his assistant's computer and see if anything's there."

"Wow, I'm still amazed."

"We could also go to Soto under some ruse that we want to do business with Afua."

"Let's keep that one on the board as a possibility. We need to get organized and write this stuff down, and you need your computer. What else do you need?"

"Super-fast internet connection and a super-fast combination and permutation calculator."

"What the hell's that thing for?"

"When I need to look into accounts, I have to do calculations to get the passwords."

"Where do we get one?"

"I have it in my room. You asked what I need, not what I don't have."

"Okay, so we can get to work, then."

"I'll go get my stuff."

Constance leaves, and I go to my desk and pull out a couple of pads. We will probably need a whiteboard so that we can both see the developing plan. I call the Office Max in town, and they have one in stock. I call out to Constance that I will be right back. She comes out of the bedroom with her equipment. I explain the need for the whiteboard. She agrees and wants to come along.

We get to the Office Max in a few minutes. As I get out of the car, I hear a voice behind me. "Greg, wait a minute." It's Robert, the IT guru. "I'm so glad to see you. I felt relieved the case went the way it did."

Constance comes around the car. "Robert, this is my daughter Constance."

Robert smiles and says, "Yes, I remember from the courtroom. Nice to see you again."

"Nice to see you too, Robert. You know, I didn't get your last name."

"Given. Robert Given."

I couldn't stand it any longer, "What brings you to Office Max?"

"I'm not too sure. I thought I would go in and buy some paper or something."

Constance laughs. "Well, I've gone into stores with less reason."

Robert looks embarrassed. He must have seen us and decided to come over. "We came here for a whiteboard," I say.

"I was impressed by your work on the case," Constance says. "I thought you made a credible witness."

"Why, thank you. I've worked with computers since I was a kid."

Constance looks at me and gives me an eyebrow arch. Usually, this means I need to say something. I don't have to thank Robert since I did that already, so I don't know what it is.

"My dad and I are working on a project. Maybe you can help us?"

I almost fall backward. Asking Robert for help was the last thing I expected her to say. "Uh, yes, we have a big project, and maybe you could help." I give Constance a cross look.

"We will discuss it and get back if you have any interest."

"What's the nature of the project?"

"We would like to get my dad's money back from the guy who took it."

"Boom. You can count me in. Do you know who it is?"

Constance doesn't hesitate. "We sure do."

"Oh, man. A project that works would be so sweet if we got the money back. You thinking a reverse look up on the transaction?"

"Exactly what we were thinking," Constance says.

"Count me in. When do we start?"

"How about right now?"

"I'm ready."

We three go into the store and get the whiteboard. I ask Robert to follow me home, but he says he has to make a couple of stops, so I give him my address. I start to give him directions, and he says he'll just put it into his GPS. He tells us he will get to us in an hour.

In the car, Constance mentions the coincidence of running into Robert. I tell her I don't think it a coincidence.

"What do you mean?" she says.

"I had a visit from an old friend while I wasn't feeling too well."

"When were you not feeling well?"

"After the trial finished. I went to get a drink and burger and fell asleep on the bar."

"What? Did you have too much to drink?"

"No, I only had a couple of sips from my drink and got real tired."

"Have you seen a doctor?"

"No need. I feel perfectly fine. That's what seems so strange. I woke up to find Keith Petros standing next to me."

"Is he the old friend?"

"Yeah, and hold on for this. He died twenty-five years ago."

"Oh, my God. Daddy. You having hallucinations?"

"That's what I thought but, believe me, he was there. He also told me you were in trouble and mentioned a third-world despot."

"Now you're pulling my leg."

"This happened, Constance. I also believe he, somehow, got Robert to go to the store at the same time as us. Remember, Robert didn't know why he went there."

"Okay, Dad, you're starting to concern me. We need to make an appointment. You've come under a lot of stress lately, and I think you're having a breakdown."

"Well, little girl, I am the dad, and I'm telling you that I'm not having a breakdown. Keith is still here, and that makes me glad."

"Okay, okay. Let's forget about it and not mention it again. Can you do that?"

"Sure. I'm just happy to know he's around."

"Dad. Please."

I let Constance have her way and promise her not to mention it again. I have a smile on my face since having Keith around feels comforting. Although I base my opinion that he is still here on sketchy evidence, it makes me feel better, so I'll stick with it.

We get home and set up the whiteboard in my office. I write at the top, *Plan for Recovery*. Constance tells me she likes the title. I tell her I couldn't stop myself from using the board, and it was all I could think to write. She laughs, and I reckon that she forgets about the Keith thing, which is good for her.

I look at the board as if it will give us a way to formulate a plan. "Why don't we put down all the things we need to decide or include in the plan?"

"I like that. Let me start. We need to know where we'll execute the plan."

"Good, and when."

Constance and I list off as much as we can think of at the time. We have about twenty items when we run out of steam. It seems a great start. As we try to come up with more, the intercom connected to the gate rings. I walk over to it and hit the talk button.

"Who's there?"

"It's me, Robert."

"Okay. Just park in the drive and come in. The front door's open." I push the button to activate the gate and return to the office. "It's Robert."

Constance nods. "I don't think we ought to tell him I was the one who took the money in the first place. He might get antsy about telling the police."

"Sure thing. He'll find out eventually, though. Before Robert gets here, I have a question."

"What?"

"When you set up the remote access to our funds, why did you use my computer? Didn't you know it would look like I took the money?"

"I'm so sorry about that, Dad. I used your computer so that I wouldn't have to worry about someone with knowledge getting in the way. I didn't consider an audit. I just thought you would be the last one to discover what I had done until I could make things right. Please, forgive me."

"Oh, honey. I didn't ask to make you feel bad. It looked like someone was trying to do me in, and I just wanted to clear the air." I give Constance a hug.

"Daddy, I have no words I can use to tell you how sorry I feel about how my problem affected you."

"It's not necessary, darling. I agree, let's not tell Robert that you took the money."

"Okay. Leave the recovery process to me. Robert can help with the scheduling and however we'll render Afua to a powerless state."

"Agreed."

The security system chime lets us know Robert has entered the front doorway. "We're in here."

"Wow, nice house. A person could get lost in here."

"Yeah, I'll give you a tour later. For now, Constance and I have been trying to flesh out all the elements we need to consider if we're to get the guy responsible for taking my money."

"By the looks of all this stuff on the board, you've made a great start."

"We thought so too. A fresh set of eyes may help. First, let me give you a little briefing."

"That would be great. I'm flat-footed here."

I invite Robert to sit and let him know we are dealing with a leader of a small country. His eyes widen with the mention of a leader of a country. I tell him about an innocent party getting forced to hack into my accounts and that we need to recover four million in World Bank funds as well as the twenty million I lost.

"The tricky part will be to destroy the credibility of the leader on the world stage. The entire project needs to get completed without exposing the innocent party who got coerced into an illegal act. Any questions?"

"Yeah, just one. Is the innocent party Constance?"

Constance and I look at each other, and the looks we pass communicate to each other that we don't know if we should admit it was her or not. I say, "What makes you think that it's her?"

"Well, having studied her work for the trial and the fact I got a small lead on the location of the original hack, I put two and two together."

Constance leans forward. "You had this opinion during the trial?"

"Yes. I traced the markers to a New York ISP, but you had cleverly covered your tracks, so I couldn't get the IP address of the computer."

"You are good," Constance says.

Robert smiles and says, "And so are you."

"Hold on," I say. "You testified that you couldn't track the address and only testified that my computer wasn't it."

"I didn't have this information when I testified. The genius of this work caused me to stay with tracking the user. It played like a chess game; I wanted to find out who it was for my personal information. Once I had formed my opinion, the trial had veered in your favor, so the conflict of helping you and destroying Constance pretty much took care of itself."

I just have to ask Robert a key question, "So, to ask you to keep our secret is not out of the question?"

"Of course, your secret is safe. Not only that, but I want to help get this guy since I believe it would take a big load of evil to force a daughter to steal from her father."

I feel relieved. "Thank you, Robert. I feel a lot better. I think you can become an asset to our plan."

Constance smiles. "That goes for me as well."

"Aw, you guys are making me blush. What's all this on the whiteboard?"

I step up to the board. "As I said, this is a preliminary analysis of what we think needs to be in any plan. We haven't done any prioritization. The items on the board are from a brain dump. Constance and I hit a dry spell. We believe your thoughts would be valuable as a third set of eyes."

"Okay, I get it now. I see you have neutralizing Afua as one of your items."

"Yes, that will prove the toughest one. Constance has the account information for the money, and it will be a matter of going in undetected and pulling it out. How to neutralize Afua remains an unknown."

"Constance, do you plan to exit the accounts the same way you did your dad's?"

"I thought I would. You have another idea?"

"As I said before, I managed to track you to your city. We will need to take one more step and leave tracks to a completely different location than where we make the withdrawal. I'm thinking of South America."

"Sounds good to me. I figured it didn't matter if I masked the actual IP address."

"Normally, I would agree with you, but we don't want any bad guys to track us, even to our city. I'm sure, with a little more time, I could have found your IP address. If we relieve some bad guys of over twenty million, they will do anything they can to find who did it."

"I agree. So, we'll add that to the plan. Nice upgrade."

I feel delighted. Robert has already proven worth the risk of inclusion. "Do you see anything else?"

"Let me see. Mmm. We should figure out a way to put the money where no one can find it except you, Greg."

"Can we open an account?"

Constance sits back and chews on a pencil. "We could do an offshore."

Robert sits quietly for a moment. "You know, moving money undetected these days makes for a real problem."

"He took the money from me. Why can't we just put it back in my account?"

"You'll still have to explain it. Don't forget, Constance moved it. You will never prove that Afua took it."

"Wait a minute," Constance says. "What if we figure out a way to set up some evidence that Afua took it, and then point the feds to his accounts? Once all gets said and done, won't the money come back to Dad?"

"That could take years until the justice department gets evidence and arranges a trial, but you *have* given me an idea. Can I write on the board?"

"Yeah. Turn it over. The other side's blank." Constance hands Robert a marker, and he moves to the board.

"What if we assume control of the account with the money? We can change the passcode, and then transfer the money to another account in the same bank under Afua's name." Robert writes, *Stay in current bank. New account.* "You will have the ability to use the new account to move the money offshore to a private account. The bank will report the movement in Afua's name. The movement in his name might cause some suspicion on the part of the government. If it works, moving the money in Afua's name might become part of the elimination of Afua as a threat. We'll need more, though. He will come a huntin' once he realizes his money has gone."

I grow excited, seeing substance forming around the plan. "Can we set it up so that Afua looks like a thief?"

"Sure, we can, but I think we'll need more."

Constance raises her hand. "Why move it to another account in the bank? Why not just change the code and empty it?"

"Yeah, good question. I thought it would look more purposeful if another account got set up in Afua's name and then transferred out. He won't be able to claim someone took it out of his account and would have a hard time explaining the second account."

"Man, that's brilliant. What kind of offshore account can we set up?" Constance grows bright eyed with excitement.

"I can set up an account that will almost not appear to exist. The drug guys do it all the time."

I can't help myself, "You work for those guys?"

"No, Greg. I helped put a few in jail, though."

Constance looks like a kid in school with her hand raising. "If you found them, couldn't others find them as well?"

"Sure they could, but they would need to have a reason. If we do this right, the feds will track Afua's money to the first offshore account. From there, it will look withdrawn. It will disappear with no tracks."

"The money will still be there, though."

"Yes, correct. It will sit in a private account accessed with the proper credentials."

"Can money get taken out?"

"Yes, and no reporting. The only thing you'll have to watch is the banking arrangement on this side of the water. They will report all transactions of ten thousand or more."

My heart takes a dive. "So, the money is useless?"

Robert shakes his head, "You can start a business and have some revenues that will make you a nice living. Let's say ten thousand a week. You need to pay taxes and report the income. Can't you consult with someone?"

"Is that illegal?"

"Well, a little. As long as you pay the taxes, who will complain because your money came from a dirtbag who took it from you in the first place?"

"Okay, keep talking. You're making me feel better."

"Yes, the act of going into someone's account is illegal, and two wrongs don't make a right. However, this guy looks like he needs a lesson."

"Well, I hope I get someone like you on my jury when I go to trial."

"You won't go to trial. Constance and I know what we're doing."

"What do you get out of this?"

Robert grins. "You can pay me in nice, repatriated cash."

"How much?"

"Would a million be too much?"

Constance and I both say "done" at the same time, so I guess the price is right. Robert wonders out loud if he, in fact, had priced himself too cheaply. We convince him he hit right on target. Then we get back to work on further details, and at about midnight, we call it quits for the night.

Chapter Twenty-one

I wake with a start. Did I hear something in my room? It might have been a dream, but the noise was as if someone walked across the carpet. The room still dark, I can hear it. Finally, it dawns on me that the noise comes from the cappuccino machine in the kitchen. Constance must be steaming milk for a coffee.

The dream included Keith telling me everything will work out okay. He seemed so vivid that I could swear he stood in my room with me.

"Keith. You here?" I feel silly asking the question aloud. With flushed cheeks, I get out of bed and take care of the morning necessities. Then I throw on a robe and do the long hike to the kitchen. I guessed correctly, Constance stands holding the steam pitcher under the wand. I ask her, "You want a latte?"

"Nope, I thought I could do a cappuccino but am not too good at it."

"Here, let me help you. I used to make these for your mother. Maybe that's why she left."

Constance laughs at my poor attempt at humor. "You two ever talk after she went?"

"No. She served the papers, and we had one conversation, and that was it. She only wants to communicate through her lawyer. How about you?"

"Yes, she and I talk about once a week."

"That's good. You should keep in touch."

"I think what she did is stinky, though."

"Aw, cut her some slack. It takes two, you know."

"So I've heard. Did you have a girlfriend on the side?"

"Well, no. I thought your mom was my girlfriend."

"See what I mean?"

"Here, a perfect cappuccino."

"Thanks. Do you see what I mean?"

"If I got carried away with the situation, I would agree with you. The plain fact is that your mother got tired of me, and that's where it is. It's like you taking my money. You had to do it, and it's over with."

"You are the most forgiving person I know. I can't imagine."

"Enjoy your coffee, and let's change the subject. When's Robert coming over?"

"He said he would get here about nine."

"Good. I can grab a shower. You want some breakfast?"

"What's on the menu?"

"Well, since we didn't get any food last night, I would think something like sausage, eggs, hash browns, and toast."

"No pancakes?"

"We can have pancakes, but I'll be honest, mine turn out like lead balloons."

"Who told you? After all those sleepover pancakes, someone must have spilled the beans."

I have to laugh. "I finally ate one when I made them for your mother, and I must say, you and your brother were real troopers to eat those things."

"Syrup works wonders. Have you heard from Gary?"

"He calls now and then. I'm not on his speed dial."

"You have an argument?"

"No. You hear anything?"

"You know how secretive my brother is. He hardly ever tells me what's on his mind."

"Yeah, we're not such a close family. I don't know how we got that way."

"Don't be silly. You just have a couple of weird kids, that's all."

"I love them, though. How do you want your eggs?"

"Nice segue away from the issue. How about scrambled?"

"I don't want to talk about the family right now. I might drop into a pile of tears. Scrambled it is."

"Poor daddy. I wish I could do something. You don't deserve to feel miserable."

"Oh, I think maybe this is God's way of keeping me honest. I have whole wheat or sourdough toast. Which do you want?"

"Sourdough. For all the years I've known you, I can't think of anything you've done that requires an attention to honesty. You are the most honest person I know."

"Thanks, honey, but there was a time in life I blamed myself for everything."

"Like your mom's death."

"Yes and even my dad's. Also, I was driving when a guy killed Keith."

"The guy was a drunk driver on the wrong side of the road."

"Yes, I know. It still hurts to think about it. Keith told me he was fine, and I should drop it."

"Why don't you, then?"

I pause over the sausage patties and give the question some thought. "I can't tell you, sweetheart. My mom and Keith have made defining characters in my life. The thoughts of each kept me from failing and had me working hard to succeed. I think, in some way, they've influenced me to try and be the best person I can be. If I were honest with myself, the circumstances of my childhood made me stronger. It took a lot to forgive my mom for doing what she did. She ceased to live when my dad died. Sometimes I would lose my breath thinking of that horrible moment when she stepped away from me and fell off that stage. It seemed almost like she wanted to die. You know the story, right?"

"I do. I've spent times in tears thinking of how you must have felt."

"Well, you can see why I forgive you so easily. You're still here, and I can talk to you and determine what you went through. My mom never gave me the chance to understand. I just assumed it was something I did."

Constance comes over and lays her head on my shoulder. "Oh, Daddy, I'm so sorry."

I pat her head. "I love you, sweetheart."

"I hope you love yourself, Daddy."

"Goodness, little one. You sound like a shrink. Here's your breakfast."

We sit at the island and eat in silence. Without Keith or my mom's deaths, I would have become rudderless. True, I didn't want to let down their memories. Though what I could have done to save my mom, I don't know, but there must have been something. She must have hated me so much to walk out on that stage and recoil from me. My mother took one of the proudest moments of my young life and turned it into a nightmare. I can't imagine what I did to her to make her want to hurt me like she did.

With regards to Keith, I've relived the accident over and over and found no avenue of escape. I even went to the accident site and tried to find a way to avoid the other car. Every move I made, the other car matched. It seemed as if he tried to hit us on purpose.

"Daddy, you planning on eating that? Your breakfast tastes delicious."

I snap out of it and smile at Constance. "Glad to hear it, sweetheart." I pick at the food; thinking of the things I regret plays hell with the appetite.

"Penny for your thoughts."

"You don't want to hear more of my crap. I got to rolling my problems over in my head. Same stuff, different day."

"Maybe you need to find a professional to talk this through."

"You may be right. More coffee?"

"Yes, please. I worry about you and this guilt thing. I deserve to be guilty for what I've done, but you? Not."

"Don't worry. I've had it with me my whole life, and no harm has come from it."

I pick up the dishes, and Constance takes her cup of coffee to the office. I rinse the dishes and put them in the dishwasher. Today, I have trouble shaking the images of my mother. I cried so many tears. Couldn't stop, although I tried. It has been a while since I've had these thoughts. Where are they coming from now? Perhaps Keith caused the pot to boil, so to speak. Once this deal is over, I'll try to find a person to talk with and maybe get a few things resolved. I can see myself going bat shit slowly, trying to get these thoughts forgotten. Now, I need to get to work. One thing for certain; I have forgiven Constance totally, and that's a good thing.

I join Constance in the office. When I look at the board, I feel satisfied we have the bones of a good plan. I should manage to put that ass Afua out of business and get my money back at the same time. My mood seems good. I like the idea of getting Robert involved and the fact that he will make a good amount of money in the process. A good payment tends to buy the kind of loyalty that gives me comfort. The security speaker buzzes. I go to it and answer. Robert has arrived, so I press the open button on the gate to let him in, and then tell him the front door is open.

Upon returning once more to the office, I let Constance know that Robert is here.

She looks up from a few papers she sits reading. "I have all the account numbers and access codes for Afua. I thought I had them, and it looks like I made some excellent notes."

"Perfect. That part of the plan will go like a piece of cake. I worry a little about taking Afua out for good. Have you thought any more about that part?"

"Yup. We can alert the World Bank that he has taken some of their money."

"Four million won't put him on any blacklist. He can just call it a mistake. We need something terrible."

"We could set up an easy trail to more thefts, and then let people know."

"That sounds like something we should think about more. I hear Robert at the front door. I told him it was unlocked, but I guess he doesn't want just to walk in. I'll be right back." After moving to the front door, I see Robert when I glance out through the side windows. I open the door and let him in. "You shy about walking in?"

"I guess so. I didn't think it would be okay."

"I told you the door was open."

"Maybe you should have said unlocked. I expected the door to stand open."

"Boy, you are literal, aren't you?"

"You could say that. Comes from years of dealing with data, I suppose."

I laugh, and we join Constance in the office. I ask Robert if he wants any coffee. He declines, and so we get down to work. I explain we need to figure out how to get Afua for good. Robert nods in agreement and looks over to Constance. She nods in agreement too.

I look at Robert, "Okay, then. Any ideas?"

"We need to get Afua in a position where he gets caught doing something totally illegal. It would help if it were also immoral, but we may not have that luxury."

"What do you mean, immoral?"

"I was thinking along the lines of underage sex or something like that."

"He's not married, is he?" I say.

Constance answers, "No, he has about three or four girlfriends. Also, underage sex is unheard of in his country. Children over there have babies at thirteen years of age."

Robert thinks a minute and then says, "So, we need to understand strongly enforced taboos in the country of Soto."

Constance tells us to hold on while she types in a Google search on Soto Taboos. "I have a list here. The taboos that are illegal are about the same as America. Drugs, prostitution, thievery. So, if we can pin some drug charge on him, that would do it."

Robert gets up and writes "drugs" on the board. "What if we could get him sideways with the drug cartel as a bonus?"

I have to interject, "Do we think he *is* trafficking in drugs?"

"Constance and I can find out for sure. All we have to do is search around for his correspondence and other files."

"Don't you think he would keep that stuff secure?"

"You and I would. There's no telling what an egomaniac will do. Maybe he's sloppy with his records. The first thing we need to do is search his phone records to see who he's talked to lately."

"You can do that?"

"Yeah, takes a few minutes, but I think we can."

"Minutes?"

"He's exaggerating, Daddy. It will take a few hours. We need to get into his computer, and then get into his email account. Most people have paperless bills, which gives us a golden opportunity to check his email, and then his records."

Robert catches my gaze, "For the next few hours, Constance and I need to get into Afua's computer and look around for what else he has there. We need his travel and a few other things."

"What do you want me to do?"

Constance looks at me in a patronizing manner. "You could pop for lunch when it's time."

"Very funny. I'll just watch if you don't mind."

"Sure, Daddy. That would be fine."

So, watch I do. The two pound on keyboards and look over each other's shoulders. They say things that I don't understand, but that make a great deal of sense to them. They exchange a few high fives that lead me to believe they feel pleased with their progress. I sit watching all of this for about four hours and, finally, interrupt them to ask about lunch. They look at me as if I have two heads and tell me to order anything. I leave and decide to go get a pizza. I would order delivery, but my favorite place doesn't have home delivery, and I can't quite get used to the cardboard pies from the chains.

I leave the house and tell them I'll be right back. I don't think they heard me or, if they did, it didn't matter. The ride to the pizza place seems pleasant, and it feels nice to get out. I get the pie, head back, and get in the house within an hour. In the kitchen, I put the pie on the island and get out plates and silverware. Then I go to the library and announce that lunch is ready.

"Um, Daddy, could you put it in the oven for a bit? We're right on the verge of finishing and can't stop just now."

"Would you like me to bring it in here?"

"No, that's okay. We'll be ready to break in twenty minutes or so."

I go to the kitchen, set the oven on two hundred, and pop in the pizza box and all. I look at my watch—I'll come back to check on the pizza in fifteen minutes. Once more, I return to the office and grab a chair. Constance sits working the keyboard, and Robert gives suggestions on keystrokes. He seems like a guide, and from the sounds of it, they've come close to the finish.

"That's it," Robert says to Constance. "We have the itinerary and his bank statements downloaded. Now, we need to exit gracefully."

Constance nods. "Okay, here's what I plan to do. I shall leave an encrypted tunnel in case we need to come back and Afua has changed his password. We won't have to go through all those combinations to crack the passcode again."

"Good idea. You do know a good forensic person will discover the tunnel, right?"

"I figure Afua won't be the one to hire such a person, and I will remove it before the events start. I just don't want to have to go through another three hours of trying to crack another passcode."

"Sounds good."

"Okay, I'm out, and his computer is back to four hours ago. He won't know we were here."

I clear my throat. "You guys want any lunch?"

They both jump up, and it's clear they feel more than ready. We go into the kitchen, and I get the box out of the oven and pull out the pizza. They dive into the food. I get grapes from the refrigerator and find out what they want to drink. Then I deliver waters all around. Both attack the pizza like they haven't eaten for weeks. I guess computer work builds up an appetite.

Finally, they slow down, so I ask, "What do we have?"

Constance says, "His entire email file and, would you believe, all his banking is on-line, so we have the bank names, and it will just be a matter of going to each bank and hacking into the accounts."

I say, "But each account will have a password."

"I bet he's not bright enough to have different passwords, so it will be a matter of trying his favorites and taking his money remotely. If we have a piece of a password, it will make the job so much easier."

"Wow." I take a bite of pizza.

Robert takes a sip of water. "Not only that, but we got some of his Excel and Word docs too. One looks interesting, as it seems like a password log. We didn't have a lot of time to look at it, but after lunch, we'll want to check it out."

We continue to talk about what these two have managed to take from Afua's computer. It sounds to me like they have about everything we shall need to make Mr. Afua a very sorry individual indeed. I ask them what else we need, and they give it some thought and come back with the opinion that there is no more needed. The answer makes me feel great. Only four hours of hard work puts us in the cat seat, and Afua firmly in the mouse's place. "Did you guys get his phone records?"

"Yup, a year's worth. Guy had a file marked 'phone records.'"

"Well done, you two. How long before you know how much more we might need?"

Constance puts down her fork. "We'll need the rest of the day to comb through what we have. Right, Robert?"

"I would say at least. We've uncovered a ton of information."

"Well, I'll just leave you two alone, then. You can analyze to your heart's content."

"Thank you, Daddy. I need another piece of pizza. It tastes so good."

"Good. I got if from my favorite place."

We finish lunch, and Constance and Robert go back to work. I feel unsure what to do with myself, so I head for a book to read. In the library, I sit in one of the big chairs. Before long, my eyelids grow heavy. I blink a few times to keep them from closing.

"Daddy, wake up. We have something to show you."

My eyes pop open like I have sat awake the whole time and can't believe I fell asleep. After a stretch, I follow Constance into the office. Robert sits by the computer and waves me over. I go and sit next to him in Constance's chair. "What do you have that's so exciting?"

"We've been into Afua's phone records for the last hour or so. He gets a regular call from various numbers attached to a burn phone."

"Burn phone? You mean a disposable?"

"Yes."

"What can we do with that? The number is untraceable, right?"

"First of all, the call comes in at the same time. Tuesdays at two o'clock Soto time."

"Okay, a regular call. So what?"

"The *so what* is a regular call from someone who doesn't want any law enforcement snooper to know who it is. It smells like a drug connection to me. Also, if we tap his phone, we can get a good idea of where the call comes from as well as who is on the other end."

"Afua is dumb enough to take these calls on his cell phone?"

"I guess he figures since he's the head of the country, no one will question him. So, I would say it's a matter of arrogance rather than stupidity. The result is the same, though. We can use the information to intercept the drop at some point and lay it on Afua."

"You don't think he does the pickup personally, do you?"

"No, of course not, but we can set it up so that he will end up right in the middle. Let's say the drug lord wants to meet in person."

"The drug lord won't co-operate."

"No, but we can imitate the guy who calls if we get a name and a recording of his voice."

"So, next Tuesday is the next time he will call?"

"Yes, if the pattern holds. We'll need to stand by with the tap in place and the recording equipment running. We have a couple of days to get ready. Also, we found some interesting stuff in his emails."

"How so?"

"It looks like several of the army officers don't feel too pleased with how he runs things. They've gone back and forth about military spending. Afua wants to cut costs, and the generals recommend another course of action. They want additional planes and troops. The generals blame tribal conflict, but it looks like they're maneuvering for more power. I think Afua wants to cut the spending as a way to keep the military down on the farm, so to speak. A military agitation might offer a way to get rid of him as well."

"I'm not following."

"If it became known by the military that Afua took money for himself instead of additional military allocations, I think it could tip the generals over, and we could have a nice coup. It will depend on how much money Afua has stolen. The twenty million probably won't do it alone. Take the drug shit, and the money stolen, and it might give a nice rope to hang him for good."

"I hadn't planned on getting him killed."

"No telling what they would do. If he resists, I don't think he will survive."

"Does he have a loyal following?"

"He has some stooges, but as far as loyalty, I don't think he has a solid base. It looks like he buys his friends."

"This all sounds quite grim."

"Don't forget, they had no election. He took power with the help of the military, and now he's turning his back on them. They will not be too kind when it comes time to take back the country."

"Any way to lure him out of the country and get him arrested on human rights issues?"

"No chance. We found nothing in the information that he has had a hand in any human rights violations. He's a thief but seems to have kept his hands clean on the human abuse front."

"I can't believe that."

"Well, we have no proof, so we shouldn't go down that rabbit trail. I can appreciate that you want to see him punished for what he did to you, but you will have no control over what happens to Afua."

I sit thinking, a phone ringing jolts me. When I look around, Constance pulls out her phone and leaves the room. I turn to Robert, "I have to release the guilt around what happens to Afua. If I get the man killed, I'll have to face my God later. Right now, we need to move forward." Constance comes back, and the color has drained from her face. "What's wrong, honey?"

"That was Peter. He got a call from Afua's thug."

"What? Why did he call Peter?"

"Afua wants another twenty million."

Chapter Twenty-two

"He wants another twenty million? Doesn't that asshole know I'm broke?"

"Daddy, please. He threatened Peter and doesn't care where he gets the twenty million. He just wants it. I believe that he assumes I can hack into a bank or something and transfer it to him."

Robert speaks up, "This won't help."

"In the meantime, they want Peter to fly to Soto and turn himself in as a hostage."

"That's crazy." I can't help yelling and throwing my hands into the air.

"Yes, Daddy, it is. The thug told Peter that if he doesn't get there by Tuesday, they will hire someone to kill us."

"Oh, brother, and to think I felt guilty about eliminating that bastard. Maybe we should call the authorities."

"Greg," Robert says. "We can't go to the authorities. We have no proof that Afua threatened Peter and Constance. He would only deny he had anything to do with the threat."

"I suppose so. Tell me what you meant when you said it wouldn't help."

"We now have a time constraint. Today is Saturday, and if Peter doesn't get to Soto by Tuesday, I can imagine we would only have a day or two after that to get everything ready."

"Can't we be ready by Tuesday?"

"If we hurry. I'm sure we can get the money from Afua's account, but part of the plan was to get the military or the authorities to jump him. I'm not sure we can make that happen."

"Do we have a way to use Peter to help?"

"Hold on, Dad. I don't want my husband in danger. A good chance exists that Afua will kill him anyway if he shows up. Don't forget, Peter is the only one besides me who knows about the thefts in the first place."

"Yeah, true. I guess him going to Soto is out of the question."

Constance folds her arms and says, "That would be my opinion."

Robert speaks up, "So, I guess we'll have to get the job done by Tuesday. We'll have to work faster."

The three of us decide that Peter should not go to Soto. I suggest to Constance that Peter books a ticket to Soto with an arrival late on Tuesday in case he is under surveillance. The reservation will at least give Afua some degree of assurance that Peter has followed the instructions. I tell her to make it refundable so that we don't have to pay needlessly for the ticket. She goes out to place the call.

"Hey," I say to Robert. "Any way to tell if we have a tap on our phones?"

"Yes, I ran an impedance test already on Constance's and mine. We're clean. You want me to test yours?"

"Sure, but I don't think I'll use it to discuss this situation. What about Peter's?"

"We haven't tested his. Better warn Constance."

"Okay." As I turn to go and find her, Constance comes through the door. "I was just going to warn you not to say anything to Peter about our plan."

"Why's that?"

"There may be a tap on his phone."

"I figured Afua's men would listen in, so I just told him to get a ticket and didn't say much more. I did tell him not to worry, and that I would try to figure out how to get the twenty million. I told him to get a refundable ticket in case I come up with the money before Tuesday. If anyone did listen, they would feel pleased with the conversation."

"Man, you are a genius."

"I wasn't born yesterday, Father."

"It didn't occur to me that the phones might be tapped until just a minute ago."

"Well, that's what happens when you get older." Constance goes back to the computer, laughing at her joke.

"Very funny. You'll get older someday. I hope you guys don't mind eating in tonight. I think we need to stay with this, and to go out will be a waste of time that we can't afford."

Constance and Robert hardly look up from the computers. They nod, so I take that as a yes. I will make some pasta and move to the kitchen to see what we have available.

As I open the door to the pantry, I feel someone watching me. A feeling I often have. I turn around but see no one there. Then, turning back to the cupboard, I pull out a bottle of olive oil and reach under the island for a pan. After placing the pan on the burner, I pour a couple of turns of the olive oil in the pan and light the burner. I turn to chop the garlic and shallots and feel shocked to see Keith standing on the other side of the island.

"You scared the hell out of me."

Keith smiles. "Sorry. I had to come and check on you."

"Well, you could have given me a warning."

"Didn't you feel my presence a few minutes ago?"

"I did, but who knew it was you."

"You better turn down that olive oil. You don't have the garlic and shallots chopped yet, and it'll burn."

"Thanks. I'm so glad you know something about cooking. I suspect that's not why you came here, though."

"So right. I have to warn you that the Afua guy is bad business. He's eliminated his competition the old fashioned way. Killed them all."

"I figured so. Any ideas on how to get him?"

"I can't get involved. If I do, I would alter the future and get my ass kicked."

"By The Leader?"

"Yup. You look well. Things must be working out."

"I'll say. The jury found me not guilty."

"I heard. That's great."

"The wife still has her bloodhound lawyer looking for hidden assets."

"Doesn't she know you don't have any?"

"She doesn't believe me. I told my lawyer to offer half of the cash and houses. She thinks I'm hiding something."

"You still think me an hallucination?"

"How'd you know about that?"

"I'm of the other world, remember?"

"Keith, why are you here? I thought you'd gone."

"I thought so too, but The Leader asked me to come back and babysit this project of yours."

"What do you mean by that?"

"They sent me to make sure you avoid any activities that might get you in trouble. You know it's wrong to steal, right?"

"Shit. You must know I've had some guilt issues around maybe getting the guy killed. You can read minds, can't you? Yes, I know it's wrong, but this guy needs to get stopped, and I just plan on getting my money back."

"I agree. I just don't want you to do anything that you'll have to answer for later. Oh, and the mind reading thing is a matter of sensing rather than literally reading."

"When you say later, do you mean in the afterlife?"

"You can put it that way if you want. There is a time when a decision on what to do with your spirit will come up. Too many mistakes and the results aren't good. By the way, only The Leader can read minds word for word."

"What happens to those spirits that make too many mistakes in life?"

"I've only heard rumors that they go to a place filled with nasty spirits and where the warmth of The Leader's presence is absent."

"No fire and brimstone?"

"Whatever that is, no. Just the absence of The Leader gives enough of a torture, which a spirit recognizes once sent away."

"So, everyone gets a taste of The Leader?"

"You have a funny way to put things, but yes, you have an interview and then the decision."

"The spirit gets interviewed?"

"Bad choice of words on my part. It's not an interview in the classic sense. The spirit is predestined and can't say anything to change the decision. The presence of The Leader is to let the spirit know how wonderful it is to be with The Leader, and then it's over for all time."

"Which religion has the key to eternal presence with The Leader?"

"My information leads me to believe that all religions teach the same tenets that, if followed, would get a favorable decision. We need to stop this discussion and concentrate on my lesson."

"Okay, just curious. How often does a mortal get to ask a spirit questions like this?"

"Maybe we'll have time for a chat again. Oh, for the record, there is no food, drink, sex, gold streets, or vestal virgins. My lesson is simple. Don't do anything against your moral character. That simple."

"If I get my money back and am not responsible for the premature death of Afua, all is good?"

"Daddy, I heard you talking from the office. Who's here?"

"I'm glad you came in. Now you can see Keith for yourself. Keith, this is Constance. Oh, of course, you know that already. Constance, this is Keith."

"Daddy? I don't see anyone. Do you feel okay?"

"I'm fine. You don't see Keith?"

"You're scaring me. No one's here."

I look around the kitchen, and Constance called it true. Keith has vanished. When I glanced over at her, he must have disappeared. Now, I look like an idiot. I look at Constance. Fear dims her eyes. Probably, she thinks I'm coming down with Alzheimer's. Best to put her at ease. "I was just talking to my imaginary pal, Keith. I was kidding about introducing you to him."

"Nice try. You need to get some rest. I worry about you. That was more than a casual pretend discussion. I don't know what to do for you. The project might be too strenuous for you."

"No. I feel perfectly okay. I'll not try to convince you that Keith is real, so let's drop it for now and let me get back to making a nice dinner for you guys."

Constance puts her arms around me, and I sweep her into a big hug. She whispers, "I love you."

"I love you, too, sweetheart."

When I release my hold, her eyes look wet. I give her a tissue, and she thanks me. Then she turns and goes back to the office. I wish she would believe me. It would take away some of her worries. Who am I kidding? Her dad is talking to some spirit who has been dead for over twenty years, and I expect her to understand. Not a chance. Maybe I'll just go with the flow and start drooling at dinner. I chase the thought away and say one last

246

thing to Keith in case he is still around. "Thanks, Keith. I know you're keeping my best interests at heart."

"You're welcome."

I whirl around just in time to see Keith fade to invisibility. This is no hallucination, and it makes me feel good to have some backup on this venture. After he leaves, I always think of things I should have asked him but never get to do it. I'm not sure he would answer a question like, "What does The Leader look like?" Or, "Is eternity forever, or is there a limit?" I make myself a promise I will try to ask a deep question about the afterlife when I see Keith again. For now, I go about fixing dinner with a grateful feeling. I pour a glass of wine, tilt it toward the last place I could see Keith, and think, here's to you, buddy.

That done, I go into the office and tell the two geeks dinner is almost ready. They look up in what has to be the first movement away from the laptops in a few hours. Robert rubs his neck, and I suggest they should take a couple of hours to relax a bit. My words must make sense to them, as they both get up from their desk and stretch.

"We have penne, salad, and wine. Follow me."

They both need to freshen up first, so I hold off serving until they come into the dining room. Once they arrive, I place a salad plate on the charger and ask what wine they would like. I pour glasses for all of us. "Now, before we start, I would like to say grace." Constance looks at me with a raised eyebrow. I have never said grace before and feel sure she sits spinning all manners of what ifs in her head. I fold my hands and bow my head. "Thank you for this food, Leader, and please protect these children in the conduct of this mission. Protect them from all temptations to act in non-accordance to your wishes. Thank you, Amen."

Constance stares at me. Robert doesn't appear to see anything out of place. In fact, he says "amen" after me and raises his head.

"We can start now," I say. I hope Constance stops staring and begins her salad.

"Okay," she says. "I'm interested in why, at this point, have you taken up prayer at meals?"

"I'm getting older, and I think I should pay attention to what will happen after my time here is done."

"You feel worried about eternity?"

"Well, yeah."

Robert tries to stifle a laugh but doesn't seem too good at it, and Constance gives him a cross look.

"Oh, Daddy. You're healthy and will live forever."

She does not know about the stroke. Did I tell her? I don't think so, and now is not the time to open that can of worms. Quiet, I merely nod and tell her we can't stay too careful.

"We've made great headway," Robert says. "We've reached the point where we can take the money with a couple of keystrokes. We also came up with an idea of sending an email to all the general officers in the army, as if it's a mistake meant for someone else."

"How would that work?"

"We have all their addresses, and all we have to do is mock up a message from Afua to a fictitious person describing some activity that we know the generals wouldn't like. Let's say promising some contracts for, oh I don't know, street construction. We could even mark it confidential and have words to the effect that the generals should not know the money is coming out of the defense fund. Might help tip the whole thing over."

"I have to voice concern about Afua's life. We don't want him killed."

"I thought you'd changed your mind about that, given he threatened to kill Constance and Peter."

"I know it sounds strange, but I had a change of heart. Call it conscience or the fact that I don't want to have this man's blood on my hands."

Constance smiles, "I understand. We'll try to be careful, but as you know, humans are not predictable."

"When will this all happen?"

"We hope to get the email out tomorrow and pull the money first thing Monday morning."

"I don't know, but I think you should pull the money first. You may tip him off."

"Good point. I wanted to take advantage of Sunday as a day Afua would probably not look at emails."

"But if the Generals jump, he will get tipped off, and who knows, he may prove successful in overcoming the general coup."

Constance adds, "Now that I think about it, if the email goes on Sunday, the generals will probably launch a military action. If we send it after we pull the money on Monday, there might be an opportunity for the generals to negotiate a change in government without violence, as Afua will be in his office. A weekday event may save Afua's life to Daddy's point."

"Good one, sweetheart. Also, Afua will still get put out of business, and the missing money will raise questions about his freedom. How can we alert the authorities?"

"We decided already to send an anonymous note to the World Bank about the four million, and also to members of their Congress and the head of the bank about the twenty."

"So, all hell will break loose on Monday, which will happen before Peter has to board the plane."

Constance nods. "We also think Peter ought to join us here. So he should take a plane ride, but it will be the shuttle to Boston and not a flight to Soto."

"Great idea. Are we good? The email to the military and the money pulled on Monday. The emails to the World Bank, Soto Congress, and Afua's bank on Monday as well."

Robert nods and Constance smiles. "We agree, Daddy."

"Excellent. Everyone finished with their salad? If so, time for the main event. While I clear and get the pasta, Robert, would you pour more wine for those who want some? I would like more. This is excellent work, and I feel so pleased. Be right back."

I pick up the salad plates and return to the kitchen. I almost drop them when I see Keith standing by the sink. "Well done," he says.

"Is there any way I can get a warning when you're going to show up? You damn near made me drop these plates."

"I guess it feels some scary seeing a transparent person standing by your sink. I take it for granted that you've grown used to me by now."

"Well, I haven't. Excuse me." Keith moves away from the sink, and I rinse the plates and put them in the dishwasher. "You think I handled the Afua thing properly?"

"I do. The important thing is that you don't try to get him killed as the end result. The Leader likes that a lot."

"The Leader knows?"

"He knows everything."

"Oh yeah, I forgot."

"Right, I'm going to fade out again. See, I'm trying to give you a warning."

"You're a real pal, Keith. Keith?" Damn, he's gone again. He must have come in to give me some encouragement, and I have to say, I feel good about our plan. With a shake of my head, I turn to getting the pasta served. I take two bowls out to Constance and Robert. "You'll find parmesan in that bowl there. Help yourself." Then I go back and get my bowl. Seated, I see that Robert and Constance have dug in already. A grin settles on my lips at the thought that I could torture them by suggesting a prayer again as a joke, but then, given that The Leader seems to know everything, I'd best not.

"This tastes delicious, Mr. Petros," Robert says.

"Glad you like it. Help yourself to the bread and pass it, please."

"Daddy, Robert and I think we can take it easy now and wrap up on Sunday."

"Agreed. It sounds like y'all have everything under control. How will you communicate with Peter on the flight?"

"He bought a burn phone and will call me and hang up. Then I'll have his number and can call him back."

"How did you get all that information to each other?"

"I told him to go to a pay phone and ring me and hang up. I called him right back."

"So, if his phone is tapped, the bad guys know he got a text from you to call you from a payphone. Any risk in that?"

"We don't think so. They could get suspicious about why I sent him to a payphone. They must know I would think his phone was bugged."

"That makes sense. Sounds like you got it all covered. When does Peter get here?"

"The flight he booked to Soto leaves JFK at two o'clock. He plans to book on Jet Blue, which leaves out of JFK. They have a one-forty-five flight that gets him here at about three."

"Okay, I'll go to the airport to pick him up when the time comes. Damn, I wish we could do this now. This waiting until Monday might prove too nerve-racking."

Constance reaches for the bread. "This pasta is to kill for. Monday will come soon enough. Thanks for offering to get Peter."

"Thanks, on the pasta. An old family recipe. No problem picking him up. It will give us an opportunity to catch up. Anyone for more pasta? I'm going to have a little more."

John W. Howell

"When's the last time you hit the gym?" Constance looks proud of her little barb.

"Very funny. It *has* been a while. I'll still have more."

When I get up, I have this feeling that I wish Constance could live closer. I enjoy her company and would like to see more of her. Maybe when this thing finishes, I'll pop for a trip, and we can have an extended visit.

On my return, Constance and Robert seem almost at the end of their meal. This causes me to rush through my second helping. It doesn't take long, as I didn't take a lot. I finish and ask if they would like dessert. Both give me the old "depends on what you are serving" look. I tell them that the only thing available is ice-cream with chocolate sauce. To my surprise, they both say okay.

I pick up the bowls and carry them into the kitchen, ready for Keith this time, but see him nowhere. While putting the bowls in the dishwasher, I have a feeling he's here but not showing himself. "You here?" No answer. I finish the bowls and get some sundae glasses down from the cupboard. Then I fill them with vanilla ice-cream and spoon chocolate sauce from the can. Most likely, I should have had in something better, but with everything going on, I forgot.

Back in the dining room, I place the sundaes in front of the two and sit again. "More wine? Or, maybe, an after-dinner drink?"

They both decline, and I sit back and enjoy watching them work on the simple dessert while going on with a discussion about tomorrow's activities.

Chapter Twenty-three

Sunday passed with a speed I couldn't have imagined. We didn't do much. I took Constance and Robert out to brunch. We spent the afternoon going through antique stores and then a simple dinner back at the house. We settled on take home from a Chinese restaurant and laughed over the fortune cookies, as they promised us a good fortune. Secretly, I hoped they would prove right, given what needs to get done. We wound down the evening watching a movie that I streamed. I wish I could remember the ending, but it must be that I fell asleep.

Both Robert and Constance feel on edge this morning. They seem quiet, but when I ask if anything is wrong, they both tell me no. We have breakfast without saying much. I reckon it's pre-game jitters and make that suggestion. They both laugh and admit I'm probably right. Their spirits pick up, and the chatter begins in earnest.

"I heard from Peter this morning, and he's all set on Jet Blue. When will you have to leave to meet his flight at three?"

"I should give it an hour. You can never tell about the tunnel. Does he know to call me when he lands?"

"Yes, I told him you would wait in the cell phone lot and to call when the wheels touch down."

"Great. We can't miss, then. You guys ready for today?"

"Yes, sir," Robert says. "We have everything set. By noon, there will be all hell breaking loose in Soto, and your money will be in the bank."

"And you'll be a million richer."

"Yes, sir." Robert smiles broadly.

"And you, my little one. I intend to make you a little richer as well."

"Don't worry about me, Daddy. Peter and I are fine."

"I know, but I want you to have some too. You must promise not to tell your mother, though."

Constance laughs out loud. "Your secret is safe with me, Dad."

"Can I watch you two work?"

"Won't be much to see. We'll type a couple of keystrokes and hit return. That will be it. You can watch if you want."

"I would enjoy that."

"Well, Robert and I would like you to join us, then. In fact, we should adjourn to the office and get it done."

We get up and move to the office. Robert and Constance sit at their computers and type in a few strokes. Robert smiles and lets me know all is complete. I look skyward and pray all will be well.

"Daddy, this new devotion seems rather strange."

"I told you about Keith."

"Yes, you did, and I thought it happened because you've come under such stress. Now, I'm beginning to believe something has happened, and you've turned to religion."

"Religion isn't quite it. I had an opportunity given to me, and I feel grateful, that's all."

"Okay, but you will tell me if you don't feel well, won't you?"

Robert breaks in, "One of the generals just sent an email to his cohorts with the phony email attached. Boy, is he mad."

A chill goes up my spine. "What's he say?"

"He wrote in Ewe, the local language of the south of Soto. Let me hit the translator. Okay, here it is."

Comrades. I must forward this email to you, which got sent to me inadvertently by His Highness Afua. As you can see for yourself, Afua plans to convert money originally intended for military appropriation to civilian projects. I can imagine he will have a big kickback from the contractors. We must do something immediately. With this in mind, I call for a meeting at 11:00 today. I know for a fact that Afua is in his office today. His presence at the government house might prove advantageous to us. Please respond with your intention of attending. The request is not an invitation and consider it an order. Commanding General Jahi.

We all sit in silence for a minute, and then Robert says, "I guess he's pretty pissed."

I have to agree. "Can we see what the others say?"

"If they respond. I don't think they will, as General Jahi doesn't sound like a person who accepts questions. I believe they will have their meeting, and that will be it."

"Anything from the bank or legislators?"

"Not directly but here is a news feed on MSN, which has a late-breaking story on a call for an investigation into the alleged misconduct of the leader of Soto. Details are sketchy, but the house of representatives has called for the appointment of a special prosecutor. No comment from Adebowale Afua's office."

"Oh, man, this looks good. It appears that all the plants have started to grow."

Constance reads a story on Yahoo aloud, saying basically the same thing as MSN. She says, "Turn on the TV. I'll bet there are more stories. Go to Fox news. They usually get on top of this kind of thing."

I grab the remote and hit power. The channel is on Fox News. I mute the broadcast so that we can monitor to watch for any Afua news but don't have to listen to other stories. As I turn to look over Constance's shoulder, a picture of Afua pops up on the screen. "Hey, look at this."

"Turn off the mute, Daddy."

I turn it off in time to hear the newsperson detail the fact that Afua lies at the center of controversy around a call for an investigation into a charge that he used government funds inappropriately. The broadcaster turns the story over to a reporter standing on the steps of the house of representatives. He speaks rapidly about how a mysterious memo got circulated to the members of the Soto Congress accusing Afua of embezzling funds. He reports that, in addition to the memo, the World Bank contacted the Chief of the Supreme Court complaining about a missing four-million dollars. He wraps up his report with a special flash that the Joint Committee of Generals is holding a behind-doors meeting. The reporter mentions that he has it on good advice that there is also another memo purporting to promise business to a contractor. The source of funds purportedly will come from the military budget. He signs off his report, and the switch goes back to the main studio. I hit mute again as the story looks like it has finished. "Man, all hell has broken loose there."

"Daddy, do you see that Afua can't possibly be killed since now the whole world knows about the situation? And if the Generals take over, it will have to be a peaceful coup."

"Yes, my darling. You and Robert have done a great job. By the way, where is the twenty million?"

Robert speaks first, "Currently, we have it in a special account in your name. I moved it twelve times. If anyone wants to trace it, then the last place that has an identifier will have them end up in the Soviet Union. It will look like the money got paid to a group of Ukrainian separatists. No one will ever try to get that money back from those guys. They will never find them, and even if they do, it will not be worth their life to ask for it back since they don't have it. As far as anyone will know, Afua is funding terrorism."

"Again, you guys are good. So, to get the money, I pay myself for consulting?"

"Right. All withdrawals will owe taxes, and you will need to report them on your federal form. In essence, this is the cost of being able to get the money."

"What about your fee?"

"Not to worry. I already took it. It didn't seem fair that you should have to pay taxes on my share."

"So, I have nineteen million in my account?"

"No, when I went into Afua's accounts, I found a spare ten million or so. I took my fee out of that."

"But that wasn't mine. I'm not sure you should have done that."

"I figured there was a cost of doing business, and Afua should pay it."

"Can you put it back?"

"Not without tipping my hand."

"Can you take a million out of my account?"

"Yes, I can do that, and it won't get charged to you tax wise."

"Do that, then, and now your fee is two million."

"Mr. Petros, I don't feel good about taking the money from you."

"Well, donate the other million to charity, then. I don't want any more than what's coming to me. I just can't accept you taking your fee from someone else."

"Okay, sir. I'll take care of it. I'm sorry. I thought you would feel pleased."

"Robert, I know you didn't mean any harm. I just have a narrow view of what's right these days. Thank you for the attempt, and I hope you understand."

"Yes, sir, I do. I admire you and don't want you to have to worry about anything."

"Thank you."

We watch the muted news for a few more minutes, and no more pictures about Afua show. Robert has a couple of emails going back and forth from the Soto Attorney General's office to the Soto State Department. The messages read to the effect that the State Department had best prepare itself for a change in government. The Attorney General has little confidence that Afua will remain in office and predicts a military takeover later in the day. The State Department protests to the Attorney General and asks if Afua can, somehow, avoid a takeover. The Attorney General indicates that the evidence looks conclusive and that Afua should resign. He will, of course, face criminal charges, but for the sake of the country, he should make it an easy transition.

Robert tells us the emails have stopped. "I think the Attorney General is trying to negotiate with the military. I have one more email to General Jahi where he has offered to arrest Afua and proceed with a criminal case if the generals turn him over to him."

Constance asks, "What are the odds?"

"I'd say pretty good. I don't think the generals have an ax to grind regarding Afua's life. They realize a peaceful settlement is the best for all concerned. Oh, hold on. MSN says Afua has resigned and is getting taken into custody by the national police under orders from the Attorney General. So, there you have it. It's over. The neutralization of Afua is complete."

I can't help but clap my hands in joy. "I am so pleased. This is the best outcome possible."

Constance jumps up and down like a cheerleader. "This is so cool. No more feeling afraid of Afua. A huge weight has lifted off my shoulders. Thank you, Robert."

"Just doing my job," Robert says. "I guess we should stay close to the news and track the progress. Oh, here's an email from the Soto State Department to General Jahi."

"Read it out."

My Dear General Jahi, "It begins." *We, in the State Department, have concerns about communication with our allies on the status of Mr. Afua. It would be helpful if you and your colleagues could arrange a press conference this evening. It would also be helpful to know exactly what you intend to do regarding the stability of the government. Please revert soonest. Regards.* "That's it."

I nod and say, "Thank you. It looks like there are cooler heads in action over there."

"Yes, Daddy. It doesn't look like Afua is in danger."

I turn to Robert, "Let me know when a reply comes from General Jahi."

"Funny you should ask. The general's reply just came in. Here's what he says, *My dear Mr. Secretary, We intend to appoint the vice president as president. Then we will call for a new election that will take place in sixty days' time. We will turn Mr. Afua over to the Attorney General so that a full investigation can take place. We believe a press conference is a good idea and request your section take on the task of setting it up. I will speak for the military, and we should have the Vice President on hand as well. We appreciate your help in this matter. It is a dark day for Soto, and we hope to move into the light as soon as possible.* ... He doesn't sign the email. That's all he says."

Constance glances at me, "It looks like they'll do this the right way."

"It does appear so."

"Whoa, here's the secretary's reply. ... *General Jahi, We are so grateful to have your patriotic support of the government. My section will take care of the details for the press conference. I will get back to you when everything is ready. Thank you again.* ... That's all he says."

"Thank you, Robert. I don't need to stay with this anymore. It looks like everything will go as I had hoped. Let's see, it's one o'clock, and I need to leave to get Peter at two. I reckon I can take a small nap before I go, or at least lay down. You two can get your own lunch, can't you?"

"Yes, Daddy, we can do that. A nap might do you some good. You've guided this process for two days, and it must have felt tiring. What about something to eat, though?"

I look at Constance to try and pick up even a hint of sarcasm. I believe her sincere. I let her know I'll grab an apple, which should be enough. I bid them adieu and go to the back of the house to my bedroom. I lie on the bed and don't try to undress. Then I think of going to the airport in clothes that not only look like they have been slept in but have. So, I slip out of my pants and shirt and set the alarm for one-fifty-five and lie down again.

The ringing of the alarm comes at me from some dark place. I reach for it and cannot believe I fell dead asleep. In need of water, I go to the bathroom, run the faucet, and fill a glass. Also, I splash my face. Then I dress quickly and move to the office. "Anything new?"

"Not really," Constance says. "A press conference will happen at six tonight. That's about it. The news stations have reported that Afua is now being held in a detention facility. They report that a hearing will occur tomorrow, where the AG will present evidence. If this were the US, Afua would have gotten released already since the case hasn't been put together yet. Over there, you're guilty until proven innocent. Hard to believe our little emails did all this."

"So, we should appreciate America is a lesson here."

"Yes, Dad. That is one lesson."

"Okay, I'm off to get Peter." I look at Constance, "You want to go?"

"I'll stay here. I want to keep in touch with everything going on. Besides, you and Peter need to bond a little."

"Okay, just thought I would ask. See ya."

"Bye, Daddy."

"Yeah, goodbye, Mr. Petros. Drive carefully."

"Thanks."

I go through the kitchen to the garage. Upon sliding into the car, I have a feeling Keith is around somewhere. I back the car out of the garage and go down the driveway. When I approach the gates, I press the remote. The gates swing outward slowly. I pull forward and stop at the street. Then I look to the right and left and then back right again, and Keith sits in the passenger's seat.

"You didn't surprise me at all. I could feel your presence."

"I knew that."

"How?"

"I could sense it."

I ask him, "Did you like the way the coup went? No bloodshed."

"No bloodshed happened as a result of what you did, and that's a good thing."

"You sound like there will be."

"I can't feel certain how the generals and others will react, but for now, everything looks okay. You can feel proud of the way it came out."

"Well, credit belongs to Robert and Constance."

"I dare say that without your guidance, the result could be different."

"By the way, I thought about some serious questions I want to ask before you disappear for good."

"You will have a little time before that happens. What kinds of questions?"

"About the afterlife. What's it like to be dead? Does some relative come and get you when it's time to go? Things like that."

"I see. You want to know more about immortality. Is that it?"

"Well, yes, that but also some specifics about the process."

"Process?"

"Yes, for example, do you know your loved ones in the afterlife?"

"Now, that question I can't answer."

"Why not?"

"I haven't gone into the full afterlife as yet. I got sent to watch over you during this hard time of yours."

"That's finished now, right?"

"I would think so, but The Leader has told me to hang on and stay with you a little while longer."

"Did he tell you why?"

"Nope, and you don't ask The Leader why on anything."

"So, you don't know if there's anyone around you might know?"

"Correct. I've met The Leader, which was a pleasure. He told me to help you, and here I am. I think once I finish my job with you, I get to go to an eternal place."

"How do you know that this isn't the eternal place?"

"The Leader told me I had to finish my task and then can look forward to eternal peace."

"And this task gives you stress?"

"I wouldn't call it stress. I don't have those kinds of feelings. He referred to the beautiful place in eternity where we dwell in His presence."

"Okay, I'll try to understand, but it gives me a tough time."

"Just think of being in the presence of someone you like and the feelings you have when with them."

"Now, you make sense. Hold on; we're coming up to the exit. I have to pay attention since it's easy to miss." I see the exit and take it. "Okay, where were we? Oh, yes, I think I get what you just said. So, The Leader is like a best friend."

"A good way to put it."

We reach the cell phone lot. "We'll have about a fifteen-minute wait. Will you know when you finish your task?"

"I think so. I'm not too clear on that. Maybe The Leader will tell me to come back to him. At least, I hope so."

"Man, there is a lot of stuff up in the air."

"Yeah, welcome to my world. It would appear an easy thing. Help a friend and then go to eternal rest. I can tell you that it's not so easy."

"You ranting?"

"Well, not exactly. Just saying."

We both laugh, and it occurs to me that it seems just as if Keith never left. I swear it feels like he's stayed with me all these years. My closeness to Keith brings up another question. "Have you been with me all this time?"

"Yes, I got my assignment a little bit after I crossed over."

"How long?"

"Time is such a relative thing, Greg. I don't know how long. Before you got married."

"You could have saved me on that one."

"Oh, please, you were happy for a number of years. Why would I deny you that?"

"Did you know it would turn out the way it did?"

"No comment. If I answer that, you'll bug me for additional answers about your life."

"I did want to know if you could see your mom or dad."

"Sadly, there is no place to meet up with relatives until you get to the eternal place."

"Maybe you'll see them when you get there?"

"I have no way of knowing. Right now, it seems like an exciting adventure. Once my job with you completes, I can go to the next level."

My phone rings. Peter tells me he has just landed. We will meet him at the Air Blue baggage claim. I figure we can wait about five minutes more and then go. That gives me time for another question or two with Keith. "So, do you think that once you finish with me, we will be able to see each other again?"

"I'm sure we will. At least, that's what I understand from my briefing in the beginning."

"Well, the hope that we can talk feels better than nothing."

"Also, don't try to convince people that we have these conversations. You will only lead them to believe that you're getting senile."

"I've found that out already. Constance thinks I've fallen off my rocker."

"Understandable. Imagine telling someone you've spoken with a person who died twenty-some years ago."

"Good advice. I'll follow it. Well, time to get Peter."

"Yes, you should go. I'll say goodbye for now. I'll see you sometime."

"I wish you didn't have to go."

"I know, but I must say goodbye."

As Keith says his farewell, he fades to transparency and then invisibility. His leaving always makes me a little sad. It leaves a vacancy in my heart that feels like a gap. Almost like hunger, only more urgent and cold. A shiver hits me as I start the car and pull out of the lot. I circle the airport, follow the signs to the arrival section of the terminal, and see the point where Jet Blue passengers can get picked up and pull to the curb. A police officer waves me away from the curb. As I'm about to pull away, Peter makes a dash for my car. Constance must've told him what car I drive. He grabs the handle and opens the door. The officer stops walking toward us and gives me a raised eyebrow. "Hey, Peter, jump in. Sorry to stay on the roll, but that nasty cop over there wants to write me a ticket."

"Hi, Greg. You can hit it; I'm in."

I smile. "It's good to see you, son."

"Same here. We've had a rough ride, and I'm glad it's over."

"That makes two of us. That little bag all you have?"

"Yeah, I travel light. I don't imagine we'll stay in Boston long."

"No, I suppose not. Now that the danger is over, you and Constance can get on with your lives. At least, we hope you can."

"Yes. Hopefully, that's true. I want to apologize for taking the money, though. We didn't know what else to do. We never thought it would lead to you getting accused of insider trading. Constance thought it would just go undiscovered and not cause a problem."

"I know. You and Constance ended up against a wall, and I'm not sure you had a choice. As I told her, I would have preferred you came to me but understand why you didn't."

"I appreciate your understanding."

I nod to Peter and think it is no use even going into the fact that Keith told me to show understanding. We talk about Peter's job, and I feel glad things are going so well.

Chapter Twenty-four

We arrive at the gates, and I hit the remote. While they open, Peter turns and looks behind us. "What're you looking for?"

He says, "I've had the feeling of getting followed."

I laugh at the idea. "That comes from being near me."

He relaxes and turns back to the front once the gates close behind us.

I say, "You've had quite a scare, so it's natural you would think people are following you."

"Ever since Afua decided to become an asshole, I've had that feeling. I don't think I imagine it. At the airport, I caught a guy staring at me, and he looked away quickly when our eyes met."

"What did he look like?"

"Hard to say. Caucasian. I know that much."

"Maybe the guy thought you were cool, and then grew embarrassed to get caught looking at you."

Peter laughs out loud. "You do know how to throw a positive spin on things."

"I'm just saying our nerves have been on edge lately, and it's natural to see bad guys on every corner."

"You're probably right. It feels good to be here." He sighs the sigh of a man who feels safe.

"It's good to have you."

We pull into the garage, and I hit the door button on my overhead console. After turning the car off, I ask Peter if he feels hungry.

"I had lunch but could use some water."

We get out of the car and go into the kitchen. I pull a bottle of water from the refrigerator. "Here you go. You can put your bag in the guest room. Constance and Robert are in the office."

Peter takes the water and goes to the guest room. I go to the office.

"Peter's here."

"Oh, Daddy, where is he?"

"He's putting his bag in the guest room."

"I'll be right back." Constance gets up and leaves the room.

I nod to Robert, "Anything new?"

"Not much. The press conference had a slight delay. It kicked off at six-thirty Soto time. A half hour after you left for the airport."

"They're four hours ahead? You know I didn't even think to work out the time difference. I wondered why things had happened so fast there. What went on?"

"I recorded it if you want to see it."

"Maybe later. For now, just give me the highlights."

"The Secretary of State opened the conference with a prepared statement that, in essence, said the President would remain under house arrest until an investigation into several irregularities completes. He indicated that the government would go on under the Vice President until a successor gets elected. All the generals sat behind the Secretary, and you couldn't miss the fact that they went there to show the country that law and order would be maintained. General Jahi didn't smile once, and I don't think he blinked either. The Vice President got up and gave a nice speech about how democracy has been allowed to work. He repeated the idea that the government would continue as normal. They allowed a couple of questions that didn't prove any more revealing. One reporter asked where Afua was being held, and the Vice President said the location remained classified. He did state that Afua was in good hands and would, in all probability, stay under house arrest for some time. A follow-up question from another reporter came to the effect of asking if Afua remained alive, and had the terse answer of yes. That was about it. The generals never said anything, and had no questions directed to them."

"Yeah, that sounds strange."

"Well, don't forget, Afua's power came from these guys, and the country still has to get used to democracy. I don't think anyone wanted to court a reaction from this team of powerful military men. They look like they have an interest in maintaining the status quo, but people still fear them."

"They killed a lot of people, as I recall."

"Ten years of civil war has its causalities."

Constance and Peter come into the room, holding hands. I make a comment about united at last, and they give me one of those fake smiles designed to let me know that I can hold my smart ass remarks to myself next time.

"I have a great idea. Well, at least I think it's great. Why don't we all go out to dinner tonight to celebrate our good fortune?"

"Daddy, that sounds perfect. Can we go to the No Name? I have this super craving for chowder."

"If you want chowder, then so be it. The nice thing about the No Name, we don't have to get dressed. We're okay as we are."

Peter says, "I've never been there but have heard about it."

"Yeah, it's one of the older places. In the seaport district, and I think you'll like the neighborhood."

"Sounds great."

"I hope you all don't mind, but I'll stay here."

"No, Robert," Constance says. "You have to come with us. I insist."

"It's such a long way from my house. I'm afraid I'll fall asleep on the way home."

"You can stay here. Right, Daddy?"

"Yes, of course. We have plenty of room and another bedroom just for you."

"Well, if you don't mind."

"No, I'm happy to have you stay. You've pretty much been here around the clock. You can take a shower, and I think I have some jeans and stuff you can put on. Stand up."

Robert stands, and he and I go back to back. I ask Constance to verify that we stand at about the same height. She does, and then I guess Robert wears size thirty- eight pants. He confirms that, and I get him a pair of jeans, shirt, and underwear. When I return, I hand him the stuff. Then I show him where the other spare bedroom is and let him know it has an en suite bathroom. Robert thanks me and goes off to change. And take a shower, I hope.

I turn to Constance and Peter, "How about you guys? You need to freshen up?"

Constance nods, "Yes, that would be nice. How long do we have until we need to leave for downtown?"

I look at my watch. Almost five o'clock. "If we leave by six-fifteen or six-thirty, we should get there in enough time to get a nice table."

"Okay, then we'll go and shower and maybe rest a few minutes."

"Good. See you later."

Once Constance leaves, I go into the kitchen and get a bottle of water. I half expect Keith to come out of the woodwork. Usually, he makes an appearance in the kitchen. Not

John W. Howell

now, though. I get the water and go back to my room. Then I
plump the pillows so that I'll have a backrest when I lay on the
bed. Once on the mattress, I lean back and take a sip of water. It
feels amazing that the threat of Afua is over. It almost seems too
easy. While I lay there lost in thought, my phone rings.

"Hello?"

"Hi, Greg, it's Jack Mathews."

"Hi, Jack, you must be working overtime."

"Yeah, you would think the law would only be in effect
for eight hours." His voice sounds weak like he feels tired of
something.

"Problem?"

"No, I wanted to let you know that all the civil actions
have now become a thing of the past."

"Good to hear. I haven't heard anything about the
divorce. You?"

"Sure haven't, but I probably wouldn't. Why don't you
call your lawyer?"

"It's one of those let sleeping dogs lie kind of things. I
guess if I don't ask, I won't hear anything bad."

Jack laughs and starts coughing. Finally, he stops and
says, "I know what you mean."

"You okay?"

"Yes, I caught a cold and have this cough that I can't
shake. I know those guys are in the office now if you want to call
them."

"I guess I should. Okay, I'll call. See you, Jack."

"Bye, Greg."

I don't want to call, but I know that's childish. I look at
my phone until I find the number and push call.

A person named Shelly answers and, after I ask for Brian,
my lawyer, she puts me on hold. Three or four minutes later,
Brian comes on.

"Hi, Greg. How are you?"

"Doing fine. How about you?"

"Great. I planned to give you a call tomorrow, so I'm glad you rang."

My stomach flips. "Any problem?"

"Oh, no. We got the list of assets from your wife's attorney, and you should schedule some time to go over it. We want to make sure you agree with everything she's listed. Once complete, we will go about making some equitable division. Also, did you know she's asking for alimony?"

"Alimony? Wait a minute; she left me. Why would she think I would owe alimony?"

"Sometimes, in these cases, you get some tax advantages to paying alimony instead of an outright cash settlement."

"I'll have to talk long and hard about that with you. I'm not sure I like it."

"Of course, we'll talk. In fact, I need to spend quality time with you to go over the decree as it has been constructed by the other side. It doesn't mean we have to accept everything. It gives a good place to start since we know now what she wants from you."

"I want to stay fair but see no reason to go overboard."

"I agree completely. Let me put Shelly back on, and she can set up an appointment, then we'll get all this straightened out. Hold on."

"Thanks, Brian." Shelly comes back, and we set up a meeting for Friday. I make it in the morning, and then decide I'll have lunch downtown. After the call finishes, I think of who I could call to join me for lunch. No one comes to mind except, maybe, Jack. I'm sure he has better things to do since my case is wrapped up.

How in the hell did Terry get the balls to ask for alimony? We had a good marriage before she decided we weren't working. Seems she ought to pay me alimony as recompense for abandonment. I'll bet she got herself a high-priced lawyer who figures I can afford any demand. I'm glad I got my twenty million—er, make that nineteen—back, and Terry doesn't know about it. Why should she? I just got it today, and I'm sure her asset list got made up before all the action on Afua. Maybe it would be a good idea to do the alimony to help offset some of the taxes on the nineteen million. Also, maybe alimony will short-circuit any argument and further discovery of assets. I need to keep the nineteen million hidden from her. I then get a flash on Keith. I'll bet he would recommend just telling her about the money and then splitting it fifty-fifty. That would be the honest thing to do, except how do I explain a magic nineteen million showing up?

Damn, this makes for a real problem. Could I, somehow, hire Terry as an employee and pay her overtime? My lawyers will have to earn their money and figure this out. The divorce has presented a moral question and gives more of a problem. I'll have to put off thinking about this until later. The Friday appointment with the lawyer will come soon enough. I make a deal with myself to forget it until then. Of course, I'll need to remember to bring it up, but that seems a small consideration.

I must have dozed off, as I jerk and instinctively look at my watch. Six o'clock. Alarmed, I jump off the bed and rush to the bathroom. My hair doesn't appear too mussed, so I run a comb through it and settle for the look. Then, splashing water on my face, I decide I don't have to shave. In all, I'm in pretty good shape to go out. A change of shirt seems all that is necessary.

Upon walking into the living room, I see everyone here except for Robert. "Where's Robert?"

Constance says, "He decided he needed to go home after all. He mentioned his dog and said to go ahead and that he'll try to make it to the restaurant."

"Aw, that's a shame. I would have liked to have him there."

"Maybe he'll show."

"Knowing Robert, once he goes home, that'll be it. Well, we might as well go. I'll drive."

Constance smiles. "I hope so since you're the only one with a car."

We get to the restaurant and receive a nice table. I tell the server that one more might join, but we will go ahead and eat. We all order a cup of chowder, and then some fish for the main course. The dinner tastes delicious, and the evening flies by. On the way home, I ask Peter, "Do you plan to stay a while?"

"I should get back to New York tomorrow."

"Want me to take you to the airport?" I hope it doesn't sound like I feel anxious to get rid of him. "I mean, I would love it if you could stay longer."

"I appreciate that, but I've fallen behind, and I can only do so much remotely. I need to meet with the clients while processing their loans."

"I understand completely. I just wish you could stay, is all."

Constance says, "I should get going as well, Dad."

"Yeah, I thought Peter's exit would trigger a stampede."

"You calling me a cow?"

I guffaw. "Yeah, right, as if I would ever get away with that comment."

Constance and Peter join me in a laugh. We pull up to the gate, and I press the remote. The gate opens at its usual slow pace, and I pull through. Then I proceed directly to the garage door. Normally, I pause until the gate closes, but my mind lagged behind on the fact that the kids will leave tomorrow. Peter brings me back when he says, "A car just came through the gate."

I turn around. What looks like a large SUV with bright lights stops behind me. "Must be lost," I say. "Stay here." I open my door and get out. I holler to the SUV that this is private property and do they need help. In the bright light, a figure climbs out of the passenger side.

273

"Mr. Petros?"

"Yes, I'm Mr. Petros."

"Greg Petros?"

"That's correct, and who are you?"

"Please, forgive my bad manners. My name is Nkiruka Simisola, and I represent the government of Soto."

"Can you come out of the bright light and let me see you?"

"Oh, my apologies." He says some words to the driver, and the lights go out. "Is that better?"

"Yes, much. What do you need from me?"

"From you, we do not need anything, Mr. Petros. Do you have your son-in-law with you? His name is Peter Cage."

"I know his name, pal. What do you want with him?"

"We just need a statement regarding the four-million dollars that Adebowale Afua took from the World Bank."

"Yes, he's with me. Can you come closer? Do you have identification?"

"Oh, most certainly, Mr. Petros. May I come closer?"

"Please do."

The man moves away from the SUV. He walks toward me with his hand outstretched. I take his hand, and he gives me a large smile. Then he reaches into his jacket and pulls out his passport. He seems to be what he says. The passport picture looks like him, and the Soto State Department issued it. The passport has a diplomatic rider and a request for all courtesy.

"Okay, this appears to be you." I hand the passport back to him. "Why don't we go inside? How about your driver?"

"Thank you for your courtesy. My driver will be fine staying with the vehicle. It is his responsibility."

"Very well. Give me a moment." I lean back into the car and tell Constance and Peter that it's okay, and the gentleman has some questions for Peter, who then wants to know what kind of questions. I suggest we all go inside, and we can discuss the whole thing there. Peter and Constance get out of the car. I introduce them to Nkiruka Simisola. Nkiruka bows slightly, and I can see he is a well-trained member of the diplomatic corps. We all go inside, and when we get there, Nkiruka seems much bigger than he appeared outside. He looked tall in the driveway, but not as chunky. This seems a bit unusual for a member of the diplomatic corps. He looks more like a prizefighter. Perturbed, I lead the group to the living room, and we all take a chair. I ask Nkiruka if he would like a drink or some water, and he declines. "I won't take too much time, but thank you for the offer."

"What questions do you have for Peter?"

"First, here is my card." He hands it to Peter. "I work in the Justice Department. We want to collect information on some of the activities of the former president. You had business with him, correct?"

Peter looks at the card, and I can tell he wonders if he should answer or not. Finally, he says, "Yes, I arranged a World Bank loan of fifty-million dollars."

"You also had charge of due diligence on the loan?"

"Yes, correct."

"When you did your audit, did you find anything not in order?"

"I did."

"Can you tell me what you found?"

"I discovered that Afua had taken four-million dollars."

"Do you know what he did with it?"

"Yes, he put it into a private account."

"How did you know this?"

"I found the paperwork in the disbursement file."

"Did you confront Afua about this?"

"Yes."

"Did you tell the World Bank?"

"No, I wanted Afua to have the opportunity to put back the money."

"Did he?"

"No."

"What did he do?"

"I don't think that has any importance to your investigation. However, I will say that he threatened me and my family if I reported him."

"I see. So, you said nothing."

"Correct."

"Doesn't not saying anything break banking laws in the US?"

"Not if I gave him the opportunity to put it right, and he does so."

"But he didn't."

"As I said, he threatened my family."

"So, you could get prosecuted should the bank choose to do so?"

"I suppose if they found out, then yes."

I can't stand it anymore. "Are you trying to investigate Peter or Afua?"

"Good question. I want to determine if Mr. Cage acted as an accomplice to the crime. So far, I would say he certainly should have said something when he first found out that Afua had taken the money."

"He told you he wanted to give Afua an opportunity to put the money back."

"Yes, but later, he should have told the bank about Afua's crime."

"Again, he told you already that Afua made threats."

"How did the threat get lifted? It appears that Afua allowed the family to live."

I have to think a minute and see no reason to mention Afua forcing Constance to come up with twenty million. To mention that could put this guy on the trail toward us. Instead, I just say, "I guess Afua felt satisfied that Peter would keep quiet about the four million."

"That doesn't sound like Afua at all. I suspect there is more than you are telling me."

"I don't think so. Peter, do you have any more to the story?"

He shakes his head. "No. That's it. I told Afua I would never tell, and he told me he would keep watching to make sure I kept my word, and that was it."

Nkiruka's expression turns dark. He opens his mouth but doesn't say anything. Instead, he gets up. "Please, excuse me. I must make a call. I will need to go outside."

"Of course, go through the kitchen, and you'll find yourself back in the garage. Your car is in the drive. I left the garage door open."

Nkiruka leaves the room. I look at Peter and raise my eyebrows. "What do you suppose he has up his sleeve?"

Peter shakes his head and fidgets with his phone. I feel unsure if it comes down to nerves or that he plans to call someone. Constance sits with her mouth pursed and looks like her mother always looked when she got pissed.

"Do we have to continue to talk to this guy?" Constance says.

I consider that for a second. "I would think not. He has no jurisdiction here."

Peter speaks up, "Probably, he could get a warrant, which could stay good when and if we travel to West Africa."

"Yeah," I say. "Remind me not to go there."

Constance relaxes her mouth and sighs. "What if he gets some consideration from our State Department?"

"Hey, kids. Let's forget this line of thinking. Nothing will happen. Shush, I hear him coming back."

Nkiruka returns to the living room, and behind him stands a huge guy, who looks like a professional cage fighter. The

277

two have frowns and appear as if they mean business. What kind of business remains unknown so far. This Nkiruka seems less and less like a member of the justice department and more like a hit man. Maybe it's his size or the nasty look on his face, but now I grow concerned.

"Allow me to introduce my associate. He is a master at lie detection. We are running short of time, and I need to get a straight story from you people. My associate is not too bright, but he does enjoy a certain amount of violence. You see, he works for a guy who works for Afua. The guy who works for Afua has reason to believe you know the whereabouts of a large sum of money that got taken from Mr. Afua's accounts."

"You can't come into my house with a thug and threaten us."

"Shut up, Mr. Petros. As you can see, I have done exactly that this evening."

"What is it you want?"

"I believe I just told you. We want to know where the twenty million went. Also, we want it back."

"What if I told you we have no idea what you're talking about?"

"I would call you a liar, and I would be forced to turn my associate loose on you to find out the truth."

Peter squirms, and Constance moves as if to get up.

"Stay seated if you please," Nkiruka says. His associate pulls a black pistol from his coat and aims it at Constance, and she retakes her seat quickly.

"No need for guns," I say. "You won't too far with this kind of tactic."

"Again, Mr. Petros, I must respectfully ask you to keep quiet."

I sit back in my chair and try to think of what we can do to save our skins. I believe that just giving them the money will not, necessarily, guarantee our safety. I shall have to think of a way to get them out of the house and to a location where I can scream for help. The late hour doesn't help either. My best case is to stall.

Chapter Twenty-five

Nkiruka goes to the dining room and pulls a chair from there and into the living room. He sits and crosses his legs. The big associate stands near the wall and folds his arms. They have prepared themselves for a long night, and I don't want to disappoint them. I ask, again, if they would like a drink, and both decline. My attempt to buy some kindness with water must have proved transparent.

"So as not to lose too much sleep tonight, I ask you, again, Mr. Petros. The location of the twenty million?"

"What makes you think I know?"

"An educated guess. When Mr. Afua got taken into custody, a quick check of his accounts came up with a twenty million withdrawal. The money got laundered so completely that we lost track of it somewhere out in the Caribbean. Now, we know that Mr. Afua stole large sums of money. We also know that he extracted a large sum by intimidating your daughter. Mr. Afua kept impeccable notes on all his transactions. Your daughter took the money from you and caused all that trouble. We think she had a way to get back the money, and that is why we have come here. We have found all the other sums that Afua stole except for the twenty million. The person I work for wants the money returned.

"So, he can return it to its rightful owner?"

"If that's what you would like to believe. You and your daughter thought no one could track the transactions. You would have been right if it weren't for Mr. Afua's black book listing the people he extorted and sums of money taken."

"Our names were in the book, and you have it?"

Nkiruka shrugs. "I guess it won't hurt to admit as much. Who would you tell? You're not going anywhere."

"What are you saying?"

"Unless I get answers, I shall ask my associate to shoot you. So, let me answer your question about returning the money to its rightful owner. Afua took the money as one of the spoils of being president. We believe that, as successors to that privilege, we should reap the full benefit of the office."

"You mean the Vice President."

"You know, Mr. Petros, the more you say, the more I think it a good idea to kill you."

"Kill me, and you'll never get the money."

"Real disturbing threat, Mr. Petros. How about if we put a bullet into your precious daughter's knee? Would that change your mind?"

I start to rise, and the big associate pulls out his gun again. I sit. Glance at Constance. An unearthly calm settles on her face. She broadcasts bravery and is trying to tell me not to fold. A glance at Peter shows him looking a little more nervous, still fidgeting with his phone. I have to think of something, quickly. No way can I continue to think of this situation in terms of affecting just me. These guys could, feasibly, kill Peter, Constance, and me. Can I make a deal? Maybe I could offer to take them to the money. I could tell them the money is in a bank that won't open until the morning. Not sure they would buy it but worth a try. I break out with a nervous tick. My eye keeps winking, and I can't get control of it. To try to massage the tick away, I put my face in my hands. If I look nervous, I will never manage to pull off lying while staring down the barrel of a gun.

"What's the matter with you?"

"I'm thinking, is all."

"Thinking? What about?"

"I will take you to the money, but I can't get at it until the bank opens tomorrow."

"You put it all in the bank? Are you out of your mind, Mr. Petros?"

"You can call me Greg, and no, I'm not out of my mind."

"What bank on this Earth would accept a twenty-million-dollar deposit without calling the IRS or the FBI?"

"I didn't deposit the money."

"Say again, Mr. Petros. I thought I heard you say you didn't deposit the money."

"That's correct, Mr. Simisola. I put the money in the bank but in a safe deposit box."

"Excellent pronunciation of my name. I don't think you can fit twenty million in a safe deposit box."

"True enough. I went to ten banks and got two boxes in each bank." I now realize I've gone way out on a limb. Somewhere, I read an ad for a duffle bag that said a million dollars in hundred-dollar bills weighs twenty pounds. The company said they had designed the bag to carry a million in cash. I figure twenty pounds wouldn't fit in one box, hence the two boxes per bank. I hope it makes sense to Nkiruka Simisola.

"When did you do this? The money went missing this morning at about eleven o'clock—seven in the morning here."

"This afternoon and this morning. I did it this morning and afternoon." I try to make the time spread as large as possible and almost locked into an afternoon. Every one of my neurons fire now. I have to stay ahead, not that I've concocted such an outrageous story.

"Are you telling the truth? My associate and I started watching your house at about three-thirty. We didn't see you come back from this bank excursion."

"That's because I'd already gotten done and back by two."

Simisola tries to figure the times to see if it is possible that I made the bank runs and returned. He touches his cheek with an inadvertent signal that he is thinking. I'll wait until he comes to a conclusion.

"Show me the paperwork and keys."

I gotta think fast. Obviously, no paperwork exists and certainly not twenty keys. I do remember I have a key to my personal safe deposit box, and this gives me an idea. "I don't have them. I put all the papers and keys into a separate box at the bank."

"So, you have twenty-one boxes. You lied to me." Peter makes as if to get up again, and the big guy gives him a sign to sit. Peter obeys immediately.

I don't want Constance or Peter to take any unnecessary risks. Since they have no idea what I'm up to. I signal for them to stay seated. "No, I didn't lie. I have a personal safe deposit box, and I put everything in there."

"You put it all in there, huh? I suppose you have a key to that box."

"I do."

"This is good for you because I was about to tell my man to take you out back."

"You want to see it?"

"Yes, of course." Simisola waves the big guy over and tells him something in their language. "Mr. Petros, please lead the way to the key, and my man will go with you. I will entertain the young people while you are away."

"There's no reason to hurt anyone."

"Do as I say, and no one will get hurt. I want that key."

I get up and lead the way to the bedroom. The big guy doesn't say anything but stays close. His breath makes the hairs on my neck stand on end. His presence makes me want to scream, let alone the fact that he carries a gun. We go into the bedroom, and I go to my bureau, which holds a little drawer where I keep things like cufflinks and tie clips. The key is on a chain, and I pull it out of a small box in the drawer. "Here it is," I say. I'm not sure whether this big person can understand English or not. He waves me to return to the living room.

I hand the key to Simisola, and he looks at it. "This is the master key?"

"Yes, if we go to that bank and get the box. All the rest are there."

"You say 'we.' Tell me why I don't just have my man eliminate you and go myself."

"A small problem of security. No offense, but the bank will match my picture on file with my face before they give me the box. You will have a tough time looking like me."

Simisola shows me his large white teeth and breaks into a laugh. "You have me there, Mr. Petros. I could never duplicate that pasty skin of yours. Mine is the skin of a warrior and yours of a slaveholder."

"I get your drift, but for the record, I have always been active in racial equality."

"Yes, most certainly you have. It is so easy for rich folks like you to be active but not get your hands dirty. We did not come here to talk about your good works on behalf of people who have a different skin color. We came here to get that money back. We will have to wait until tomorrow to go shopping, so to speak. Of course, it means we will need to stay here with you, so you can make no attempt to escape and warn anyone."

"You know that Afua took that money from me, don't you?"

"Yes, of course. I like to think of it as reparation for the injustice of you being so rich and the rest of the world so poor. It makes it so much sweeter to relieve you of its evil."

"Does Afua know you're going after the money?"

"He doesn't know anything right now. He will go to prison, and what does he need with twenty million in prison?"

"So, the corruption continues."

"The generals will get their military budgets to spend. The country will have a new president, and everyone will be happy, including the new president and myself. We have worked hard for happiness and deserve it."

"You are a thief."

"Oh, that's rich, Mr. Petros. You take money from Afua and have the nerve to call me a thief?"

"The twenty million is mine. I earned it."

"Mr. Afua earned it as well. I earned it too. So, we all earned it, and it will be my pleasure to get it back and spend it."

I sit back in my chair and see no need in getting this character agitated. A glance over to Peter shows that he has stopped fooling with his phone. Constance sits with her hands in her lap, looking as if she's in the park on a lovely day. I think, for now, we have containment of the emergency. It appears that Simisola believes me that the money is in ten banks, and he feels satisfied that he and the big guy there will manage to retrieve it tomorrow. What does he plan to do until tomorrow morning? Then he speaks and leads me to believe he reads minds.

"You three will stay in the master bedroom. My associate and I will remain outside the door, so if you try anything, we will be there to punish you. Do you understand? I will need to take your phones, please."

The big guy comes around and takes all of the cells and lays them on a side table. "Also, Mr. Petros, do you have a hammer and nails?"

"In the garage."

"Take my associate and show him where."

I get up, and the big guy follows me. He must like intimidation, as he stands way too close, again making my hair stand on end. We go to the garage, and I get the hammer and a can that has nails in. I hand them to the big guy, and he shoves them back at me and waves me inside. I guess I'm the worker, and he is the manager.

Once back in the house, I hold out the tin. "Here."

Simisola says something I can't understand, and the big guy takes the hammer and nails from me. He goes out of the living room, and then turns toward the master bedroom. Simisola and I stand looking at each other. I hear pounding, and finally, Simisola tells me the big guy is making sure that none of the windows will open from the inside. I have to admit; he takes every precaution. Eventually, I would have thought about climbing out a window, but for right now, I didn't think of it.

The big guy returns, and Simisola gives us a signal that we all should go to the master bedroom. Constance gets up slowly, and Peter holds out his hand for a boost up. Constance obliges and pulls him to his feet. I can't tell which of the two is strongest.

"Can we get some water?" I ask.

"Isn't there a sink in the bathroom?" Simisola says.

"Yes, but some cold water would be nice."

"Okay, go and get a few bottles. We will stay here and make sure you return. You have one minute until my man shoots your daughter in the foot."

I hurry to the kitchen and go to the refrigerator, where I pull out three bottles and turn to leave. As the door of the refrigerator closes, movement from the kitchen window catches my attention. I go over, and Robert pops up from crouching under the sill. He points to the door, and I go there and let him in. Then I put my finger to my lips so that he won't make any noise. He hands me a phone and whispers, "Keep it on vibrate. I will call you." Then he ducks down behind the kitchen island and waves me back to the living room. I return and tell Constance and Peter that we should go to the bedroom.

"Before you go, does this house have a security system?"

"It does."

"What happens if you don't set it each night?"

"The security company sometimes calls to see if I have a problem, but more often than not, nothing."

"Please, set the system. We don't want any visitors. Oh, and Mr. Petros, please set it so that the motion detectors get disabled. You know how to do that, don't you?"

"Yes, I can set the system without motion detectors." I go to the keypad by the front door and set the system. Simisola looks to the corner of the room, and then waves his arm. The motion detector goes out, indicating it had picked up the motion. No alarm sounds. He smiles broadly.

"I like people who follow directions. Let's go to the bedroom."

We all walk to the master, and Simisola goes into the bathroom and looks around. He seems satisfied that we have no way out of there. He then walks to the table by the bed, takes the telephone, and rips it out of the wall. "I don't want your rest disturbed," he says. He follows his joke with a deep laugh. For certain, he enjoys his own humor.

He looks at me with what I would describe as an assistant principal glower. "I don't want to have to hurt any of you. I shall close the bedroom door when I leave, and I don't want anyone to touch even the knob. Do you understand?"

"I understand completely." I feel the weight of the phone in my pocket and pray it doesn't go off before Simisola leaves. He takes one last look at each of us and signals the big guy to follow him out. Mercifully, they are gone.

"Do you have a plan, Daddy?"

I put my finger to my lips and nod. Then, holding up two fingers, I move as far away from the door as possible. Constance and Peter follow. I whisper that we should all go into the bathroom and close the door. Constance and Peter let me know they understand, and we all head to the en suite. Once inside, I close the door and put my ear to the wood to see if it is possible that Simisola has come back to the bedroom. Satisfied that we have relative security, I say, "We need to keep our voices down. Robert is in the house, and he gave me this phone." I show them the cell. "He will call, and we will work out a plan."

"How did Robert get into the house?"

"I let him in when I went to get our water."

Constance wrinkles her nose. "How did he know to come over to the house? I thought he'd gone for the night, seeing as he didn't show up at the restaurant."

Peter raises his hand. "I sent him a text that we were in trouble but not to call the police."

"Good job," I say. "I thought you just sat fiddling with your phone."

"I guess that's what Simisola thought as well."

Constance gives Peter a hug. "I'm so proud of you."

Peter smiles. "What's next?"

"We wait for Robert's call. The phone is on vibrate, and Robert will probably call when he thinks it safe to talk. I would guess, after one of those guys goes to sleep."

Constance yawns. "I wouldn't mind getting some sleep as well. I didn't get much last night. I couldn't stop thinking about all the stuff in the office. Do you think those two have any skill at computers?"

"You worried about them going through the files?"

"No. They won't get to the files unless they have some knowledge. Do you know if they do?"

"I wouldn't think so. I reckon that someone else in Soto managed to look at Afua's computer. Simisola was here in the US and didn't have a chance to get into the computer."

"Not unless he could log in remotely."

"Oh, crap. If so, are we in more trouble." I hadn't thought of a remote login.

"I don't think so. I built good firewalls. I feel sure they can't get through. It might take half the night just to break the code to sign on to my laptop."

"Don't scare me with questions like that again."

"Sorry. I didn't mean to."

"It's okay. I just don't need any more problems right now. My ruse about the safe deposit boxes will fall apart as soon as we get to the first box, so I hope Robert has an idea. We're done here unless you or Peter have a question. If not, let's go into the bedroom, and you can have a lie down."

Constance shakes her head and looks at Peter. He shrugs, and I take it they have no further queries. When I open the door, I feel a rush of cooler air from the bigger room. Constance goes to the king bed and stretches out. Peter looks at me as if to ask permission to join her. With a wave of acknowledgment, I sit in one of the chairs at the bottom of the bed. I pull the phone out of my pocket and place it on my leg. Then I close my eyes and, before long, feel myself drifting. I keep jerking awake and feeling somewhat surprised to find that I have, in fact, fallen asleep. So I don't miss Robert's call, I want to stay awake. You would think that would be an easy task given the severity of our situation.

Something hits the carpet. I almost jump out of the chair when I realize it's the phone, which just fell off my leg. Hurriedly, I grab it and can feel the vibration. I connect and whisper, "Hello?"

"Greg, it's me, Robert."

Robert whispers into the phone too, and it makes it a little hard to understand him.

"Where are you?"

"I found your attic on the second floor, and I'm in there. It offers the only spot where I thought I could whisper without them hearing."

"Good choice. The installation is quite thick in there, and it's almost soundproof."

"Okay, good. We should wait for these guys to fall asleep. Then I will come out of here and hit the big guy on the head and take his gun. It will all be over for the other then."

"Can you see in there?"

"I have a little mag light, so I can see a little."

"Look around. I think I have a croquet set up there. One of those mallets would make an excellent weapon."

"Okay, hold on. I'll look."

"The last time I saw the set, it was on the left near the rear of the space."

"Okay, I'll go there." A few minutes of silence ensue, then Robert says, "I see it. What color do you think would be best?"

"No time for jokes." Though he did make me smile.

"Okay, I got it. Now all I have to do is wait. Once I think it's clear, I'll sneak out of the attic and creep down the stairs."

"Do you see a way we could distract these guys from in here?"

"It would be easier if I knew exactly where they'll be."

"Do you know the location of the master bedroom?"

"Yeah, right off the living room."

"How about we pretend to feel sick or something and get these guys to come to the bedroom door. Would that help?"

"Yeah, I would say better than trying to find them in the dark."

"Let's do it, then. Give me five minutes or so. Is your phone on vibrate?"

"Yeah."

"How about I call you back when I'm sure they've both come to the bedroom door."

"What if they go into the bedroom?"

"Even better, as their backs would face the door. You would have an opportunity to whack them good."

"Let me ask one more time. Shouldn't we call the police?"

"Nah. These guys would spook and maybe shoot one of us. Let's call them after we get control of the situation."

"Okay, you're the boss."

"Fine. See you in a few."

The line clicks off.

Chapter Twenty-six

I cut off the phone and let Constance and Peter in on the plan.

"I'll call these guys to the door. You two should go to the bathroom, so we'll have enough room for Robert to get a good swing. I have a feeling that the big guy won't go down easy."

"Daddy, it's too dangerous. What if Robert misses or something?"

"Yeah," Peter says, "I don't think this is such a good idea. Sounds half-baked to me. Let's just call the police."

"You know why we can't do that? We have a guy out there with information that Constance pulled twenty million out of Afua's account. Don't forget, he's a member of his country's justice department and has political and diplomatic protection. I just don't want to chance it until we get free."

"What will you do when we do get free? Won't it be the same thing?"

"Simisola will listen to reason and go back to Soto without the money. If we call the police, that will force him to tell his story. Without the police, no harm done, and I can make the case that instead of getting charged with breaking and entering, he might as well go home."

"I see. You make it sound reasonable."

"So, you're in?"

Peter heaves a heavy sigh. "Count me in."

"Great, thank you. Now, you two go into the bathroom."

They follow my directions and move out of the bedroom. I go over to the door and listen. I don't hear anyone nearby. Nervous, I punch in Robert's number but will wait to hit send until I feel sure they stand by the entrance. Then I pound on the wood and yell to Simisola to open the door.

"What's the problem?" Simisola talks through the door, and I'm not sure the big guy came with him.

"Could you come in here? I don't feel well and need to get some medicine."

"Where do you keep it?"

"In a locked cabinet in the bathroom, but the key is on my car key ring." This excuse made for the only thing I could think of at the last second.

"I'll get the key ring and will come right back."

I still can't tell if the big guy stands out there or not. It seems I'll have to open the door and see for myself. Slowly, I turn the knob and pull open the door. The big guy stands there, and I feel so shocked that I forget to call Robert. Time is running out, so I decide to hit the big guy with a tackle as if grabbing a football. I need to hit him low and dislodge the ball from his hands. In this case, it could be a gun. I'm not sure he has it pulled out. Then he shifts, and I have to move. Panicked, I drop the phone and hit the big guy full in the stomach with my shoulder. Then I do a twist roll and bring him down. He falls, and the air rushes out of his lungs. He will have a problem getting up. To make the chore even more difficult, I lay on him. He pulls his gun out of his coat. I must grab his wrist, or I will get into serious trouble. Not giving myself time to think about the consequences, I jump to one knee, just in time to hear the explosion from the end of his arm. He got a shot off, and I have to stop the next one. I reach for him. A white-hot rush engulfs me somewhere near my heart, followed by a bolt of red behind my eyes and a signal to my brain that something has gone seriously wrong. My brain catches up, and I now realize I got hit. The pain causes me to slump over the big guy, no longer capable of preventing the next shot.

"What have you done?" Simisola screams.

The big guy attempts to drag himself out from under me while explaining that it happened by accident, and he didn't mean to do it. Simisola calls him a few names, and then helps him up. I groan when the big guy's last move causes my head to drop onto the floor.

"We need to shoot all of them and get out of here." Simisola uses a voice two octaves higher than normal. I sense panic and hope that Robert can do something since I am incapable of moving. Though bleeding a lot, I can't do anything about it and feel weaker by the second. A skirmish breaks out nearby. Robert must have come down from the attic after hearing the shot. His mallet connects with the big man, and he falls directly beside me. Then comes a sickening pumpkin cracking noise, so I know he hit Simisola as hard as he hit the big guy, but Simisola's head, not as hard, explodes. Simisola falls on top of the big guy. His face turns to me, and I can see the shocked look in his eyes.

"Daddy. Oh, my God. Robert, call 911, quick."

Constance rolls me onto my back. I don't want to but can't keep from moaning. "Oh, Daddy. You'll be all right. Robert is calling 911. Stay with me, Daddy. Please, Peter, get a towel. So much blood. We have to stop it."

"Constance," I say. "It's okay. Keith's here. He'll take care of everything."

"Daddy, please stay with me. Keith's dead. Daddy, please, look at me. Don't leave me, Daddy. No, Daddy, please, breathe. Open your eyes. Daddy, please don't leave me. We need each other, Daddy. I love you. Oh, my God. Where is the towel, Peter?"

"Let go, Greg," Keith says.

"Hi, Keith. Is this it? Is this why you had to stay here all this time?"

"Yes. My job is to take you to The Leader."

"I feel so sorry for Constance."

"She's okay. Now, come on. Let it go."

"Daddy, who are you talking to? Please, open your eyes. Please, Daddy."

"Constance. I love you. I'm going with Keith now. Please, let me go."

Constance looks up, and I think she sees Keith standing above us. The hurt and pain leave her face. She leans closer and whispers, "Oh, Daddy. Daddy, all my love goes with you. Goodbye."

"Goodbye, sweetheart."

"Take my hand, Greg."

I reach up and take Keith's hand. The pain stops, and I feel wonderful. I get up and walk with Keith, still holding his hand. Constance cries loudly and calls for me. I know she will do fine. Keith and I need to go to The Leader. Once there, I will get my directions, and then maybe I can return and help Constance adjust. I love her so much and can feel only that love. No sorrow. She no longer needs me. I gave her everything she needed, and I feel good about that. "We going to The Leader?" I ask Keith.

"Yes. I hope to be able to finish my assignment and then go on to the eternal life. The Leader promised that if I did my job well, the reward would be mine. You may have an assignment, but we'll find out."

"What about those horrible people who Robert killed?"

"They won't bother anyone anymore. The police will arrive, and Robert will explain that they held you hostage. He will tell them a story about coming over and finding them in the house. Then he will show how he hid in the attic. They will ask if he knows why they went there, and he will say he doesn't know.

295

He won't get held, and the deaths will be ruled self-defense given that you got killed by one.

"The investigation will go on for a while in an attempt to determine why the diplomat came into your house. Of course, no one in the new administration in Soto will say anything. The book that Simisola mentioned is destroyed, and the Vice President won't chase the twenty million. They won't harass Constance again."

"That's a relief."

"You could feel that outcome yourself, right?"

"Yes, I could feel that." I look at Keith, "What will happen to us? Will I see you again?"

"I'm not sure. If not, will it bother you so much?"

"Now that I think about it, I have great love in my heart for you that can never be taken. I hope I can see you again. If not, I know you are happy and that you have pleased The Leader, and that is all that counts."

"Atta boy. That's how you're supposed to feel."

"There's not much more to say. Oh, wait. Do you think Terry will still get a divorce? We never signed the papers."

"No, Greg. She's now a widow, and Constance, Gary, and she will be your heirs according to your will."

"Well, I hope Constance keeps the nineteen million a secret."

"Do you really?"

"Now that you've said that, I have to admit something's come over me that makes me hope she tells her mom. It wouldn't seem right to keep it from her."

"And so, your spirit life begins. We've said it all. It will be The Leader's turn now. I love you, Greg."

"I love you, too, Keith. I'm ready. Lead the way."

End

From the Author

Thank you so much for reading Circumstances of Childhood I hope you enjoyed the story. It would be nice if you could give the book a review on Amazon. This is one way authors receive feedback from their readers and are so thrilled to find out what you think about their story.

You can also catch up with **My GRL**, **His Revenge**, and **Our Justice** by going to my author page on Amazon. Here is the link.

https://www.amazon.com/author/johnwhowell

You can contact me at my e-mail address johnhowell.wave@gmail.com

You can also reach me at johnwhowell.com

My next novel, a collaboration with Gwen Plano, author of **Letting Go into Perfect Love** is titled **The Contract** and should be out mid-year 2018.